THE CASE OF THE
REINCARNATED CLIENT

THE CASE OF THE REINCARNATED CLIENT

From the files of Vish Puri, India's Most Private Investigator

Tarquin Hall

Severn House Large Print
London & New York

This first large print edition published 2020
in Great Britain and the USA by
SEVERN HOUSE PUBLISHERS LTD of
Eardley House, 4 Uxbridge Street, London W8 7SY.
First world regular print edition published 2019 by
Severn House Publishers Ltd.

British Library Cataloguing in Publication Data
A CIP catalogue record for this title is available from the British Library.

ISBN-13: 9780727892799

Severn House Publishers support the Forest Stewardship Council™
[FSC™], the leading international forest certification organisation. All
our titles that are printed on FSC certified paper carry the FSC logo.

Typeset by Palimpsest Book Production Ltd.,
Falkirk, Stirlingshire, Scotland.
Printed and bound in Great Britain by
T J Books Limited, Padstow, Cornwall.

*In memory of Mrs East and in celebration
of true originals everywhere*

One

Vish Puri tried taking a deep breath to calm his nerves, just as Dr Mohan had advised him to do during times of stress. But it was a struggle: his chest suddenly felt tight, as if he was at high altitude.

Only his mother had this effect on him. And there was no doubt he'd heard her out in reception.

'Chubby's very much there, na?' she'd asked, her shrill voice carrying through his office door.

Elizabeth Rani's response was drowned out by the curse Puri uttered under his breath: 'By God, what now, *yaar*?'[1] But he knew it would be only a matter of seconds before his intercom buzzed and his executive secretary announced – with tickled glee, for she adored Mummy-*ji* – his mother's wish to look in on her son.

For a moment, Puri contemplated the possibility of escaping out over the roof, where he could access the fire escape on the adjacent building. To do so would involve passing in front of the reception window, however, and he would be spotted for sure.

Besides, it had been only half an hour since

---

[1] The equivalent to 'pal', 'mate' or 'dude'. See glossary for further definitions and explanations of Indian-English usage.

1

he'd polished off an excellent *rogan josh* and a couple of naans, and he wasn't altogether convinced he would be able to pull himself up to the small toilet window, nor that he would fit through it.

There was no point pretending that he was on an important call and couldn't be disturbed, either. Mummy would simply wait him out. And if he tried to explain the truth – that in thirty minutes he needed to leave the office for two urgent meetings, the first with his lawyer and the second with Mr Ram Bhatt, a recent client, who had sounded anything but satisfied on the phone – he would only get a lecture about working too hard and not looking after his health.

Worse, she might pry. Mummy was forever trying to find out what cases he was working on and had an uncanny knack of drawing out the details. Take the last time she'd visited the office, for example. Puri had just finished a meeting with a prospective new client. A middle-aged air hostess who'd been fired from her job because she'd gained weight, she wanted to avail of Most Private Investigators Ltd.'s services for the purposes of gathering evidence of wrongful dismissal (the reason given by her employer being that her 'reflexes were impaired'). Unfortunately, the meeting had not been a total success and the air hostess had left the office in a flood of tears. Thus when Puri's mother had, by chance, passed her on the stairs and the two fell into conversation, Mummy-ji became embroiled in the whole business, committing the firm to taking on the case without so much as a by your leave.

2

Puri had objected strenuously, of course. His mother had no right to speak with his clients, let alone get involved with their – *his!* – cases. She had played hurt. And then, predictably once home, Puri had received a ticking off from his wife, Rumpi. He only had himself to blame. If he'd shown the prospective client more sympathy and not referred to her as a *trolley dolly* or suggested that beyond a certain age an air hostess was, surely, better suited to doing the check-in, then she wouldn't have left the office so upset. Mummy-ji was only trying to help. Her heart was in the right place. The usual.

Puri took another deep breath and exhaled. 'Face the music, Puri-*sahib*, that is only way,' he murmured to himself.

Invite Mummy in, hear her out, and then show her the door with a gentle reminder that he was not to be bothered at his place of work unless it was an emergency. And by emergency he did *not* mean a 'hit-and-run job' on Mrs Pathak's poodle or the theft of Ninu Auntie's (alarmingly large) stash of Xanax.

Buzz went the intercom.

Puri raised himself from his chair and made a quick survey of his office, checking for anything lying around that he didn't want his mother to see. He'd been reviewing the matrimonial case file for Mr Ram Bhatt in anticipation of their meeting later and it was lying open on his desk. Hurriedly, Puri closed it and made for the door.

Mummy was still chatting with Elizabeth Rani. 'Ah, there you are, Chubby,' she said, as if his whereabouts had been in any doubt. 'Just thought

3

I'd come by. So many days have gone past since last we met, na?'

In fact, it had only been four days. But for an Indian mother, that was a lifetime, Puri reflected as he greeted her.

'Wonderful to see you, Mummy-ji. Looking so nice, I must say.'

He made a gesture of bending down a few degrees as if to touch her feet, as was customary, knowing that she would raise him up by the shoulder – and that his paunch would prevent him from reaching the floor, anyway.

'I'm not interrupting something important?'

'I'm wanted at Patiala House, actually, Mummy-ji,' he said, checking his watch.

But she either ignored him or didn't hear. 'Just I was reading about that Muradnagar murder – the double one,' she said. 'Must be the woman was having an affair.'

Puri knew full well that Mummy was fishing, mentioning the high-profile case on the off chance that he was involved. 'Some *chai vai*, Mummy-ji?' he asked as he returned behind his desk rather than sitting next to her.

'Nothing,' she said and sat down on the chair opposite his desk, ensuring as she did so that the back of her light-green *kurta* didn't crease.

'You've taken your lunch, is it?' he asked.

'Just I've come directly from my Ladies' Club biannual new members luncheon.' She sounded faintly irritated, as if he should have known.

Puri's leather executive chair wheezed like an asthmatic as he lowered himself into it. Mummy was poised on the front of her seat, straight-backed,

4

with her handbag in her lap. The manner in which she held on to the straps with both hands conveyed a steely determination, as if Puri needed reminding.

He was going to need a cup of chai – *strong* chai.

Leaning over his desk, he pressed the talk switch on his intercom and spoke into it. His voice was louder than necessary, a habit from those bygone days before the mid-Nineties when all Indian phone lines crackled like Geiger counters and crossed lines had been the rule not the exception.

'Madam Rani, some chai if you please.'

'Right away, sir.'

He took his finger off the switch with a flourish, evidently well pleased with himself for his ability to make use of such a marvel of the modern, technological age.

'So – tell me,' he said, sitting back in his chair.

'One matter is there, Chubby – top priority,' replied Mummy, suddenly brisk and business-like. 'Obligation is there on my part and the responsibility lies with you, also.'

Puri could feel his chest tightening again. 'Mummy-ji, I'm not following, exactly,' he said.

'You have gone the family business way, after all,' she replied.

He rolled his eyes. 'Mummy-ji, let us do without the drum roll, if you please.'

She gave a tut. 'Chubby, don't do impatience, na. I was getting to the crux,' she scolded. 'Now, where was I? Oh yes, regarding your responsibility. This is a matter regarding your papa-ji, Om Chander Puri. Some information has come

5

to light. Thus I'm doing my duty and looking into the matter.'

Puri held up a hand. 'Don't tell me this has got to do with the Shandu Shetty homicide.' He was tempted to add, *And I'm well aware of Papa-ji's full name, thank you.*

'Not at all, it is concerning another case all together,' she said. 'You remember Riya Kaur? She got murdered during the riots.'

By riots, Mummy was referring to the Anti-Sikh Riots of October-November 1984 when more than 3,000 Sikhs were massacred by Hindu mobs in Delhi in the wake of the assassination of Prime Minister, Indira Gandhi, by her Sikh bodyguards.

'From what I can recall, Riya Kaur was a young mother resident in Rajouri Garden. She went missing during the riots and the circumstances pointed to her having been taken from the house by the mob in the dead of night, though like many hundreds of others her body was never identified let alone located.'

Puri had a flash of his father sitting at the table in the kitchen of the old family home in Punjabi Bagh a few years after his forced retirement from the Delhi Police, speaking about the case, his features suffused with sadness.

'Papa-ji took on the investigation after Riya Kaur's father filed the missing persons and appealed to him personally,' Puri added.

'The two were known to one another from childhood,' interjected Mummy.

'Bobby, then Papa-ji's junior partner, worked on the case, also, but it remains unsolved – and, for all intents and purposes, a *missing persons*,' Puri stressed.

'Suspicion fell on the husband, Mantosh Singh,'[2] said Mummy.

'No charges could be brought.'

'He murdered her, rest assured. Just some proofs were absent.'

'By *proofs* you're referring to the woman's body itself, I suppose?'

'Come, Chubby, a body is not everything,' she said.

Puri felt his head swimming. How had he allowed himself to be drawn into this ridiculous argument? What was she getting at, anyway? And where was his chai?

He glanced over at his blood pressure machine. It was the briefest of glances, but his blunder didn't go unnoticed by his mother.

'Chubby, what is *that*?' she asked, squinting at the apparatus.

'What is what?' he asked, playing dumb.

'It is for measuring blood pressure, na?'

'Yes, Mummy-ji, if you must know, my blood pressure has been somewhat elevated of late. And speaking frankly, the last five minutes have not improved matters.'

---

[2] Sikh men and women rarely use the same last names after marriage (in accordance with the instruction of the tenth Sikh guru (1666–1708)). Men apply *Singh* and women, *Kaur* i.e. in the modern context, married couples are known as Mr Singh and Mrs Kaur. This practice was implemented to emphasize gender equality and to do away with names denoting caste.

'Chubby, how many times I'm telling you, diet is required? Obesity is there.'

'And how many times I've told you that detective work is not for mummies?' Puri shot back.

She was silent for a moment before answering. 'Many times you've told me, if you must know. Never mind that I've offered valuable assistance in times past, to you and Om Chander Puri. You've forgotten the Butter Chicken murder case, for example?'

A knock on the door left Mummy's question hanging in the air.

Puri bawled a gruff, 'Enter!' and the office 'boy' (who was in fact a grown man of twenty-six) came in bearing the tea.

The crockery on his tray rattled in the stony silence as he crossed the room and approached the desk.

He had brought two cups. The first he placed on the desk in front of Mummy, the second in front of Puri, along with a plate of custard-cream biscuits.

Once he was gone – backing out of the door like a courtier in a throne room – Puri picked up his cup and sipped zealously at the hot, milky chai. A quick glance up at the clock on the wall between a prominently displayed selection of framed awards and accolades and photographs of him with various personalities (including a beaming Dalai Lama and faintly perturbed-looking Amitabh Bachchan)[3] told him that ideally he should be on his way in five minutes.

[3] Bollywood superstar.

'I'm due at Patiala House, then a meeting with a client,' he said. 'What is this all about, Mummy-ji? Why rake over the past? Nothing is to be gained. It is a cold case, as cold as . . . I don't know . . . a fridge!'

'What if I told you some crucial new evidence has come to light?'

'What evidence?'

'I'll tell you in due course. First thing is first. To solve the case, the Riya Kaur file is required.'

'The official file?'

'Precisely.'

'From the police department's archives?'

'Correct.'

'You wish me to enter the building and simply ask for the official file to be handed over, is it?'

'Such a small thing for a great detective, na?'

Puri almost smiled at her gall. 'Flattery will get you nowhere, Mummy-ji,' he said. 'Now . . . I suggest you tell me what all this new evidence is you think you've discovered.'

'First, you must promise to get hold the file, Chubby. For solving the case once and for all, it will be indispensable. My memory is not what it was.'

Puri tried to explain that it was no small thing to get hold of such a file. It would be risky – an offence under God knows how many acts. If caught, he could face prosecution. The police chief would lock him up and throw the key in the Yamuna.

But it did no good – Mummy was relentless, and it wasn't long before Puri found himself agreeing to do 'his best' and 'try' to get her what she wanted.

With this, she stood and began to leave.

'Aren't you forgetting something?' he asked.

She looked puzzled.

'The evidence?'

'Oh, yes, sorry, yaar, so forgetful I'm getting.' She took her seat again. 'See, Chubby, the fact is that, regarding the Riya Kaur murder, one witness has come forward.'

'What kind of witness?'

'A human one, naturally. You think it could be a dog or a monkey or some such?'

'Nothing would surprise me.'

'Well, she is very much a woman.'

'And?'

Mummy gave him a blank look. 'That is all – a woman,' she said.

'A member of the family, a servant, neighbour . . . butcher, baker, bloody candlestick maker?'

'Language, if you please.'

'Well?'

'She is related to Riya in a way, yes.'

'And this woman claims to have witnessed what, exactly?'

'Everything.'

'Meaning?'

'She saw what happened with her own two eyes.'

'Saw what exactly?'

'You wish to know her testimony, is it?' asked Mummy with a sigh. 'For that, Chubby, some time will be required and you've a meeting to attend unfortunately.'

10

Puri placed both hands palms down on the desk, as if he needed the support to steady himself.

'Just answer me this: the female, your *witness*, is she willing to go on the record, to testify in the court?'

'That could prove . . . complicated.'

Puri took a deep breath and exhaled, determined to remain cool, though he felt like he could explode.

'Mummy-ji, tell me who this witness is, exactly and precisely, or I will *not* get you the file. Final.'

'But you promised!'

'You've one minute, then I'm terminating this conversation. No discussion.'

'Very well,' she said, composing herself. 'If you must know, Chubby, the witness is in fact Riya Kaur herself.'

'She's alive? You've met with her?'

For a fleeting moment Puri felt hopeful. His father's failure to solve the case had troubled him to his dying day. The case had been a personal one. Riya Kaur's father was his close friend.

Was it possible that Mummy had got to the bottom of it once and for all?

Her reply – 'More or less' – brought him back down to earth with a thud, however.

'*More or less?* How someone can be alive *more or less*, I ask you?'

'Simple, na,' replied Mummy. 'Saanvi is the reincarnation of Riya Kaur.'

Puri closed his eyes. 'By God,' he breathed. 'You're saying some woman is claiming to be Riya Kaur?'

'Not some woman, Chubby, if you please. *Saanvi*. She is '84 born.'

'And you plan to present her into court, I suppose? "Your Honour, this is the woman who went missing all those years back. We recognize that she looks *nothing* like Riya Kaur and that she is *not, in fact*, Riya Kaur at all. But if it please the court, we ask Your Honour to indulge this little fantasy!"'

Mummy's face flashed angry defiance. 'Saanvi is the one, rest assured,' she said. 'So many details she knows. Like the colour of Riya's wedding sari. How she could know such a thing?'

Puri stood up and began to gather his things: keys, wallet, the Ram Bhatt matrimonial case file.

He grabbed the custard creams as well.

'So, you'll get hold of the file tomorrow?' asked Mummy.

Puri ignored her.

'Chubby, you gave your word!' came her voice as he exited his office.

He closed the door behind him and paused, holding on to the handle as he weighed the wisdom of leaving his mother in his office (where she was now free to snoop) with the prospect of throwing her out (whereby he would have to endure more of her ridiculous nonsense).

His indecision lasted but a couple of seconds, and he passed quickly through reception and down the stairs.

It would be up to Elizabeth Rani to evict Mummy from his office.

The prospect of this caused him to give a loud

12

guffaw. 'Pigs might fly. Cows, also,' he mumbled to himself as he made his way through the bustle of Khan Market.

Two

On the drive over to the Delhi High Court, Puri munched on his custard creams and tried to put his mother out of his thoughts. He checked his messages, looked over the Bhatt matrimonial case file, pondering what cause his former client might have to be unhappy about the investigation Puri had carried out on his behalf, called his tailor to ask when his new safari suit would be ready, though he already knew the answer, and checked his messages again.

Mummy-ji's words kept coming back to him, however, and soon, despite his best efforts, Puri found himself railing against her theory. Though as a Hindu he believed in reincarnation and the notion that the soul is eternal, he found the idea of someone recalling events from a past life preposterous. Clearly this Saanvi, the young woman Mummy was touting as Riya Kaur born again, was deluded or worse.

'Such a nonsense,' he cursed.

But for all his indignation, a voice (which perhaps belonged to the little boy who had once looked to his mother for support and guidance for everything and could not bring himself to accept that she might be wrong) whispered the possibility that maybe – just maybe – there might be something – some kernel of truth – in what Mummy was suggesting. Did it not warrant investigation? Did he not owe it to Papa-ji to find out?

This dissent from within fuelled his irritation still further and in retaliation Puri resolved to break his word and not get hold of the Riya Kaur case file for his mother. 'Final, decided, no discussion,' he said out loud suddenly, somewhat to the consternation of his driver, Handbrake, who gave him a brief, quizzical look in the rear-view mirror.

Puri checked his messages again, found yet another unsolicited SMS from a real estate company offering to sell him a condo in Goa, and stared out the window of his faithful Hindustan Ambassador. Though it was only four o'clock, it looked uncommonly dark outside, as if the city was experiencing a prolonged eclipse. He wondered if perhaps his window might be dirty – it did not take long for a fine layer of sand and dust to settle on everything in Delhi these days, hence the common sight of private chauffeurs incessantly wiping down vehicles wherever they were parked – or whether the smog was gathering again.

In winding down the window to check, Puri was reminded of just how efficiently the new bulletproof glass he'd installed last year[4] insulated him from the noise of the city's frenzied traffic. Turning the handle was akin to increasing the volume dial on a stereo system, and Puri

[4] Following an attempt on his life by the don of the notorious Red Onion Mafia.

14

winced as he was fully exposed to the full quadraphonic tumult of ragged honking and straining engines.

By now the Ambassador was edging through the congestion on India Gate Circle, a battle-scarred bus belching black exhaust on one side, a cluster of three-wheeler auto-rickshaws that moved like a darting school of fish on the other. Puri strained for a glimpse of India Gate, the British war memorial that had long since become a cherished landmark of the Republic and more recently a promised land for selfie-stick salesmen. The lights had not yet been turned on, however, and the monument was barely visible, merely an outline with no detail. This was more than could be said for the dome of the president's palace and the *chattris* of North and South Block, which, on a sunny day, stood sentinel at the end of the long imperial avenue known as Rajpath. The buildings had been wiped from the landscape by a dense bank of smog. Puri even had difficulty locating the sun, scanning the sky until he found what looked like its replica in a shadow-puppet play, a small mellow disc behind a gauze curtain.

Puri didn't have to check the latest air pollution levels to know they had gone through the roof. His eyes were beginning to sting and the pleasant aftertaste of the custard creams had been replaced with the bitter zing of lead. Possibly this was another ignominious record for Delhi, now one of the most polluted cities in the world. 'Gas Chamber' was a term that often featured in people's vocabulary these days and one that Puri did not find all that far-fetched. Diesel emissions from millions of new cars on the roads and thousands of polluting trucks moving through the city at night, particles thrown up by construction sites, tens of millions of fireworks lit on Diwali, and the burning of stubble in Punjab after the harvest were all contributors to the poisonous air cocktail. It didn't help either that every morning, without fail, in every residential area and market across the city, thousands of sweepers armed with stiff bristled *jharus* swept up all the smut that settled during the night, driving great clouds of it back up into the air.

Clearly something had to be done. But the politicians seemed to have little appetite for drastic reform. And from what Puri could make out there seemed to be barely any pressure from the public to improve things. The poor had more pressing problems to deal with, while the growing, affluent middle classes were, on the whole, indifferent. Times were good, after all. The economy was growing at a rate that the rest of the world envied. Not in his lifetime had Puri seen such optimism about India's future. 'What's a little bad air?' he'd heard many say. The effects were being overblown in the media. Every industrializing economy faced such issues. Look at Britain – the mills, the pollution of the rivers, the London smog that killed thousands. All that got sorted out eventually. Besides, Indians are much hardier than others.

'*Sawan ke andhe ko sab hara hi hara nazar aata hai,*'[5] went the saying, Puri reflected.

[5] 'One who goes blind in spring, sees only greenery all around.'

He wound up his window again, satisfied that the glass was clean and that his driver had not been shirking his duty, and wiped his streaming eyes with his handkerchief. Out of the corner of his eye, he noticed a traffic cop standing on an island conducting the rowdy ensemble of vehicles. He was wearing a pollution mask, a paper one, and Puri was reminded that Rumpi had urged him to wear one as well on days when the levels were 'extremely hazardous'. The residents of Beijing were all wearing them, she'd argued. But he'd rejected the idea. Not on the grounds there wasn't a problem; Puri was no pollution denier. He had petitioned his member of parliament to scrap diesel vehicles and written a long letter to the honourable editor of the *Times of India* on the need for better public transport in Delhi. *While the Metro is an undoubted success on every measure*, he'd written in reference to the city's new rail system, *bus services in the city are not in the least bit satisfactory and are not for use by the faint-hearted, the drivers often being reckless at best.*

No, Puri refused to wear a mask on the grounds that it wasn't practical. Every time he needed to make a phone call would mean removing the damn thing. Plus he'd look ridiculous. And it was bound to make his moustache itchy.

The Ambassador stopped in front of Patiala House, formerly the Delhi residence of the maharaja of one of India's wealthiest princely states, or kingdoms, and since 1978 the site of the Delhi High Court.

'I'll give you a missed call,' Puri told Handbrake,

which meant that the driver was to wait nearby, probably down some side street, until summoned by a single ring on his mobile phone.

Puri stepped out of the car, brushed some custard-cream crumbs from his lap, and then headed through the main gates. It was rare for him to come to the courthouse without first taking the precaution of donning the garb of a lawyer – white shirt buttoned at the top with no tie, a black jacket, black trousers and half-moon glasses – and in his trademark Sandown cap and safari suit, he felt exposed and vulnerable. There were, after all, quite a number of individuals who visited the court on a regular basis on account of his professional efforts, and he preferred to avoid any unpleasant entanglements with such types. This included serial carjacker Aqil Nasir, alias 'Baba', who Puri had tracked down after Baba snatched his neighbour's BMW at gunpoint (thereby collecting a two *lakh* reward from the police for his capture in the process) and whose trial was ongoing. Puri was fairly sure that Mrs Dadwal, who was undergoing lengthy divorce hearings and blamed Puri for the end of her marriage (not without cause as it had been he that had proven she was having an affair with her yoga instructor)[6] might well be in the courthouse as well and would

---

[6] Mrs Dadwal, who was in her late forties, was found out after she fell pregnant. She had thought this impossible as her fallopian tubes had been tied. Ironically, the contorted yoga position she was taught by her lover (and which Puri's operative captured her practising on camera with his active assistance) caused the tubes to come untied.

18

not hesitate from giving him a piece of her mind.

But he was in luck. The timely arrival in a police van of a student union leader from one of the major universities charged with some perceived slight against 'religious sensibilities' caused considerable excitement among the waiting camera crews and photographers who jostled for comment and pictures, while a number of rabble-rousing lawyers who had taken exception to the accused's statements lobbed their shoes at him.

Only the freelance typists seated behind the row of rickety desks arranged beneath the huge *peepal* tree that stood to the right of the main building remained indifferent to the hubbub and continued to bash away at their archaic machines with a certain rhythmic reliability, adding relentlessly to India's prodigious paperwork.

Puri was able to pass unnoticed into the labyrinth of lawyers' 'chambers', which were in fact little more than prefabricated huts, some no larger than cubicles, with flimsy metal doors not much thicker than gym lockers.

The cramped premises occupied by *Balbir Aggarwal and Associates, Advocates* was utilized as efficiently as that of a submarine – more so perhaps, given that two lawyers and a clerk occupied the space. Anyone moving along the narrow spaces between the furniture had to do so with sideways shuffles. The shelves were stacked with leather-bound legal tomes two deep; the files were kept above a false ceiling through which, upon request, they were lowered on a homemade pulley system; the bench upon which clients perched during meetings was hollow and, occasionally, visitors were asked to stand up while court forms or items of stationery were retrieved from beneath their seats.

'Mr Puri, *saar*! Make yourself comfortable, et cetera!'

Balbir Aggarwal did not stand to greet him; the low ceiling and his height (he was six feet tall exactly) deemed it unwise. And such a formality would have been redundant anyway. In Puri's words, he and his lawyer had, 'practically gone the marriage way'. They never spoke less than three or four times a day; rarely did a week go by without the two of them appearing in court together. Only physical intimacy was lacking between them, as the detective often joked.

'Why the urgency?' Puri asked, careful not to knock Balbir's framed law degree off the wall with his paunch as he shuffled to the client's bench.

'Some good news, which required delivering to you in person,' said Balbir with a grin, the LED lights above glinting off his head's shiny, barren dome.

'Good news?' Puri sounded sceptical.

'Well, as you yourself have so often observed, in life one should always expect the unexpected, et cetera.'

Balbir reached over his desk and brought his hand down hard on a counter bell, which gave a loud *ding*. This was his signal to his clerk, who sat not more than four feet behind him, to order tea.

'Concerning Puran Chandra,' said the lawyer.

Puri gave a start. 'That bloody *goonda* – what about him?'

'He's settled his account.'

Puri gave another start. 'Not possible.'

'Until two hours back, I would have agreed with you. Then one of his lackeys appeared out of the blue – no warning, no explanation, in quite a hurry it seemed. Hands me a plastic bag full of cash and explains Chandra requested him to deliver it to me in person. Asks me to sign a chit and leaves, et cetera.'

Puri frowned. 'How much he gave you exactly?'

'Seven lakh, twenty-five thousand.'

'The full amount in totality?'

By way of an answer, Balbir retrieved a large, old-fashioned iron key from his desk drawer and turned forty-five degrees in his chair to face his antique, cast-iron British safe (of which he was very proud, never failing to point out to fellow admirers that it was from Liverpool). It gave a clunk and a creak before disgorging the afore-mentioned plastic bag.

Puri emptied the contents: a dozen or so wads of one-thousand-rupee notes bound in rubber bands tumbled on to the desk. He weighed one of them in his hand and then thumbed the notes.

'All present and correct, I take it?' Puri asked, still suspicious.

'Hardly seems likely that he would pay you of all people in counterfeit notes,' commented the lawyer.

'I'd not put anything past him,' said Puri as he tugged out a random note and inspected it against the light. 'This is a man who sold his own sister's property from under her, including all the furniture and fittings.'

The note proved genuine, however, and he returned it to its respective wad.

'Why now, after so much of time?' he mused. 'It has been owing for what?'

'Three years, four months,' said Balbir.

'All of a sudden, out of the blue, no explanation?'

'Possibly my countersuit struck a chord, et cetera,' suggested the lawyer with a sanguine smile.

'My friend, you did everything appropriately and correctly, not to mention diligently and professionally, also,' said Puri reassuringly. 'But it goes against his character to settle in this way. You remember what trouble I faced with him?[7] No, there is something more to this matter. Could be he requires my services again? Or he's found the God and is feeling so much of remorse for past misdeeds.'

Laughter filled the little office, and then the courthouse chai boy came through the door carrying a couple of small glasses of dark, muddy chai.

'Well, here's to one lawsuit down, twelve to go,' said Puri, raising his glass.

'Better make that unlucky thirteen,' said Balbir.

---

[7] Puri had been pressured into working for Puran Chandra by a minister in the previous government. Chandra had paid half the detective's fee in advance, but withheld the balance on the pretext that his name had appeared in the newspaper in connection with the case (which had been unavoidable).

'Don't tell me there's another one!'

'Your former client Mr Ram Bhatt filed a case against you this morning.'

Puri gave an exasperated sigh. 'By God.'

'He's demanding a return of all fees paid *and* damages amounting to one *crore* rupees.'

'*One* crore! But that would be the ruin of me!'

'He claims the matrimonial investigation conducted by your firm into his daughter's fiancé, Vikas Gupta, was, and I quote, "highly deficient". After only two months, the marriage is on the rocks; the bride has returned in the past day or so to her father's house. Ram Bhatt holds you accountable for the failure of the marriage, et cetera, *and* for "ruining his daughter Tulsi's life" and damaging the reputation of the family, et cetera.'

'Why's he holding me responsible, exactly?' asked Puri with a puzzled frown.

'He hasn't specified in his written complaint. The details will be made clear on the first day of hearing, at which point the court will decide the merits of the case. A date has been set for two weeks from now. Meantime, I suggest you fill me in.'

Puri explained that it had been a straightforward matrimonial investigation involving two affluent Delhi families.

Ram Bhatt's daughter, Tulsi, was highly eligible – twenty-four, attractive, slim with a 'very fair complexion' and a degree in business management; 'the boy', Vikas Gupta, was twenty-seven and came from a 'status family', the father being a successful manufacturer of textiles.

23

'Tulsi and Vikas saw one another at a wedding, went on a date to see a movie, after which Gupta's parents approached the Bhatts and suggested the two tie the knot. Naturally before he was prepared to give the final go-ahead, Bhatt wanted to take the sensible precaution of having his prospective son-in-law vetted,' explained Puri.

Bhatt signed up for the full five-star service and Puri set his team to work, turning over every aspect of Vikas Gupta's life and looking into his family's affairs as well.

'Our investigation was thorough in every which way,' Puri went on to explain. 'We set a honey trap for the boy using one of my operatives and he passed the test. The investigation turned up nothing else incriminating. We gave Gupta a clean slate. Moreover, Bhatt signed the standard contract, which as you're very much aware includes an indemnity clause.'

'Naturally I will argue that the claim is baseless in the event we're required to submit our arguments,' said Balbir.

Puri gathered up his things and the bag of cash. 'Meantime, I'll do my best to persuade him to drop the case and settle things somehow.'

The lawyer looked concerned. 'You plan to meet with Bhatt?'

'He called me two hours back summoning me to his place for a meeting at six o'clock sharp.'

'Not with his lawyer present, I trust?'

Puri assured Balbir that if there was even a 'sniff' of another lawyer he would bow out of the meeting.

'Perhaps he's bluffing, filing the case to soften you up, et cetera,' suggested Balbir.

'Let us hope. God knows my lawyer bills are high enough as it is,' said Puri, sucking in his paunch as he shuffled sideways out of the office.

Three

'He's torturing me, Mr Puri! Every night. There's no stopping him. I've tried everything!'

Tulsi Bhatt was sitting at a long, shiny mahogany table in her family's dining room, flanked by her parents. Her eyeliner was smudged with tears, compounding the image of misery.

Puri, who sat opposite her, made the mistake of saying, 'Come, my dear, you've been married all of two months, only. Surely it is too soon for the ringing of alarm bells.'

Tulsi gave a start, mid-sob. 'I should just put up and shut up, is that what you're suggesting?' She dabbed the end of her crimson nose with a wad of damp tissues. 'Be the dutiful wife? Pretend there isn't a problem? You realize that I haven't slept in weeks?'

'Where marriage is concerned, in early days . . . often there are creases to be ironed out, we can say,' said Puri.

'Creases? *Creases?*' Tulsi shot her father a look of exhausted exasperation.

In turn, Ram Bhatt glared at the detective across

the table. He had a bloated face that made him appear deeply unhappy at the best of times.

'I hold you responsible for this mess, Mr Puri,' he said, jabbing a finger in the detective's direction. 'You told us everything was *bilkul theek*. Vikas Gupta is of sound character – guaranteed, pukka, no issues.'

'Sir, with respect, our enquiry discovered nothing to suggest the boy was an unsuitable match for your daughter,' Puri stated calmly. He referred to the file and read from the summary: 'No prior marriage. No criminal record. No drugs. No gambling. No debt. No smoking, use of drugs or alcohol and all. Close family relations. Cohabits with parents and grandmother. Foreign returned – attended a prestigious US college. Hobbies include cricket, driving around a Royal Enfield, watching movies. One former girlfriend, but that is all.'

'Except that is not all,' interrupted the father. 'Your investigation overlooked his snoring! How, I can't imagine. The boy could wake the dead! Never in all my years have I heard anything like it. He grunts, wheezes, snorts, makes gargling noises. At times it sounds like there's a chainsaw being used in the room! Had you brought this *defect* to our attention – had we *known* – then we would *not* have agreed to the marriage. Thanks to you, I have flushed eighty lakh down the toilet on the wedding and now my daughter is damaged goods.'

Tulsi gave a loud wail and blubbered, 'I. Am. *Not. Damaged. Goods*. Papa!'

'Who is going to marry you now? Ha? Answer me that!'

Tulsi's mother, who Puri judged to be a kind, sympathetic woman but more or less voiceless when her husband was present, put an arm around Tulsi's shoulder, whispered something comforting in her ear, and chaperoned her out of the room.

'Sir, kindly explain one thing,' said Puri once the door had been closed, 'what has been done to alleviate Gupta's snoring?'

'*Everything*, Mr Puri!' Bhatt sighed. 'Ayurvedic remedies, throat sprays, nasal strips, sleeping tablet, chin straps, laser treatment. He has tried gargling with garlic, tried tongue exercises, slept upside down on some contraption. There's not an expert or hypnotist in town he hasn't consulted with. They have tested for allergy, deformity in the nose, childhood trauma, recommended various mattresses, pillows . . . Nothing has worked.'

'He's tried a little warm ghee before bedtime?' suggested Puri.

'Yes, Mr Puri, I believe he has tried *a little warm ghee*,' Bhatt said impatiently.

Puri ignored his sarcastic tone and asked, 'You've heard him at night, sir – yourself?'

'Yes, yes, Tulsi has videoed him.'

'She's not exaggerating somewhat?'

'Once Vikas gets going, the lamp on the side table rattles and shakes as if there's an earthquake. One expert monitored his snoring during the night and said he had never recorded such levels. They were off the scale. No one could sleep through it. So, no, she is not *exaggerating somewhat*.'

'What does Vikas have to say about it all?' asked Puri.

'He claims he was never aware that he snored and his family is adamant he didn't have the problem – that it only started after marriage. But I don't trust them. Either they're lying or they're up to something.'

Before elaborating, Bhatt went over to the door, opened it a crack to check that no one was listening on the other side and came and sat down next to Puri.

'I suspect that this might be a ruse on the family's part to wreck the marriage,' he confided, keeping his voice down.

The thought had occurred to the detective as well, but he had dismissed it already as far-fetched. 'Sir, why they would go to so much of trouble?' he asked.

'The dowry for one. It was not an insignificant amount.'

The paying of a dowry by the daughter's parents to the son's remained a common practice despite being illegal in India, hence Ram Bhatt's furtive tone. In the event of Tulsi leaving her husband, the sum (generally paid in cash and jewellery, though it was not uncommon among the wealthiest these days to include the odd BMW) would be forfeited.

'The Guptas are not short of a few crore,' pointed out Puri.

'Perhaps they're facing difficulties we're unaware of. Or perhaps it is the case that Vikas has had a change of heart after consummating the marriage. He gave Tulsi a test run for the first few nights but didn't like the ride. Either that or he has taken a fancy to another model – one with higher horse-power or better suspension maybe.'

Puri was slightly thrown by all the motoring metaphors and frowned as Bhatt went on.

'The bottom line is that Vikas might be faking all the snoring somehow, to drive away my Tulsi,' he said. 'I leave it up to you to find out. You're the private investigator. Report back to me in a week.'

'Sir, with respect, if Gupta and his family are attempting to annul the marriage I can hardly be held to account.'

'That is where you are wrong, Mr Puri. As I intimated previously, I hold you fully responsible for this mess. Get to the bottom of it or, rest assured, I will hound you through the courts till your dying day. That is all.'

Puri was shown out. As he made his way to the front door, he could still hear Tulsi's crying coming from upstairs.

Handbrake took the expressway from Delhi South to Gurgaon[8] where Puri had built a house among mustard fields in the Nineties and now found himself surrounded by a burgeoning satellite city of skyscrapers and malls, towering housing blocks and elevated Metro lines carried on great concrete plinths.

At a few minutes to seven, he stepped in through the front door of his house to find the hallway filled with a heady concoction of pungent

[8] Gurgaon was officially renamed Gurugram in 2016.

aromas. He slipped off his shoes and put on his *chappals* as his finely tuned nose went to work trying to identify the various components: roasting cumin was one; he could make out the distinct tang of *hing*, which suggested that there was *moong daal* on the boil; and strongest of all was the unmistakable smell of fresh roti.

The effect was intoxicating and, like a lovesick teenager, he made his way slavishly to the kitchen. There he found his wife standing at the stove cooking a roti over a naked flame. The heat had caused the unleavened bread to inflate like a puffer fish. With both sides nicely browned, she placed the finished product on the marble counter to her right where she dabbed a little ghee on to one side. All the while she was humming an oldie to herself: '*Yeh shaam ki tanhaiyan . . . aise mein tera ghum . . .*'

'Good evening, my dear,' Puri announced himself.

'All well? *Khanna* is almost ready, you must be hungry.'

Rumpi had started on another roti and shot him the briefest of smiles. 'What's that, Chubby?' she asked, spotting the plastic bag, which he'd put down on the kitchen table.

'An outstanding debt got settled today. Why it should be so, I cannot say. Something of a mystery, in fact.'

'I see,' said Rumpi in a tone that suggested that she wasn't the least bit interested in the details. 'Well, don't leave it there. You know how nervous I get when there's money in the house. Go put it in the safe.'

'Yes, my dear, I was about to do just that, actually. Where is everyone?' By everyone he meant the two ladies who worked for them, and Sweetu, the houseboy.

'Sweetu has been driving me absolutely potty – going on about some chit fund scheme. I couldn't listen to another minute of it. I packed them off to see a movie.'

'*Achcha*,' replied Puri as he made his way over to the stove. 'So it would seem you've found a way to get me all alone, is it?' He placed his hands gently on her waist. 'I trust your intentions are honourable?'

'Quite honourable, Chubby, I can assure you,' she admonished him, coyly.

He planted a kiss on her neck just below one ear, savouring the smell of mustard oil in her hair.

'Chubby, please, you want me to burn the *jeera*? Stop trying to be the Casanova and go and freshen up.'

Puri made his way upstairs where he put the cash in the safe before washing his face and tending to his moustache, which had gone a little droopy. He splashed on a little of his favourite Sexy Men aftershave and changed into a freshly pressed kurta *pyjama*. It occurred to him that Rumpi was deliberately buttering him up and would, by the end of the evening, ask him to get out his chequebook or try to talk him into taking a holiday. She had got rid of all the staff for the night and cooked some of his favourite dishes, after all. The final clue would be if she had cooked *kheer*, his favourite dessert. But it didn't bother him, a bit of cat and mouse with Rumpi was always good fun, and he returned to the kitchen with his stomach growling in anticipation.

Rumpi ate little meat these days and thus the meal was pure vegetarian – moong daal as he had already surmised, smoky *bainghan bharta*, which went perfectly with a little of his wife's tangy cauliflower pickle, a few rotis and, last but not least, one of his own green chillies, raw. The talk was all of family and neighbours – Rumpi's mother had undergone a hip-replacement operation a couple of weeks ago and taken a short walk this morning; their eldest daughter had called to say that their grandchild, Aarav, had a cold; Mr Jadhav, the nosy neighbour, had circulated another of his community 'newsletters' in which he railed against 'undesirable elements' playing outside his house: namely the children of casual labourers living on nearby construction sites. As for Rumpi, she had spent much of the morning volunteering with SayTrees and had helped plant a half-a-dozen Neem saplings.

Predictably, Mummy had also called, around thirty minutes after Puri left her at the office.

'Sounded quite upset, I must say,' said Rumpi.

'Mummy-ji was accorded a most warm welcome, I can assure you,' said Puri, sounding defensive. 'Then, and not for first time by any and all means, she crossed the line, started going on about some woman who claims to be the reincarnation of a missing woman. I've enough on my plate just now without another goose chase of the wild variety. Thus I wished her good day and went on my way.'

Rumpi stared at him in silence, her eyebrows slightly elevated – the knowing look that communicated the futility of not being totally straight with her.

'OK, fine, I walked out and left her in the office,' admitted Puri.

This prompted Rumpi to remind him of the wisdom of not allowing his mother to get to him: 'She's only trying to help. You never know, she might be on to something.'

He gave a snort.

'I was just reading the other day about a girl born to parents in Himachal who was able to describe every detail from her previous life – her toys, village, everything. When she was finally reunited with her parents from her previous life, she recognized them instantly. Knew their names. Besides, it's not as if Mummy's always so wide off the mark. She did get hold of your wallet after you were pickpocketed.'

Puri bristled at the mention of this incident.[9] 'My dear, I was hot on the trail, I can assure you. It was a question of time, only, before I got hold of that charlie. I was involved with another investigation – a most complex one during which I faced some considerable danger to life and limb and all.'

'Chubby,' Rumpi said gently, reaching out and placing her hand on his. 'What's the harm? Mummy won't be around forever. She's getting

---

[9] See *The Case of the Love Commandos.*

quite frail, in case you haven't noticed. It means so much to her to have your support. Try to see it from her point of view. She wants her son's help. Were her husband still alive perhaps it would be different.'

Puri brooded while Rumpi cleared the table and then suggested he go into the lounge.

He had just sat down on the couch when his phone rang. It was Balbir.

'You've seen the news?' he asked. His voice was heavy with concern.

'What news, exactly?'

'Switch on the TV right away.'

Puri turned on Action News!

The screen flashed with bright graphics, icons and slogans. *Breaking News* burst from the middle of the screen like the title of a Hollywood superhero movie, accompanied by a *whoosh* sound.

Fighting Corruption was the banner across the top of the screen.

At the bottom a tickertape message read, *Fake currency menace . . . Government fighting against black money.*

The prime minister was speaking – standing at a podium with the Indian tricolour behind him. An address to the nation, it appeared.

Puri turned up the volume. He listened to the PM for a minute or so – he was speaking in Hindi – before asking Balbir what it was all about.

'As of midnight, all five-hundred- and one-thousand-rupee notes will no longer be legal tender,' he said.

'Come again?'

'The government is cancelling the five-hundred-and one-thousand-rupee notes, and in the coming days it will be making new five-hundred and two-thousand notes available,' explained Balbir. 'After midnight you won't be able to spend the old ones. There will be some exemptions from the sounds of things – for seventy-two hours you'll be able to buy medicine, tickets on government buses, pay utility bills, that sort of thing. But beyond that any of the obsolete cash will have to be deposited with the bank and exchanged for the new tender. But if you deposit two and a half lakh or above, you'll come under investigation. The PM says the aim is to flush out black money and what he's calling the 'fake currency menace'. It's a brave move if you ask me, though one that will cause some disruption to all our lives. I myself am sitting on several lakhs et cetera.'

Rumpi entered the room, bearing a bowl of kheer on a tray.

Puri was staring at the TV, trying to follow what was being said.

'Something wrong?' she asked.

'Bloody rascal,' said Puri.

'Pardon?'

'That Puran Chandra. He got a tip-off from some insider. That is the only explanation for him suddenly paying up in this way. There's been leakage.'

'I'm not following, Chubby.'

'Basically, my dear, it would seem that I've been given the shaft.'

Rumpi offered him the tray. 'Here. I made kheer,' she said, with a defeated sigh.

Four

The figure emerging from the mist looked like a warrior monk with a shaved head and a black, flowing ponytail. He was wearing a simple dhoti. His chest was half bare. Three white wavy lines marked his forehead. His impenetrable eyes and an inscrutable countenance denoted an individual of long experience and deep wisdom. Though advanced in years and carrying a staff, his every step conveyed vitality and purpose.

Puri was eating a chicken frankie, a messy affair. He hid it behind his back, suddenly ashamed of himself. With his other hand, he tried to wipe away the green chutney around his mouth. The napkin had a smooth sheen, the type that seem designed not to absorb. Much to his frustration, Puri found himself in a less than presentable state as he bowed before the master.

'Follow me,' instructed Chanakya, Puri's guru, for it was he.

Chanakya, India's Machiavelli, led the way along the base of the battlements of Pataliputra, the ancient capital of the Maurya Empire. Soon, they entered a thick jungle. It was lush and green and filled with animal calls. Spears of light pierced the gloom. Puri began to notice, however, that this was no ordinary jungle. The leaves were in fact one-thousand-rupee notes.

Looking up, he watched bank tellers swinging from creepers. The snakes slithering along the branches all had the same human face – Puran Chandra's.

Presently, Chanakya led him into a small clearing. In the middle stood an angel with the blanched white face of a young woman. Its head was turned down to the earth with closed eyes in a pose that denoted despair. Its wings were unfurled, arching over its back, each feather aglow with celestial light.

Puri approached, hesitantly, shielding his eyes, wishing he had brought his aviator sunglasses.

The angel raised its head and its eyes opened. They were like black bottomless wells, terrible to behold. Puri felt rooted to the spot, almost overcome by a rush of wonderment and terror.

The angel lifted one arm and, with an exaggerated motion, pointed with a long, slim finger down at the earth.

Puri found that there was blood bubbling up out of the ground as if from a spring at his feet.

Horrified, he began to back away, seeking an explanation from Chanakya, but his guru had vanished.

He started to run back through the jungle, which was now ablaze.

Puran Chandra snakes darted through the undergrowth, trying to escape the smoke and flames.

Puri fled, too, running faster and faster. He felt like his heart was going to burst. And then he tripped over a branch and let go of his chicken frankie.

He watched it fly through the air in slow motion, trying desperately to reach for it.
'Nooooo!'

Puri woke late, feeling disorientated and out of sorts, and not just because of the nature of the dream, which had been disturbing on all levels.

After the prime minister's unprecedented announcement, he'd realized that Puran Chandra's seven lakhs was not the only cash he was saddled with. Rumpi, it turned out, had won three lakhs at her kitty party on Saturday. The Puris, who did not use debit or credit cards owing to an inherent distrust of banks (and for professional reasons, Puri not wishing to give anyone the opportunity to track his transactions or whereabouts) had various other sundry cash at home: the monthly allowance for the running of the house; some 90,000 that Rumpi had put aside in order to get the house painted next Diwali; the odd few thousands squirrelled away for a new pair of shoes. Add to that the float of five lakh that Puri kept in the safe at the office, and he was looking at a grand total of some seventeen lakh, all in the now obsolete five-hundred- and one-thousand-rupee notes.

Technically, there was nothing stopping Puri taking all the cash and depositing it in his bank account. Thereafter, if the government was to be believed, he would be able to withdraw the new five-hundred- and two-thousand-rupee notes. But Puri feared that if he were to make such a large deposit, he would trigger an investigation into his financial affairs. The fact that he had nothing to hide and had done nothing illegal would make not the slightest bit of difference. The income tax inspectors were a corrupt bunch and they were bound to seize upon such a large deposit as proof of nefarious activity. The threat of a hefty fine and an intrusive audit would follow. And the only way to make it go away would be to supplement the inspectors' meagre state salaries. In the event that he refused – which Puri would do so unhesitatingly – his case would drag on for years. More lawyers' fees, more paperwork and more court appearances, in other words. They might even bring criminal charges against him for money laundering – *they* being his enemies in the establishment, including several high-ranking bureaucrats who could make his life very difficult indeed.

'In such circumstances, my hard-earned reputation, which is second to none, would go for a toss,' Puri had told Rumpi last night as he'd made a number of phone calls, trying to find ways to 'launder' the cash without breaking the law.

Buying gold was the quickest, easiest option. But he'd been unable to reach the one gold broker he trusted to make a transaction over the phone before the midnight cut-off.

It was not until two o'clock that the broker finally returned his messages. After apologizing and describing how his place of business had been stormed by frantic customers bearing duffel bags, suitcases, and pillow cases stuffed full of cash, he offered to sell Puri the gold he needed and to backdate the transaction. But the detective turned him down flat.

'Law is law,' he said.

Puri's principles also disallowed Rumpi's suggestion of appealing to his childhood friend, Rinku, for help. The old rascal would take care of the problem courtesy of the *hawala* network or some other illegal means, and Puri would have no truck with such activity.

There was nothing stopping Puri from paying the household staff six months of their salaries in advance and asking them to deposit the cash in their own bank accounts, however. Together with the two and a half lakh he could deposit in his personal account and another two and a half he could place in his business account without risking scrutiny, this would account for around eight lakh. Of the remaining nine lakh, he might be able to pay some to his office staff. But he had no idea what he was going to do with the balance. Perhaps his senior operative, Baldev, aka Tubelight,[10] would have some suggestions?

Time spent attending to his prize chilli plants on the roof and taking a refreshing bucket bath ensured that, by the time he reached the kitchen, Puri was beginning to feel more himself again. Rumpi had made him a couple of *aloo parathas*, which he devoured hungrily between gulps of strong, sugary chai, while voicing his views on the prime minister's bold initiative.

'Personally I admire what all he's trying to achieve – takes balls,' said Puri. 'God only knows

[10] Puri uses nicknames for all his operatives. Tubelight is so called because he's a heavy sleeper and takes a while to flicker into life in the morning.

action is required, corruption having infected every part of our society. Some economists are saying the shadow economy now accounts for fifty per cent of the entire economy as a whole.'

'Yes, Chubby,' said Rumpi as she brought him some garlic pickle.

'Question is, will the sharks escape the net?' Puri continued. 'The fact that Puran Chandra got a tip-off in advance is not a good sign. Only time will tell, my dear.'

'I'm sure you're right.'

Puri cleared his plate and hurried to the door, eager to be off, calling over his shoulder that he would be back as early as he could manage.

It was only after the Ambassador had pulled out of the gate that he remembered Rumpi's meal last night and the kheer. Whatever she wanted to discuss with him would just have to wait, he decided. She would understand given the circumstances, which were hardly of his making, after all. In a couple of days things would get back to normal and then he would make some time for her.

Finding the traffic on the expressway refreshingly light – many people had taken the day off work to sort out their cash woes it seemed – Puri asked Handbrake to turn on the radio. Unsurprisingly, the airwaves were jammed with debate on the PM's 'demonetization' initiative or 'notebandi' as it was being referred to colloquially. The media was on the whole applauding the prime minister who had 'stunned the nation' with a 'bold' step. One commentator described the shock move as a 'surgical strike' against money hoarders and terrorists who had 'flooded India' with fake notes. Scrapping eighty-five per cent of the country's currency overnight would cripple the shadow economy and unmask 'lakhs of tax dodgers', commented one expert. 'The black buck stops here,' said another.

But there was the odd voice of dissent. Most of the country's illegally generated revenue was not held in cash, but rather in *benami* properties, bullion and jewellery, one leading economist pointed out. The government's policy was ill considered, in his view, and would have little impact on those determined to hide their assets. The average Indian citizen, however, was going to suffer in the coming days and weeks. 'India is a cash economy with eighty-five per cent of the total population working in the unofficial sector,' said one university professor. 'This demonetization gambit will affect the *aam admi* needing to get his pregnant wife to hospital by car or the mother trying to feed her children and suddenly finding that her money is not accepted at the milk stand,' she predicted. 'Those with the means and with access to credit and the banking system will ride out the chaos, while, as ever, the vast majority will suffer hardships.'

Handbrake was a case in point. He possessed only a couple of hundred rupees in small denominations, he said; later that day, he needed to buy his son, who suffered from thalassemia, his medication.

Puri assured him that he would help and not to worry. But when he checked his wallet he found that he only had two one-hundred-rupee notes and a few grubby tens. He had brought with him Puran Chandra's seven lakh to put in the office safe, and now he checked the bundles in vain for any one-hundred-rupee notes among the five-hundreds and thousands.

In doing so he was reminded of his dream – of the strange money trees and the cash catching fire – and he found himself pondering what it meant.

Somehow – he couldn't tell why – he had a strong feeling that the dream was connected with the Riya Kaur case and that Chanakya was urging him to get involved. It wouldn't be the first time his guru had turned up in one of his dreams and pointed him in the right direction.

Another thought niggled at him as well: Mummy might just have stumbled on to something and – worse – in spite of her unorthodox, haphazard methods, she might just stumble upon a concrete lead.

It was primarily this fear – though admittedly Rumpi's point that Mummy deserved and needed his help played a factor as well – that caused him to call her around fifteen minutes later (that is after doing some deep breathing exercises first).

'Mummy-ji? Good morning, Chubby this side,' he said. 'Yes, yes, all's well. You've seen the news? You're facing any difficulty?'

Mummy had a stash of one-hundred-rupee notes at home, she assured him. She always kept such a reserve, having lived through the government demonetization of 1978. If he needed some small denomination notes she would be sure to bring him some.

Puri had to admit that he had been caught 'somewhat short'.

'A couple of hundred bucks would undoubtedly come in handy. Most kind of you,' he found himself saying. 'Now regarding our discussion yesterday—'

'Best thing is for you to meet Saanvi for yourself and make up your own mind about her,' interrupted Mummy.

'Meet her in person?' asked Puri, feeling wrongfooted.

'How else, Chubby? Now you listen, na. I've arranged for her to come to Café Coffee Day in SDA[11] Market at two o'clock.'

'So soon?' he asked.

It was now approaching ten o'clock so the meeting was still four hours away, Mummy pointed out.

'Very well, Mummy-ji,' Puri conceded, unable to think of a viable excuse for not taking the meeting.

'And you'll bring the Riya Kaur file?'

'I'll endeavour to get hold of it this morning, only, but no promises, ha. A favour will have to be called in.'

Puri was about to hang up, but his mother insisted on another moment of his time. Had he spoken to his brother, Bhuppi?

'Two, three days back? Why exactly?'

He listened for a moment and gave a low whistle. 'By God. I'll call him directly.'

Puri ended the call and dialled his elder brother.

[11] Safdarjung Development Area in south Delhi.

He was aware that Bhuppi had sold one of his investment properties recently and that 60 per cent of the total had been paid to him in 'black'. What he didn't know was that the money, close to one crore, was still 'lying idle' at home – not under the mattress exactly but stuffed inside it.

To make matters worse – at least from Puri's perspective – Bhuppi had called Rinku and asked for help.

'Bugger says he'll turn it into white but will be requiring forty per cent commission! What the hell? You'll talk to him, Chubby? Tell him I'll require a better rate for old time's sake?'

'That one is a rocky road. You know the *funda*,' breathed Puri.

'Just ask him, *yaar*. He can't refuse you.'

'Bhuppi, when you'll learn? In life there's always a price to pay.'

'Sure, Chubby, but it is negotiable.'

Puri reached the office and, after putting Puran Chandra's cash in the safe and counting the petty cash, which amounted to a few thousand rupees, most of it unfortunately in five-hundreds, he asked Elizabeth Rani to instruct all his staff – office and field – to be at the office at four o'clock.

He called Facecream, his Nepali operative, personally, however, and explained that he also wished to speak with her about taking on the Vikas Gupta snoring investigation.

Finally, he considered how best to get hold of the Riya Kaur file.

Puri was completely persona non grata at Delhi Police Headquarters these days – he had shown up the charlie who posed as the head of the force on one too many occasions – and though he liked to think that, if he so chose, he could sneak into the records office in disguise, the hard truth was that there were too many officers milling around who might see through his get-up. This would undoubtedly lead to his arrest – at which point the chief would take considerable delight in locking him up and misplacing the key. Calling on his father's ex-partner, Bobby, was not an option, either, as he was retired and would have to go through official channels to come by the file, a process that would take days, perhaps weeks.

There seemed nothing for it, therefore, but to call upon his inside man, Inspector Jagat Prakash Singh, with whom he had an understanding – a 'mutual arrangement of the back-scratching variety', as Puri put it.

Their arrangement worked as follows: Puri secretly consulted on some of Singh's tougher cases. And, when the circumstances proved necessary – i.e. when the official force was required to make a case stick or when it seemed best to keep Most Private Investigators out of the headlines – Puri invited the inspector to make arrests at the conclusion of one of his own cases and allowed him to take credit for his work. For this, Singh passed him information, got the odd test carried out in the police laboratory or ran some fingerprints through the system. He was also kind enough to 'gift' Puri the odd bottle of Royal Challenge whisky.

Needless to say, the two were careful never to

be seen together. Which was why, when he called Inspector Singh and explained that he needed one of his father's old case files 'at short notice', Puri suggested they meet at 'their safe house' – so called not because it was a safe house used for stowing witnesses or for the purposes of surveillance, but because it was a safe environment in which the two of them could do business and talk freely.

A perfectly normal residence with a little courtyard in front lined with potted marigold plants, it was the home of Singh's maternal uncle. A widower who lived alone, having refused to move to Canada to join his two sons owing to the freezing weather and lack of edible food, Uncle-ji spent most of his time sitting in his front room watching cricket with the volume up high.

Inspector Singh was a frequent visitor so the neighbours found nothing untoward about the uniformed officer pulling up in his official car. Better still, Puri was able to enter the house from the narrow *galli* that ran behind it. And with Bengali Market close, Puri never arrived empty-handed.

On this occasion – by now it was twelve thirty – he came bearing cups of chai and a box of *jalebies*.

'Inspector-sahib! *Kiddan?*' greeted Puri.

Inspector Singh was a thickset man, over six feet tall, with a large jet-black beard. Despite his size, he always ate surprisingly sparingly, taking only a small, curly section of the sticky, deep-fried sweet and sipping his chai like a child savouring a hot chocolate. His abstemiousness tempered Puri's usual intemperate inclination, yet inevitably, as the two men caught up with one another's news, the takeaway box was emptied.

Given the risk of leaving incriminating, syrupy fingerprints on the Riya Kaur file and the limitation of licking off the residue, Puri had to give his hands a thorough wash with warm water and soap in the kitchen sink before taking possession of it.

Not that there was much to be found between the ends of the worn, dog-eared binder.

The First Information Report (FIR)[12] was pinned inside along with a couple of search warrants, and several forms pertaining to evidence that had been catalogued and stored.

The investigating officer's reports, notes, transcripts of interviews with witnesses and the victim's nearest and dearest – everything vital pertaining to the investigation, in other words – were missing.

'There *has* been trouble with termites in the building,' said Singh by way of an explanation, though he sounded unconvinced himself.

'Termites, is it?' asked Puri, almost mockingly. 'Come now, Inspector, let us not beat around any bushes: we both know this was the work of rats.'

Singh said with weariness, 'There are quite a few to be found scurrying around the building these days.'

'All the senior ones have access to the archive, I take it?'

---

[12] A written document prepared by the police when they receive information about the commission of a cognisable offence. Essentially a complaint of an alleged crime.

'Any investigating officer can walk straight in. Technically, we're supposed to fill in a request form—'

'But few bother. And clearly smuggling a file out of the building undetected does not pose too much of a difficulty as you have proved today, only.'

Puri inspected the spine; it was a good inch-and-a-half wide and showed all the signs of having been wrapped around a thick wad of documents.

'Why not dispose of the file altogether?' he mused.

'Destroying it entirely would raise suspicion in the event of the case being reopened, sir. This way it can be put down to the usual "storage malfunction".'

Puri finished his chai, wishing there was more.

Inspector Singh shifted in his chair and frowned.

'You're wondering what reason someone would have for looting the file, so to speak?' said Puri.

'At the very least it would seem that someone has something to hide. Did your father form a theory as to what happened to the woman?'

'It was not a case Papa-ji spoke of to me in great detail, Inspector. 1984 haunted him – of that much I am certain. The things he saw with his own eyes during those terrible, dark days, I shudder to imagine. All I know are the basics: that Riya Kaur's father came to him personally and begged him to locate his daughter, dead or alive, and that Papa-ji suspected foul play on the part of the husband, Mantosh Singh.'

Puri reached for the file and flicked through

the few remaining pages again with a prolonged frown.

'Let us hope Bobby, my father's ex-partner, can recall all the details of the case,' he said. 'I seem to recall Papa-ji telling me that what evidence was found – some blood in the *dickie* of the husband's car – raised the possibility that Mantosh Singh murdered his wife *before* the riots started on 31 October.'

'I take it the body was never recovered?' said Inspector Singh.

'Correct – and Riya's father died a few years later a broken man.'

They both fell silent and the sound of excited cricket commentary over the roar of a crowd spilled suddenly into the room.

Inspector Singh stared down into his chai. 'Dozens of bodies went unidentified during the rioting,' he said. 'Many were dumped in the Yamuna.'

Puri had not been in Delhi during the riots[13] but knew that the inspector had lost family in 1984. Few Sikh families in the capital had escaped unscathed.

'Hard to imagine such organized violence breaking out in Delhi today. Seems like a lifetime ago,' Puri said.

'It was hard to imagine such a thing in those days, also, sir,' said Inspector Singh.

He heaved his great frame off his chair, crumpled his cup and dropped it in the dustbin. The

---

[13] He'd been serving in Military Intelligence at the time elsewhere in India.

jalebi box followed. Then he filled a couple of glasses of water from a Bisleri bottle, placed one before Puri and drained the other.

'Regarding Mantosh Singh – you'd like me to do some digging, find out what I can?'

'Any assistance would be much appreciated, Inspector-sahib. Meanwhile I'll endeavour to find out whether any of Riya Kaur's relatives are alive and able to help with any and all information.'

Puri picked up the file, promising to get it back to the inspector by early afternoon.

Inspector Singh saw him to the back door. 'Sir, one thing: why the sudden interest?' he asked. 'You have a new lead, perhaps?'

Puri hesitated. He could hardly tell the truth about the reincarnated witness. Nor about his dream.

'Actually, Inspector-sahib, I'm looking over the case as per my mother's request,' he confessed. 'In old age she has become somewhat obsessed with Papa-ji's cold cases.'

Inspector Singh's face lit up at the mention of Puri's mother. 'Ah, well, she has a nose for these things,' he said.

Puri's eyebrows rose like hackles and he demanded to know how the inspector knew his mother.

'I thought you knew, sir. It was she who suggested I approach you that first time – regarding the Johar Kidnapping case.'

Puri could barely disguise his surprise. 'But how did you two come into contact in the first place?' he asked.

'I served as a junior detective for three years

in Punjabi Bagh and Mrs Puri became my number-one local source for information,' explained Inspector Singh. 'No one could sneeze in west Delhi without her coming to know. Often she brought crimes to my attention. Thanks to Mrs Puri, I was able to book one bank robber and a murderer. But I didn't realize that the *two* of you collaborated,' said Inspector Singh, grinning through his beard.

'From time to time it becomes necessary,' said Puri carefully.

'Must make quite a team.'

'We're not exactly a team, Inspector-sahib. I remain very much in charge. Though I believe strongly in the institution of family, I'm a professional after all and she . . . well, when all is said and done, she is a mother, first and in life. We all bear certain responsibilities.'

'Absolutely, sir, understood,' said Inspector Singh, with a faintly bemused expression.

Five

Puri had to get out of the car across from SDA Main Market and dodge a maelstrom of vehicles swarming along the road like blood cells and viruses locked in battle. Beyond the main gate lay a congested car park and a few concrete blocks arranged around a small, pedestrianized plaza. The detective had always known the market as a convenient place to purchase essential items such as milk and vegetables, pots and pans, and his favourite tipple, Royal Challenge. The Singh Tyre House and the Jain Departmental Store[14] had been there for as long as he could remember. Both were busy with labourers lugging stock in and out, voices raised as inventories and orders were checked and loaded into the backs of trucks. Stacks of dusty merchandise and trampled cardboard boxes occupied the pavements in front of these establishments; the terrain beyond was scattered with plastic chai cups and *beedi* and cigarette butts.

The local authority, which shared the same indifference to aesthetics, had ensured that the fabric of the place was in a constant state of disrepair. Blight infested the walls. Gordian knots of wires and cables hung from the sides of buildings. A few trees and shrubs planted in an enclosure in the central plaza looked like singed survivors of Hiroshima.

Yet deeper within the market, trendy cafes, restaurants and bars had supplanted many of the old shops. Their bright, vivid facades, which held the promise of frothy Italian coffees, cheese-stuffed pizza crusts and Belgian beer on draught, looked almost miraculous, as if transformed by pixie dust.

Puri found the contrast between the old, creaking India and the slick consumerism of the new surreal. The clientele, mostly students at the Indian Institute of Technology[15] nearby, were a

---

[14] Indian English for 'a department store', though Jain Departmental Store sells only beer, wine and spirits.

[15] India's answer to MIT.

puzzling spectacle for him as well. Though they ranked among the brightest minds in the world and were destined to go on to design micro-chips and spacecraft, the young men were dressed in tatty T-shirts and ripped jeans that appeared on the verge of dropping down around their owners' ankles. He frowned at the easy mixing of girls and boys away from home. And when he passed through the market's small central plaza and spotted a gang gathered around a *momo* stand – headphones draped around their necks, mobile phones constantly at the ready, a couple of the boys smoking in the company of females – he shuddered to think that his youngest daughter might get involved with such types. Surely the least he could expect from a future son-in-law would be for him to tuck in his shirt.

Puri entered Café Coffee Day – 'A Lot Can Happen Over Coffee!' – equally ill at ease amidst the manufactured corporate world of faux-leather armchairs and sepia prints portraying life in Italy as one long coffee break followed by rides through Rome on Vespas. Still, he knew from past experience that he was expected to join the queue at the counter (and not barge to the front or go to one of the tables and snap his fingers for service) and stand (impatiently) in line.

The young man who served him bore the brunt of Puri's displeasure. 'Hi, saar, how you're feeling today, saar? All good, saar?'

Undaunted by the detective's scowl, he recommended the special.

'Saar, why not try our Revive With Butterfly Pea Flower cold drink?'

Knowing from past experience that the chai was undrinkable and cost ten times the amount he'd pay at a roadside *dhaba*, Puri ignored the barista's entreaty, and ordered a dip tea. He was about to order a chilli cheese toast as well (which the chain had rebranded as a 'Toastizza') when he realized that he only had a single one-hundred-rupee note left in his wallet and that it wouldn't cover the bill.

By the time Mummy arrived a full fifteen minutes late, he was feeling ravenous.

'So many traffic snarls,' she said by way of an excuse. 'Saanvi is on the way. You got the Riya file, is it?'

Puri's revelation that it had been stripped bare was met with grim disappointment.

'Everything looted?' she said, sounding helpless.

He handed her the file, making clear that he needed it back. 'What was it you were hoping to find?' asked Puri.

She ignored him as she looked over what remained of the paperwork. Puri had to press her for an answer again.

'Must have been something specific you were looking for,' he said.

Before he was able to get an answer, however, a woman, who must have been Saanvi, came hurrying into the cafe and over to the table.

Though markedly thin with a gaunt face and nervous, flitting eyes, her dress sense was bright and bold, with feather earrings and rainbow-painted nails. Pink leggings and a pair of black Tomboy boots strung with multicoloured laces flashed beneath an orange kurta. Puri judged her to be from a middle-class family, her accent and diction denoting south Delhi. That she was single was obvious, too. There was the absence of a wedding ring or *sindoor*, and she possessed a patent adolescent quality. In the time it took for Puri to be introduced and to regain his seat, he had formed an impression of a woman who, though in her early thirties, had yet to grow up. This was further evinced by the puerile wonder with which she glanced around the cafe, eyes twinkling at the brightest detail; the jiggling of her leg beneath the table; the manner in which she looked to Mummy-ji, searching for succour when grappling with an answer to a question – even one as straight forward as what she'd like to drink.

It took her several minutes to peruse the menu and make up her mind. Puri then had to borrow a few one-hundred-rupee notes from his mother (which she gave him gladly, though not without again touting her sagacity in having kept a stash for such a rainy day) before enduring another encounter with the same, irksome barista – 'Why not try the Vegan Shake, saar? Very tasty, saar!'

'So, tell me, how all you two came to meet?' he asked brusquely once he returned to the table, his patience beginning to fray.

'Oh, that's easy, Uncle-ji,' smiled Saanvi, though she looked again to Mummy for encouragement before going on. 'It was Maaya who introduced us!'

Puri sent his mother a frown. 'Maaya?'

'The one doing hypnotism.'

'She specializes in taking patients back to their past lives and remembering who they were and what happened to them.' Saanvi beamed.

'It is known as past life regression therapy,' clarified Mummy.

'During my second session, Maaya discovered that I'd been murdered – and suddenly a lot of things made sense,' said Saanvi.

Puri mixed disbelief and incredulousness into a prolonged frown, as he fought off the urge to make his excuses and leave. There was an awkward silence.

'Previously Saanvi was having nightmares – terrible they were,' said Mummy.

'Yes, I used to have the same one over and over again,' said Saanvi, her leg jiggling faster now, her fingers nervously intertwined. 'Should I describe it for you, Uncle-ji?'

Puri's nod was vague encouragement to go on.

'Well, see it started with this man's voice shouting at me, telling me to stop crying. I can't make out his face. I feel lost. I don't know where I am exactly. Then I'm being carried. I try to get away, but I can't. Something's holding me tight. I'm put in this dark place. I'm all on my own, cold. I'm crying and crying. There's this deep, deep sadness. And then there's something over my mouth. It's strong, holding me down. I get this feeling like I'm suffocating. I start gasping for air. My lungs feel like they're going to burst.' She paused. 'That's when I wake up.'

Saanvi's leg settled back into a slower, gentler motion.

'Anyway,' she said with a frivolous giggle, as if suddenly trying to make light of it all, 'one day I got talking with my friend, Sheikha, and she told me about Maaya. See, Sheikha had discovered that she was a Maratha warrior in one of her past lives. It helped explain why she had all this latent aggression. After a few sessions she was like a new person. So I thought I'd give it a try. Low and behold, when Maaya hypnotized me, she discovered that something terrible had *actually* happened to me. She realized my night-mares weren't just dreams, they were things I had experienced – they were *memories* from a past life. So, she started trying to figure out who I was and what had happened. In that way she promised to get the nightmares to stop.'

Puri didn't let on that he'd had dealings with a hypnosis therapist before. The case involved a father accused of sexually abusing his daughter, a crime she alleged after being treated for repressed memories.

The allegations, which Puri proved to be fabri-cations (or rather twisted inventions), had almost destroyed the family.

If this past experience was anything to go by, Maaya was manipulating Saanvi and probably charging a small fortune in the process. But how had Riya Kaur come into the frame? The case was not a famous one. And how the hell had Mummy got caught up in all this? Was she going senile?

In trying to tackle the first question, Puri was initially thwarted by a sudden whoop of joy from Saanvi, prompted by the arrival of her order: a giant Cocoa Fudge Sundae.

With wide, unbelieving eyes, she took a long spoon to the chocolate sauce and ice cream, and gave a long, satisfied, 'Mmmm.'

Puri regarded the delicious-looking concoction with a pang of jealousy, but persevered. Why did Saanvi believe she was Riya Kaur?

'That's another easy one,' said Saanvi, licking chocolate-coated lips. 'When I was hypnotized, Maaya asked me my name and I told her.'

'You told her your full name?'

'Oh yes,' said Saanvi without hesitation. 'I told her I was Riya Kaur.'

'During further questioning, Saanvi said she lived in Rajouri Garden, also,' said Mummy. 'She described the gate to the property where she lived and other such details – the dog barking next door, exact layout of the house and so forth.'

'You had read about the Riya case somehow? Knew some person or other familiar with the events?' asked Puri.

'No, nothing like that, Uncle-ji,' said Saanvi good-naturedly.

'Surely it's possible Maaya planted these details in your memory somehow while you've been under her influence,' suggested Puri.

Saanvi broke into a ripple of laughter. 'No, it's nothing like that, Uncle-ji, believe me. All Maaya has done is helped me remember my past life.'

Puri reflected for a moment. 'If that's the case, then you should have no trouble telling me what happened to Riya and we can clear up the mystery once and for all,' he said matter-of-factly.

'It's not that simple, I'm afraid. Maaya's having to take me through events slowly – with the help

59

of my spirit guides. Another couple of sessions and we should have all the answers.'

'And you, Mummy-ji? How did you come into the picture?' asked Puri.

'Maaya did research and found out that Om Chander Puri was the investigating officer on the case. Turns out her mother is old friends with Smita Jain who plays bridge with Gita Tiwari.'

Puri gave a knowing nod. He should have known: the old Auntie Network again – a back channel of influential ladies in Delhi, better plugged in than Interpol, the CIA and James Bond put together.

'Isn't this wild, Uncle-ji?' said Saanvi with a grin. 'To think that I was murdered in my last life and your father investigated what happened to me – and now here we all are, working to solve the murder together?'

Puri's expression hardened. 'Saanvi, kindly understand one thing: I've not committed to reopening this case. I've agreed to meet you as something of a courtesy. That is all.'

But the honest truth was that Puri was intrigued and not about to leave it there. Where there is smoke there is definitely fire, he reminded himself. Besides, he could not help but feel protective of Saanvi. She was naive and vulnerable, and clearly Maaya, the past life regression therapist, was taking advantage of her.

What, though, of Saanvi's family? How did they fit into all this?

'It's just me and Papa.'

Puri asked about her mother.

'She died – a car accident on the road to Vrindavan.'

He asked if her father had accompanied her during the sessions.

'He thinks it's all hocus-pocus. Sheikha came with me the first time. And Mummy-ji has sat in on the last two.'

A frown swooped on to Puri's brow. 'You went?' he asked his mother.

'I wished to see Saanvi under hypnosis for myself, na,' was her explanation.

Puri wondered if she had tried this regression hypnosis as well. Perhaps Maaya had managed to get some kind of hold over her.

'You know what?' said Saanvi, suddenly enthused. 'You should come, too, Uncle-ji! I've got my next appointment at three o'clock. It's round the corner. I'm sure Maaya would love to meet you. Oh please?'

Puri, caught off guard, took a moment to reply. 'Some work is there, actually,' he said, without being specific.

'Better you return to the office, Chubby, and I go with Saanvi,' said Mummy. 'You and Maaya will not see eye to eye.'

Clearly she didn't want him coming along. And that sealed it.

Mummy suggested they cover the short distance to Maaya's on foot, but Puri preferred to drive and keep his car close by.

It was but a minute's journey down a long, leafy street lined with large villas and modern blocks of flats all with high walls and gates in front with security guards passing the time of day in the sunshine.

They passed a dance school offering *kathak* classes, a playground ebullient with laughter and squeals, and a press *wallah* working at a stand by the side of the road, gliding a big metal iron heated by smoking coals over crumpled cotton shirts.

Soon, they turned into a cul-de-sac – a temple with a soaring white dome dominating the far end.

Maaya's house was about halfway down on the right, a whitewashed villa dating back to the Fifties.

A brass sign on the pillar read, *Maaya Shruti: Past Life and Regression Therapist.*

Saanvi was about to press the doorbell on the gatepost when there came a shout from across the road.

They turned to find a tall, agitated man exiting a car. 'Wait there!' he ordered and started towards them.

'Daddy? Oh my God! What are you doing here?' asked Saanvi with alarm.

'I should ask you the same question. I forbade you from coming here again to see that woman,' he said, approaching fast.

'But—'

'But nothing!' He reached for her arm, but she struggled free, pushing his hand away.

'I'm telling you – you get into the car this instant! I'm taking you home and that's that!' he shouted.

Saanvi stamped her foot. 'You can't do this,

Daddy. You've no right. I can see who I want, when I want.'

'While you are living under my roof, you will do as I say!' He had her by the arm again. 'It is for your own good. I'm trying to protect you. Now get in the car!'

Puri stepped forward and said, 'Sir, I would not wish to come between a father and his daughter—'

'Then don't!' snapped the father. 'This is a family affair! I don't know who you are but stay away from my daughter.'

He turned hard, forbidding eyes on Saanvi. 'I won't tell you again. Come!'

'Daddy, please. I want to stay, to see Maaya, *Didi*. You can't make me leave!' she said, breaking into sobs.

But it was no use. Puri and Mummy were powerless to intervene. They could only stand by and watch as the father marched her to his car and opened the door.

Without a glance back, she climbed on to the back seat and sat crying with her face in her hands.

A moment later, the car pulled away with a violent crunch of tyres.

Six

As Puri and Mummy approached Maaya's door, he was conscious of having already formed a negative impression of the therapist before meeting her. And this made him wary. Prejudicial thinking clouded an investigator's judgement, something his father had drummed into him from an early age. 'An open mind pays off in time,' Puri could hear him saying.

Once shown into the house by the maid and finding himself in a spacious living room furnished like a maharaja's harem with low-set divans and silk cushions, he found adhering to this old adage was going to prove challenging.

Puri could not help but scowl at the garish oil paintings of earth maidens, Om symbols, and third eyes with moonbeams shooting out of them that dominated the walls. The titles of the books on the shelves – *Oracle of Visions*, *The Soul Shift*, *Core Light Healing* – brought some sharp eye-rolls, too. And the piped electronic mantra-chanting fusion music put his teeth on edge.

It almost came as a relief when Maaya came down the stairs to greet them and he found her to be exactly as he had pictured her.

Pretty and petite with a long mane of shiny black hair, she wore a tasteful embroidered cotton kurta, black leggings and brown leather sandals that showed off nails painted glossy maroon.

With a chiffon *dupatta* floating back evenly over her shoulders, she went straight to Mummy and greeted her with both hands held out in front, delicate fingers flashing astrological gemstones.

Even her voice matched Puri's expectation: it was dreamy and affected, like a medium at a séance.

'How awful! That poor, dear child. I do hope

64

she's all right?' Maaya gushed after listening to Mummy's account of what had happened to Saanvi. 'Is there anything to be done?'

'Better we wait and see, na? No doubt she will contact me before long. The dust will need settling first.'

Maaya released Mummy's hands and turned to Puri.

'Now,' she said, eyes flashing with anticipation. 'This is a true honour. The great Vish Puri, here in my house.' She pressed her hands together in a *namaste*. 'I must tell you that I'm a great fan, Mr Puri. I read all about you in *India Today* when they published that big profile a few years ago. Your involvement with the Panchen Lama case[16] was extraordinary. The way you outwitted the Chinese agents. I have rarely felt so proud to be Indian.'

Being especially susceptible to praise, Puri almost succumbed to her charm, before responding formally, 'Yes, well, most kind of you . . . a pleasure to make your acquaintance, also.'

Maaya motioned her guests towards a set of three black bamboo divans caparisoned in Nepali mandala textiles and brightly coloured silk cushions.

A square coffee table in the middle flickered with scented *diyas* beneath a chakra gemstone tree.

'It would seem solving mysteries and detective work runs deep in your family, Mr Puri,' Maaya

---

[16] Maaya is referring to Puri's involvement with the hunt for the child Panchen Lama.

commented. 'Your father was a decorated police officer, I understand. And your mother tells me she has solved several mysteries herself. I must say I find her extremely inspiring. I hope I'm half as sharp and active at her age.' She sent Mummy a winning smile. 'The energy that flows from her – her aura – is positively luminescent. I could bask in it all day.'

'Personally I cannot comment on her aura, but Mummy-ji has always been a motivated person, we can say,' said Puri.

He lowered himself down on to one of the divans, unwittingly crushing a couple of silk cushions beneath his weight.

Maaya continued to gush about the thrill of being involved with a real murder investigation, but soon Puri made it bluntly clear that his time was precious.

'It is my understanding you've been seeing Saanvi for some weeks now,' he said, having decided not to take notes as he would normally do during such an interview, thinking it would send the wrong message – that he regarded Maaya as being credible.

By now she was sitting on her own to the left of him, her slim legs tucked beneath her, feline-like. 'Yes, I believe it has been a month or so,' she said.

'Saanvi described to me having so many night-mares,' he said.

'Not exactly nightmares, Mr Puri. They were memories resurfacing, manifesting themselves as dreams. Like so many people she was unaware that they pertained to her past life. You see, Mr

Puri, we believe that the Universal Energy binds and sustains us all in our present lives, but when our energies – destructive thoughts and emotions like pain and trauma – get stuck in the past, they act as a drain upon the present. It's my job as a practitioner to go to the source event in the earlier life and unravel the experience. In Saanvi's case, I have been able to prove that she was murdered and is still suffering from the trauma of that horrific, violent event.'

Puri bristled. '*Prove*, madam? I fail to understand what proof you've discovered exactly?'

Maaya's full red lips stretched into a smile. 'You're sceptical of my methods, Mr Puri?' she said.

'Madam, where investigation is concerned, cold, hard facts are required. A case cannot be made on gut feeling and wishy-washy thinking. What you're describing is pure fantasy.'

Maaya regarded him silently, her smile replaced fleetingly by one of mild irritation. 'I didn't realize this was to be an interrogation, Mr Puri,' she said. 'I thought perhaps we might be able to pool our talents to find out what happened to Riya Kaur. You might care to know that I've been able to help a number of clients solve crimes and mysteries that occurred in their past lives. I have received a master's in clinical psychology from King's College, London and my PhD from Princeton.'

'Through hypnosis, Maaya provided the location of a family's hidden fortune in jewellery,' piped up Mummy, who was sitting on his right.

This earned her a firm rebuke in the form of

a hand thrust up in her direction – a reminder of her promise on the doorstep not to interrupt him.

Maaya, in turn, offered Puri a mild reprimand of her own. 'I believe your mother is only trying to be helpful, Mr Puri – and what she says is perfectly true. I was able to use past life regression to help a client locate a hoard of jewels. It had lain hidden in the ground for forty years. The grandfather of that particular family buried them prior to being killed during Partition. The case has been well documented. And now I would like to put a question to you, Mr Puri, if you will allow me. Do you believe in reincarnation?'

Puri gave a nod. 'Naturally.'

'Then is it really so hard to believe that we carry with us the memories of past lives?'

'In my experience, memory is a most unreliable faculty,' he said. 'It can be tampered with and affected by external influence. Thus someone watching TV can come to believe that a certain character's experiences are in fact their own. Books can do the same, actually. In Saanvi's case she wants to believe her issues come from a past life, so she is open to suggestion.'

'Perhaps you should watch the video recordings of her sessions,' Maaya suggested gently. 'I'm sure Saanvi would have no objection. I can assure you they show very clearly that there has been no suggestion on my part. Her ability to describe the events in Riya Kaur's life is irrefutable.'

Mummy chimed in again. 'I told you, na. Saanvi described Riya's house, its layout, a tree in the garden that got chopped down years back.'

Puri peered at her with myopic distrust. 'How do you know there was a tree?'

'One of the neighbours told me,' said Mummy with a shrug.

'By God, you've visited the place?' he breathed.

'I went to take a look around. Why not?'

'No doubt you've gone through the newspaper cuttings, also?'

'Mr Puri, I think I can see where you're going with this,' interrupted Maaya. 'Let me assure you that the details in the newspaper reports have only served to confirm Saanvi's memories – not the other way around. I have not tampered with her memory, as you suggest. Also, when all is said and done, Saanvi is a grown woman. Surely she has the right to make her own choices, don't you think?'

'Who all is paying for her sessions? Tell me that. They cannot come cheap,' Puri shot back.

'For my services, I charge rupees three thousand per hour,' replied Maaya. She paused to allow Puri a moment's perceived triumph before torpedoing him. 'But as Saanvi is not employed, I have been treating her free of charge.'

'Is it?' said Puri, uncertainly. 'Well, no doubt she will be back for more.'

'I certainly hope so. Her therapy is not yet complete. A couple more sessions and we will know the truth about what happened to her. In this way, Saanvi will find peace.'

'I'm sure,' said Puri, sounding far from convinced.

He pushed himself up off the divan and stood,

leaving the two cushions looking as if they might never recover.

'Thank you for your time, madam, but I believe I've heard all I need to hear, for now at least. Come, Mummy-ji, let us be on our way,' he said, brusquely.

Maaya led the way to the front door. She opened it and they stepped out into the bright sunshine.

'Thank you for coming, Mr Puri,' she said again, pressing her hands together in a namaste. 'Would you like me to have copies of Saanvi's tapes sent over to you?'

'By all means and I'll try to find the time to take a look,' said Puri with indifference.

'Your office is in Khan Market, I believe – above Bahri Sons.'

'You certainly seem to have done your research, madam. Good day to you.'

Puri knew that if he and Mummy had a debrief right there in the street, he might lose his temper and say things that he would regret, so he suggested they talk later instead and hurried towards his car.

Once safely down the street, the Punjabi expletives came thick and fast – and it was with considerable effort that Handbrake kept his eyes on the road (and a straight face).

He was still ranting about Maaya (surely one of the most manipulative, conniving females he had ever encountered) and Mummy (whom he couldn't believe was being so gullible) when they reached Khan Market.

By now Puri was famished. And though he knew his staff were waiting for him, he headed

70

straight for Khan Chacha and found just enough cash by rummaging through his wallet and pockets for a mutton *kathi roll*, which he ate with his customary extra helpings of tangy green chutney.

In this way, the storm passed, and as he walked the short distance to the office, eating a *kulfi faluda*, he was able to reflect (fairly) dispassionately on his encounter with Maaya.

One thing was clear: she had brainwashed her client. To hell with preconceived ideas, he was sure of it. All those so-called memories had been culled from the newspapers and movies and carefully planted in Saanvi's memory while she was hypnotized.

But why? He wondered if Maaya's motive might not be blackmail. She would use Saanvi to identify someone she claimed had murdered Riya Kaur and then threaten to go to one of the twenty-four-hour news channels and destroy their reputation unless they paid up. Editors these days loved such stories. The more unsubstantiated the better. He could see it now: *Victim Murdered In Past Life Tells All*.

Or was it personal? Did Maaya have her own secret connection with the Riya Kaur case? Was she after revenge?

Clearly, Saanvi's father wanted nothing to do with Maaya. Was he being rightfully protective? Or was he afraid of something coming out in the wash?

Puri decided he could go no further until he had familiarized himself with the Riya Kaur case. For this he would need to speak with

Bobby. He also needed to get to the bottom of why Mummy wanted the file so badly. What had she been hoping to find?

He decided to call her and set up another rendezvous for tomorrow.

Her phone rang a few times before he got a recorded message from the network provider. It sounded as if it had been voiced by an Indian version of Eliza Doolittle, each consonant over-emphasized. 'This number is not available at the present time. Please try again later.'

Delhi's 'connectivity' was hugely oversubscribed and the mobile network had become extremely unreliable of late.

He tried again and this time got a message saying, 'The number is either switched off or not reachable at the present time.'

On the third attempt, the Indian-Eliza-Doolittle voice told him, with finality, 'This number does not exist.'

An SMS failed to reach Mummy as well.

Back in the office, Puri called for his executive secretary. 'Seems I've been caught on the hop and placed in a sticky position, so to speak, Madam Rani,' he told her once she was seated, before explaining that his former client Puran Chandra had paid his bill in cash ahead of the prime minister's demonetization announcement.

In short, he was advancing her six months of her salary, he explained.

'Thank you, sir,' she gushed.

'Most welcome,' said Puri, with a magnanimous gesture.

Tomorrow she could take the day off and all she had to do was go to the bank and deposit the money into her account.

At the sight of all the cash, however, a frown swooped on to her brow and hovered there.

'Something wrong, Madam Rani?' he asked.

She hesitated. 'Well, sir, you see—'

'Allow me to assure you that everything is above board, pukka, no issues,' said Puri.

'Naturally, sir, I would never think otherwise, not for one moment. I know you to be a man of the highest integrity,' she said. 'No, it's not that . . . you see . . . well, I feel somewhat embarrassed having to admit this . . . but I've been saving to help Kapil, my nephew. He needs an operation . . . a delicate one. Seems he and his wife cannot—'

'You've been keeping this cash at home, only?' interrupted Puri, who was squeamish about hearing people's personal details.

'In my locker, yes. I counted it last night, after I heard about the PM's notebandi announcement – and, well, the total amount is two lakh, forty thousand total.'

'Naturally you want to deposit it in the bank and you're concerned that further cash would raise a question mark with the bank and all.'

'I'm sorry, sir.'

'Understood, Madam Rani, no apology required,' said Puri.

She apologized a few more times nonetheless before asking for permission to take tomorrow morning off in order to go to the bank. After apologizing yet again in advance for the inconvenience her absence would cause, she returned to her desk.

Mrs Chadha, who manned the phones in the communications room and was often required to use her gift for impersonations, came to see Puri next. She, too, turned down his offer of six months' salary in advance on the grounds that she had already agreed to deposit two and a half lakh in her personal account on behalf of her eldest son. She, too, asked to be excused from work the next morning.

Puri had no luck with his other permanent office staff, either. Even the lazy office boy, whom he'd dubbed 'Door Stop', turned him down. He had been sending half of his salary to his parents in their 'native place', a remote village in Jharkhand; being the only member of his family who could read and write (Puri having sponsored him to attend literacy school), he needed permission to travel there to open his first bank account, though to do so would require the requisite paperwork, including a birth certificate (and to get one would require paying a bribe to a local official, which might prove challenging seeing as he only had fifty rupees in legal tender).

With his undercover operatives, however, Puri met with some success. This, perhaps, was the more improbable outcome. Tubelight, for example, heralded from a clan of hereditary thieves and the concept of a bank account with all the requisite paperwork was anathema.

'How you'll deal with so much of cash?' asked Puri, curious.

Tubelight scowled playfully. *'Jugaar ho*

jayega![17] he said. He gestured to the remaining lakhs on the desk. 'I can take the rest off your hands, boss. You can have it all back once the banks issue the new notes.'

'I won't have dealings with any *charsobees*,' said Puri.

'Nothing like that, boss. My cousin-sister's husband has got a wedding hall. Weddings are exempt from the notebandi – if it can be proved they were booked, then they can be paid for in old money. My relative can say you made a booking for your daughter's wedding a few months back and you can pay for the event in cash.'

'That's your plan?'

'Me?' Tubelight gave a sardonic snort. 'I've got my own problems, boss.'

All the members of his family had been caught with large amounts of cash. His answer was to turn to the farmers in his ancestral village.

'Farmers?'

'They don't pay income tax and few have bank accounts,' Tubelight clarified. 'I'm getting them to open accounts in their names – all benami – then deposit two and a half lakh each. They take a small cut, then refund me later. Want me to line up two or three for you?'

Puri thought on it for a minute or so. In India there was a limit to how clean anyone could remain. There was no point pretending otherwise. At times, a bribe simply had to be paid to get the job done. But this was not the kind of illegal

[17] 'The work will get done, one way or another.'

75

he could live with. Tubelight was describing a money-laundering scheme, essentially. Puri would have no truck with such activity.

They turned to other business.

Puri wanted full background checks on Maaya and Saanvi.

Tubelight looked doubtful.

'Some issue?' asked Puri.

'Everyone's having an off tomorrow.'

'The work can't wait – top priority.'

Tubelight sighed. 'Right, boss, I'll manage somehow,' he said as he hurried off to get the work started.

Flush, the young electronics and computer whizz, was next.

He had no issue with taking the cash, either, and though he tried to explain that money could easily be 'booked' through some online foreign exchange site in the Maldives, none of the jargon made any sense to Puri and he cut him off mid-ramble.

'One more thing is required – tracking the location of two mobile phones.'

'Nothing simpler,' said Flush, and asked to be given 'the digits'.

The first number was Saanvi's. The second was Mummy's which he knew by heart but went through the motion of having to look it up.

'I should assign the second trace a case number?' asked the operative.

Puri hesitated. 'This one's off the books, so to speak.'

'You know which platform the subject uses?'

'Platform?'

'Android, iPhone, Windows, Blackberry?'

'It's an older model – basic.'

'Means I'll have to hack the provider's network, locate the nearest base station to the signal and upload the GPS spyware encrypted via the—'

'Just go!'

Facecream, Puri's young, enigmatic Nepali operative arrived after everyone else had left for the day.

She turned down the offer of an advance without giving an explanation why, though she alluded to the fact that she was going to need to visit her homeland in the not too distant future to sort out some 'financial matters'.

Puri was under the impression that she was unable to visit Nepal safely due to her earlier involvement with the Naxalites. She had once told him how, as a teenager, she had become involved with the revolutionary Maoists and, after growing disillusioned with all the violence, fled the country. True, a lot had changed since then. The civil war was over, the Communists now participated in the democratic process. Perhaps the old ghosts had been laid to rest. But he knew not to pry. Facecream was, in Puri parlance, a 'privately minded person'.

He did feel entitled to ask after Deep, the young boy whom she rescued from the village in Uttar Pradesh where she worked undercover during the Love Commandos case[18] and subsequently adopted, however. Puri had ensured that he got

[18] *The Case of the Love Commandos.*

77

enrolled in a good Delhi public school and even put him to work under her supervision a couple of times.

'He's doing well, studying hard for his exams,' she said before they turned to the snoring case – and not without a few smiles.

Facecream remembered Vikas Gupta from the matrimonial investigation they'd conducted into his background. She had been used as bait to test his character. Puri had arranged for her to bump into him in the elevator of a five-star hotel one evening and, though she had been wearing a bandage dress with a slit up the thigh and told him that she was all alone and afraid of the dark, he had acted the gentleman.

'Is it really *that* bad – the snoring?' she asked.

'I'm told he could wake the dead,' said Puri.

'Has he tried wild yam root?' she asked. 'I've heard it can work wonders.'

'I'm told anything and everything has been done to cure him.'

Puri went on to explain about his former client Ram Bhatt's threat to sue the firm, the ruin that would bring, and the need for them to get to the bottom of what was going on. This would have to be done without his or his daughter Tulsi's knowledge and without Vikas Gupta's, either.

'No one is to be trusted,' he said.

'You think someone's trying to wreck the marriage?' asked Facecream.

'All I know is this: prior to marriage Vikas Gupta was not a snorer. Had he been, it would most definitely have come to our attention.'

Step one was to have a snoop around the couple's bedroom and try to ascertain if something the family had overlooked was causing the snoring.

'Then I want full surveillance, round the clock,' said Puri. 'Ascertain who comes and goes from the house, also. Remember: if we don't get to the bottom of what all is going on here, Ram Bhatt could bring down Most Private Investigators once and for all.'

Seven

Dusk was no longer a distinct period in the twenty-four-hour cycle during the winter months in Delhi. It had been reduced to an almost imperceptible interval when the sky turned from kitchen sink water grey to neon-lit night with a streak of turmeric yellow etched in the smog to mark the passing of the sun.

Mummy had to check her watch to confirm the time – by now almost six – and commanded her driver to, '*Jaldi!* I don't have all day, na! Don't do dilly-dally!'

She had employed a number of drivers in her time and had little patience for any of them, but this one deserved an award for being the most useless of the lot. He was always falling asleep in the car (when she'd gone to do some shopping at the Great Mall of India before Diwali, he went down into the underground parking and fell into a semi-coma on the back seat, leaving her stranded with her shopping for an hour), and was constantly 'doing chitchat' on his phone. He had to be Delhi's slowest driver, as well. But most infuriating of all was his habit of pretending to know where he was going when he didn't have the foggiest. This usually resulted in Mummy having to navigate, while the driver received her instructions and chastisements in smouldering silence.

'Why you're turning here, na?' she scolded him now. 'What I told you? Left *then* right!'

Mummy had driven to Rajouri Garden from Maaya's.

With the file purged of all the interview and witness notes along with the name of a key witness, the Singh family cook – whom Mummy remembered her husband mentioning when he'd discussed the case with her all those years ago – there was nothing for it now but to engage in some good old-fashioned footwork.

In her experience, local *sabzi* wallahs were generally the best source of intel in any given neighbourhood. There was rarely a housewife, maidservant or cook whom they didn't know in their patch and what they weren't told, they overheard. Gossip was as integral to their trade as stocking shiny eggplants, big bunches of fresh coriander and plenty of green chillies.

Mummy spotted the sabzi wallah who plied the streets of Rajouri Garden F Block making his way out of the area in the direction of the main road and ordered her driver to pull over ahead of him.

'Wait here and don't do chitchat and be *vella*!' she instructed as she left the car.

Mummy received a reluctant, indolent look in return and the usual, disgruntled grumblings about how madam didn't understand that he couldn't park anywhere and it was getting late and he wanted to go home.

'No argument! This is your duty, na!' Mummy scolded him and left him sitting there, brooding.

She pulled her short wool coat, which she wore over a chunky cardigan and a long kurta, tight around her, tugged down the flaps of her monkey cap so that it covered both her ears, and adjusted her thick wool socks, which were a style especially designed for aunties so as to accommodate toe loops on chappals.

It seemed colder for this time of year, though she wondered if her arthritis, which had been mild until now, was getting worse.

The cart trundled towards her with its owner, pushing from behind, backlit by the headlights of fast-approaching cars.

Though tired after a long day that had begun before dawn and facing an arduous trek through brutal traffic and pollution ahead of him, the grizzled old sabzi wallah was only too happy to stop and part with some of the last of his vegetables.

Soon, he was telling Mummy all about Mantosh Singh, Riya's husband, who still lived with his family in the same house in F Block.

Sahib remarried in the late Eighties, the sabzi wallah divulged while weighing a kilo of blighted tomatoes on the old pair of scales, a few odd bits

81

of iron serving as weights. This second wife had given him three strong sons, the second of whom had married recently. The bride was from Ludhiana and was a '*pataka!*' She was said to be smart, too – 'convent-educated', no less.

The sabzi wallah flashed a gap-toothed smile as he described with a mix of wonderment and something approaching pride the opulence of the wedding at a big banquet hall in Sainik Farm (though, evidently, he had not featured on the guest list). 'It must have cost sahib crores,' he said. But then what was money to such people? It flowed to them from Lakshmi like water from a pump. Sahib owned two big sari emporiums nowadays, the largest of them in South Extension. He drove an 'Au-die' and took his wife shopping in *Angrezi* countries.

'The family used to employ a cook,' said Mummy. 'A Sikh lady, short and plump.'

'Ha, yes, I know the one,' said the sabzi wallah. 'She left seven, eight years ago.'

Did he remember her name? Mummy asked.

He thought for a moment and then began to bemoan the fact that his memory was not what it was.

'Before I would never forget a name, but now . . .'

He bagged a kilo of *bhindhi* for Mummy, then added, 'I remember she lived in East Delhi.'

At around the same time that Mummy was carrying out her investigations in Rajouri Garden, Puri passed down Nelson Mandela Marg, past the three malls – great mock Floridian temples to consumerism draped in giant banners advertising perfumes and designer jeans – and reached Vasant Kunj, a predominantly residential area made up of 'sectors', 'pockets', 'enclaves' and 'housing societies'.

Entry was restricted to each by barriers and guard posts, one entrance barely distinguishable from the other, bar their alphabetical designation.

Beyond the barrier to Sector Three, Pocket Five, it was hard to tell the low-rise apartment blocks apart, either; the plethora of parked cars and the gathering darkness blurred the lines still further.

Puri had been visiting the place since his father's junior partner had relocated here in the early Nineties, and though he wasn't sure that he had ever known the precise address, he could have found the door blindfolded (or so he liked to think).

A ring of the bell brought Bobby's daughter-in-law to the door in her apron with news that Bobby had gone for his evening walk. She offered to call him, but Puri was confident this was unnecessary. The retired additional deputy commissioner of police didn't move quite as quickly as he once did and would not have strayed far; besides, everyone in the neighbourhood knew him. Indeed, as Puri made his way between the apartment blocks and small communal gardens that softened the stringent architecture and brought a sense of welcome calm, he quickly picked up the trail. Two aunties returning from the Mother Dairy stand with fresh paneer had passed Bobby not ten minutes earlier walking in the direction of the mandir; a group of kids playing cricket with a tennis ball chorused that, yes, Uncle-ji had passed that way; a blind man taking a stroll with a maidservant leading him by the arm said he had spoken with Bobby not five minutes ago.

The final breadcrumb proved to be a chorus of laughter coming from a small park reserved for residents.

A group of men sat playing cards in the glow of one of the lollipop lights that lit the jogging track.

Bobby, who sported a big, bristly salt-and-pepper moustache, stood over them with rounded shoulders, hands held behind his back and taking a keen interest in the game.

Spotting Puri's approach, he stepped away from the group, though provoking guffaws and roguish smiles with some parting banter.

'VP, nice surprise, ha! All well?' said Bobby as he walked over to him.

'Fit and fine, never better, Uncle-ji.'

'Rumpi, the girls . . .?'

'Thriving. First class. How are your knees? Still paining after the operation?'

'Pah! Never better. I bowled on Saturday! Two for twenty-nine!'

They found a quiet bench in the park and, as the last of the light faded from the sky, Bobby took an illicit cigarette from the top pocket of his shirt. It was slightly crumpled and he tried to smooth it into shape before lighting up.

'I take it this isn't a social visit,' said Bobby,

exhaling a plume of smoke. 'I don't suppose it has anything to do with the Riya Kaur case?'

'Mummy's been to see you, is it?' guessed Puri.

'A few days back.'

'She told you why the interest all of a sudden?'

'Mentioned something about a new witness,' said Bobby.

'More or less,' said Puri before explaining her mad theory.

Bobby gave a hoot. 'A witness who says she was murdered in her past life. I've heard some things in my time, but that, I believe, is a first, VP.'

'And with any luck, a last,' intoned Puri.

A couple of aunties brisk-walked past them on the jogging path, one of them dabbing her sweaty face with a tissue.

The shouts of the boys playing cricket nearby crescendoed suddenly. Apparently a player had been run out.

'Still . . . that nose of hers . . .' said Bobby, dragging leisurely on his cigarette. 'Sir often commented on it – used to say that she didn't miss a thing. He could never hide so much as a surprise birthday present from her.'

'Papa never encouraged her. And he would not have approved of her roaming around.'

'Things were different in those days, VP. She had a family to raise, a house to run. Her time is her own now. You shouldn't be so hard on her. The fact is sir respected her opinion and welcomed her insights. In fact, there were a few hard nuts she helped him to crack.'

'Now and again, maybe,' said Puri uncharitably.

'The Rope Trick case, for example. It was Mummy who suggested the killer walked on his hands to enter the room.'

Puri was thoughtfully quiet for a moment or two. Three crows were jabbing at a greasy take-away box that had spilled from a bin not far from where they sat.

'What all she was after, Uncle-ji? Mummy – why did she come to see you exactly?' he asked.

'She wanted to know about the cook who was employed by Mantosh Singh's family. She was a witness to what happened the night the mob came. Mummy remembers sir speaking about her when they talked over the case – and I got the impression her "witness" has mentioned her as well.'

'By God,' breathed Puri.

The crows had managed to get the takeaway box open and were fighting over some manky, gnawed chicken bones.

'What did you tell her – Mummy, that is?' asked Puri.

'That after thirty years my memory is not what it was. I remember the cook. I took down her statement. She was short, plump, Sikh, but as for her name and address . . . well, when it comes to that kind of detail I'm more like Motu-Patlu[19] these days.'

Bobby finished his cigarette, crushing the filter beneath the heel of his shoe.

---

[19] Motu and Patlu first appeared in the Hindi comic strip, *Lotpot*. Always involved in simple plots and mysteries, the characters were depicted as bumbling idiots.

'There's something more to this otherwise you wouldn't be taking such a keen interest,' he guessed.

Puri gave a nod.

'I happened to get a look at the Riya Kaur case file and it seems someone in the department has been doing the housekeeping, so to speak. All the notes, transcripts, reports have been removed.'

Bobby looked surprised. 'Mantosh Singh covering his tracks, perhaps? He's grown extremely wealthy from what I understand. Must have contacts. It would not be hard to pay off someone to cull the file.'

'These things don't happen by accident, that much is certain,' said Puri.

A couple more crows had joined the others and were fighting over the chicken bones – a stridency of caws and beating wings.

'Without the file, I'm at something of a disadvantage regarding the details of the case,' added Puri.

Bobby put up his hands in a gesture of regret. 'Then you'll have to settle for the memory of this old man.'

The Riya Kaur case, Bobby recalled, had been opened at the insistence of Riya's father, who became convinced that his son-in-law, Mantosh Singh, murdered his daughter one or two days before the assassination of Indira Gandhi on 31 October, 1984 and buried the body himself.

'Officially sir was the investigating officer, of course. He deposed Mantosh Singh. Otherwise,

I did all the footwork. We had our hands full after the riots.'

'Mantosh Singh was your main suspect?' asked Puri.

'The only suspect, yes.'

'Why exactly?'

'His car survived the riots – the mob didn't set fire to his garage for some reason and it was parked inside. Upon inspection, I found a few specks of blood in the dickie along with a shovel and some loose dirt. This presented the possibility that he'd murdered his wife a day or two before and buried the body as Riya's father believed.'

'Naturally Mantosh Singh denied it.'

'Naturally – he claimed he'd had to clear a blocked drain in front of his shop and cut his finger.'

'Your next step would have been to ascertain the whereabouts of Riya Kaur in the days prior to the assassination.'

'The answer was that she'd been in her room and hadn't left after giving birth to her second child – a boy, I believe – a few days earlier. The servants said they'd seen her, of course – the cook included – but when pressed, they confessed none of them had been *inside* the room.'

'Her parents visited after the child was born?'

'Yes, I believe he was delivered on 26 October and they were there the next day.'

'Why she didn't return home for the birth?'

'The baby was premature.'

'How were relations between Riya and Mantosh and her in-laws?'

The short answer was not good. 'I think they

were cruel to her, the mother-in-law in particular,' said Bobby.

Puri took out his notebook and started to jot down some details and then went back over the dates, writing:

26 Oct (?): Birth, boy, second child, premature.

27 Oct (?): Riya Kaur parents visit.

From 28 Oct: Riya Kaur whereabouts unconfirmed.

31 Oct: Indira G assassinated, rioting follows.

Puri looked up. 'Questions,' he said. 'Number one, why did Mantosh Singh claim his wife remained in the room after giving birth?'

'He said she was depressed. The family doctor confirmed she was on medication.'

'When did he say he'd unblocked the drain exactly?'

Bobby sucked in his breath. 'I *think* a day or two after the birth, but don't quote me on that.'

They turned next to the events of 31 October and 1 November.

They broke down as follows: on 31 October, Mantosh Singh went to work as usual in his father's sari store in Connaught Place.

When news began to circulate of Indira Gandhi's assassination at the hands of her two Sikh bodyguards,[20] both Mantosh Singh and his father, fearing the worst, shut up shop and returned home.

---

[20] This was in retaliation for the assault by the Indian army on the Sikhs' holiest site, the Golden Temple in Amritsar, to rout out Sikh separatists, in June 1984.

By evening, reports reached them of outbreaks of violence directed at Sikhs across the city.

By the morning of 1 November, gangs were roaming the streets, dragging Sikhs from their homes and murdering them in cold blood.

Mantosh Singh and his father elected to shave their beards and long hair and discarded their turbans.

In the evening, a mob surged through the usually quiet, residential streets of Rajouri Garden, a predominantly Punjabi, Hindu neighbourhood. Young men armed with knives, iron bars and cans of kerosene had already targeted a couple of other Sikh households, murdered the male members of the family and, in one instance, abducted the women.

'Mantosh Singh and his family were some of the lucky ones,' explained Bobby. 'There's a galli running behind their house and no one was keeping watch over it. They managed to slip out the back unnoticed and from there went directly to the old Rajouri Garden cinema.'

'It was Muslim-owned, I seem to remember.'

'By old Karim. He took them in and hid them in the basement.'

'The family entailed who exactly?' asked Puri.

'Mantosh, his parents, Riya's two children – the girl and baby boy. The servants fled with them as well.'

'But not Riya Kaur?'

'Mantosh maintained that after gathering everyone at the back gate, he returned to the house to fetch her. He said the medication had made her sleepy and she hadn't come downstairs of her own accord. But by then it was too late: the mob broke into the compound and he fled.'

'Did anyone corroborate his version of events?'

'No one contradicted him, put it that way.'

'And the house was set alight?'

'After being looted.'

Puri wrote for a minute or two in his notebook, then said, 'If Riya was still alive on the evening of 1 November when the mob came – if Mantosh Singh did not in fact murder her as her father affirmed – then it's possible she was taken from the house by the mob,' he said.

'That always seemed to me the most likely scenario. And I'll tell you why. A few hours after the family reached the cinema – in the middle of the night, in other words – Mantosh Singh left and was gone for around an hour.'

'How did you come by that information?'

'The cook told me,' said Bobby with irony.

'No wonder Mummy is searching for her.'

Puri paused for a moment. 'I take it Mantosh Singh claimed he went back looking for his wife?' he asked.

'Right, made a big drama about risking his life searching for her.'

'You didn't buy it?'

'He struck me as a cold, ruthless man. I was never in any doubt that he was capable of murder. What's more likely is he went back to make sure the job got done. By then his neighbours were lying out in the street, burnt and mutilated. It's entirely possible Riya Kaur was among them. By the time her father came looking for her three days later, the corpses had all been taken away.'

Puri sank back on the bench. 'I'm beginning to understand why the case didn't get solved. Where to start? The blood in the dickie might be a red herring. Mantosh Singh did indeed cut his finger while clearing a drain. Perhaps Riya was indeed medicated and unable to escape the house? And there's one other possibility we should not discount – that Riya escaped of her own accord after Mantosh Singh and the rest of the family fled the house.'

'Not likely, VP,' said Bobby. 'Gangs of killers were scouring the neighbourhood. And if she was helped by someone, a friendly neighbour, then why has she never turned up?'

'You found no other trace of her whatsoever?'

Bobby paused. 'There was her *chunni*. It was spotted by her father when he started searching for her a few days later.'

'Where did he find it?'

'In the drain in front of the house – a yellow chunni. It was identified as belonging to Riya by one of the servants. There was blood all over it.'

'Riya's blood?'

Sadness suffused Bobby's features. 'Who is to say, VP?'

Malis, though solitary figures and not in Mummy's experience as prone to gossiping as sabzi wallahs, were often retained by the same families for generations and had proven reliable informants in the past. The Singh family's gardener, however, had no recollection of the plump Sikh cook – but then again he didn't seem to recollect much of anything, and Mummy suspected that his interest in horticulture extended to smoking certain varieties of flora.

Her conversation with the pressing wallah, whose stand was positioned between two trees at the end of Mantosh Singh's street, proved fruitless as well, the man having taken over from his father, who had died in a train crash four years earlier.

She had better luck with the local knife-sharpener wallah, whom she came upon by chance one street over from Mantosh Singh's residence while he was making his evening rounds.

He had stopped his bicycle in a layby and pulled back its old-fashioned stand so that the back wheel was lifted an inch or so off the ground. Within this wheel was mounted a second, smaller wheel and to this was attached a belt that drove a circular stone mounted on the handle bars; thus the knife-sharpening wallah was able to sit on his bike and remain stationary while whetting the various knives and implements brought to him by servants from nearby homes who answered his call. '*Chakuuuu! Chhuri!*'

Of course he'd known the plump Sikh cook, he told Mummy, once she'd struck up a conversation. She had worked for Mantosh Singh for thirty years and been one of his best customers.

There was a catch, however.

'I always knew her as Cook Madam,' he said. Did he know where she lived, at least?

'She was from Trilokpuri, though she moved after the *danga*. You should ask sahib, he'll remember. He gave her money, enough to buy a house.'

Mummy showed surprise. 'A house?'

'She worked for him a long time,' said the knife sharpener. 'What can I say?'

Mummy did not try to speak with Mantosh Singh, of course; to do so would have alerted him to the fact that she was looking for the cook, who had witnessed the events of October and November 1984 and might well be able to implicate her former employer in the murder of his late wife. Instead, she decided to venture over the Yamuna to East Delhi. There was a gurdwara there, and she felt sure that the custodian of the temple would know of the cook.

At the mention of Trilokpuri, however, Mummy's driver pleaded a number of excuses for not driving to the area.

It was late.

Think of the traffic on the bridge!

It was dark.

He did not know the way.

He was hungry and had only 'taken' one cup of tea since four!

Finally the real reason came out: Trilokpuri was dangerous. There had been fighting in the streets only a week or so ago, he insisted. *Muslims* had instigated the violence, he added, emphasizing the word with ugly contempt.

Mummy's ears burned at this and she gave him a proper dressing-down. All of us are equal in the eyes of God, she admonished him. She would not put up with such prejudice from him or anyone.

'Drive me there this instant or your job is getting over, you duffer!' she threatened.

But it did no good. Madam could not force him to venture into such a dangerous part of the city late at night when his duty was 'getting over', he argued.

'If you refuse me, I'll terminate you, na!' she said.

He looked nonplussed and he and Mummy spent the journey home to Punjabi Bagh in stony – deafening – silence.

To appease Bobby, who insisted he stay for dinner, Puri agreed to go in for 'one peg only'.

The talk in the Singh's living room, where one glass of Royal Challenge translated into three and platefuls of chilli *pakoras* and aloo *chaat*, was dominated by demonetization. The banks and ATM machines would all open in the morning. Long queues were expected. Word had leaked out that there'd been a delay in the distribution of the new five-hundred- and two-thousand-rupee notes. Many people were already finding it hard to pay for the basics. Bobby's daughter-in-law was among them, having spent her last few rupees on milk. But overall, the country seemed behind the prime minister's initiative with the twenty-four-hour news channels still praising it as a 'big-bang reform', a 'surgical strike', and 'shock and awe!'

It was not until they were back outside and stood admiring Bobby's small but immaculate patch of lawn (which he treated like a rare silk Persian carpet that no one was permitted to tread upon) that Puri returned to the case.

'One thing is there: for all the lack of evidence,

it was not like Papa-ji to drop a case entirely. After retirement, he worked on two cold cases. We collaborated on one, in fact. But he never revisited this one.'

'No other witnesses came forward, no body was discovered . . . there was nothing to go on,' said Bobby.

'Or perhaps he didn't want to revisit 1984. Perhaps he wanted to forget. He told me once that India died that week.'

'I heard sir say the same. But thanks to his bravery, more than a dozen families were saved. He risked his life – and his career. He did his duty while many of his fellow officers stood by and watched innocent people being killed. He was a hero, VP. They should have pinned medals to his breast. But sometimes, heroes go unrecognized and unrewarded – and the bad guys win the day.'

Puri was about halfway home when Flush called.
'Tell me.'

The young operative sounded flustered. 'Boss, that second number you gave me – can you tell me to whom it's registered?'

'Why exactly?'

'Well, I've uploaded the GPS spyware and I've hacked into the nearest base station—'

'Proper English, yaar!' interrupted Puri.

'Sorry, boss . . . So, basically, it seems like the subject is using some kind of hardware that's blocking the signal.'

'Not possible. The individual in question is' – Puri chose his words carefully – 'an everyday person. Her handset is ancient, held together with sticky tape.'

Flush thought for a moment. 'I guess there could be a problem with the antenna and it's picking up interference. It would have to be something transmitting on a low frequency close to the phone.'

Puri pictured Mummy's phone, which she kept in her handbag. What else did she keep in there?

The answer came to him.

'Don't tell me,' he said before suggesting Mummy's hearing aid, which she often refused to wear, as the culprit.

'That would explain it, boss!'

'You're telling me all your protocols-this-and-GPS-that have been rendered useless by an old lady with a standard hearing aid?'

Puri disconnected the call and a smile crept across his face.

'By God, Mummy-ji, no one stands a chance,' he murmured.

Eight

Puri got home at around ten thirty to find that Rumpi had gone to bed. He had to rouse one of the servants to heat up his food. And after polishing off a plate of *rajma chawal* with raw red onion sprinkled in salt and *amchoor*, he spent thirty minutes watching the news.

The next morning – Thursday – he was ready

97

by seven thirty and hurried downstairs, anxious to be out the door.

'I would not be requiring my breakfast this morning, my dear!' Puri called out to his wife as he put on his shoes.

His words brought Rumpi hurrying from the kitchen. She was wearing an apron and her hands were covered in sticky gobbets of *atta*.

Her voice held thinly veiled exasperation. 'Off to work so soon?' she asked.

'It is most imperative I get to the bank,' he explained.

'You can't make ten minutes for me? I'm making aloo paratha,' she said.

Usually the promise of a hot, fiery paratha, all buttery and served with fresh *dhai* and mango pickle, would have been enough to persuade Puri to drop pretty much anything, but he stood firm.

'I had better get a move on, actually, my dear,' he said with regret.

Rumpi gave an '*Arrey!*' and her arms flopped to her side in a gesture of defeat. 'I don't know why I bother, Chubby, I really don't!' she said and stormed back into the kitchen, slamming the door behind her.

Puri stood there for a minute or so, staring at the door, contemplating what to do. Long years of marriage had taught him that he would be well advised to try and clear up the matter straight away. Showing a little contrition would no doubt help. But he resisted the voices of reason and sound judgement. If he didn't get a move on, the whole day would go for a toss. Rumpi simply didn't understand the kind of pressure he was under, what with so much responsibility and all.

Puri reached Khan Market at eight twenty to find the ATM machines still switched off and long queues formed at the four banks. The line at his own bank was already far longer than he could have anticipated, stretching along the length of the pavement and doubling back again through the car park. At a rough estimate, he calculated five to six hundred people waiting patiently ahead of him, watched over by the Delhi police. A mix of young and old, men and women, they were all drawn from the lower strata of Indian society – domestics, drivers, office peons, shop assistants, rickshaw wallahs and the odd student. There was not a single representative of the typical well-to-do middle-class fellow customers with whom Puri regularly rubbed shoulders inside the branch – bureaucrats, merchants and traders, builders and property brokers, factory owners and wholesalers, accountants and lawyers.

No doubt such types had use of debit and credit cards so their need for cash was not as urgent, yet he could not help wonder how many of those in line had been sent as proxies for their employers.

This gave him an idea: he would get Door Stop to stand in line for him, and hurried to the office to give him his orders.

Puri had forgotten that he'd given his staff the day off, however, and found the premises locked.

So rarely did he open the door himself, he wasn't sure which keys on the big clod he carried around with him worked on which lock.

He was trying to figure it out through trial and error, his back turned to Middle Lane, when a figure approached him from behind.

'Mr Puri – I want to speak with you.'

The detective turned to find himself face to face with Saanvi's father.

'Mr Srivastava, is it?' Puri asked, fumbling with the keys.

'*Doctor* Srivastava. And I want to know where my daughter is!' he demanded.

'She's not with you at home?' asked the detective with concern.

'You take me for a fool? I saw you with her yesterday – you and your mother. I'm aware that she has been one of the ones leading Saanvi on.'

Though Puri found his tone highly objectionable, he kept his cool.

'I'm not aware of Saanvi's location, that I can assure you two hundred per cent,' he said.

'What about your mother? Is my daughter with her?'

'Not that I'm aware. Then again, whom Mummy-ji sees and where she goes is her business, only,' answered Puri, though he almost choked on the irony of this statement. 'Surely, sir, your daughter, being a grown woman, is deserving of certain freedoms herself, also?'

Dr Srivastava's eyes flashed with anger. 'I will decide what is best for Saanvi! I'm her father! I don't need a lecture from some interfering *jasoos*!' he shouted.

Puri met his outburst with pitying eyes. 'Sir, kindly get control of your temper. It is unbecoming of a man of education such as yourself,

100

and will not help your cause at all. Frankly speaking, I'm somewhat allergic to being spoken to in such a manner.'

The rage lingered on Dr Srivastava's face a moment longer but then gave way to a fleeting hint of regret.

'You're a father yourself, I take it?' he asked, his tone still terse.

'I've been blessed with three daughters in total, yes.'

'Then you'll understand that I would do anything to protect Saanvi.'

'*Anything* is a big word.'

'You're not understanding me. Saanvi is not a well person. Her mental health is extremely fragile. She requires specialist care and medication. Recently she's been behaving erratically again. I suspect she's stopped taking her pills. That being the case, there's every chance she could suffer a major relapse.'

'Relapse?'

'Saanvi's like a schizophrenic, Mr Puri. She doesn't understand reality the same way we do. She hears voices . . . experiences hallucinations . . . can manifest multiple personalities. The antipsychotic medication helps, of course. And she *was* seeing Dr Anjali Mittal, an eminent psychiatrist, before she was lured into all this past life hypnotism mumbo-jumbo.'

Srivastava's smartphone rang suddenly, punctuating his words. He was startled for a second, then tugged the handset out of his pocket with an expression of anxious expectation. This turned instantly to piqued disappointment.

'Go away!' he bawled, tapping hard on the face of his smartphone to reject the call.

He thrust the phone back into his pocket and gathered his thoughts. 'Look, Mr Puri, I just want Saanvi back home. She requires the help of trained professionals, not amateur dilettantes and hippy dippy therapists. Saanvi's past is nobody's business.'

Puri was about to suggest they go up to his office and talk the matter through calmly and constructively, but Dr Srivastava turned and strode off down Middle Lane.

The detective watched his back until he was out of sight, unsure of what to make of him.

As a father himself, he felt sympathy for a fellow parent seeking to protect his sick daughter. His distress was understandable too. Perhaps even his anger. But was he being over-protective? Had he smothered Saanvi – or worse? Was Dr Srivastava anxious not so much for his daughter, but for himself?

As soon as Puri was up in his office, he called Bhuppi, who'd been trying to reach him during the past ten minutes or so.

'Mummy-ji reached home late last night and now she's ailing – got a head cold,' reported his brother.

'Where she went, exactly?'

'Who knows, Chubby! I've sent her to her bed and called the doctor. Jassu's making her *khichdi*. That's not all: seems Mummy fired her driver.'

'Another one bites the dust,' sighed Puri. 'This one lasted – what? – two months, maximum?'

'Six weeks, three days. Sure, he's a bit of a *pakau*, but still . . .'

'What happened exactly?'

'He's telling me Mummy wanted to go to Trilokpuri during night-time. Can you believe? Anyway, naturally he refused. Something's going on I should know about?'

'Seems Mummy-ji's been going over one of Papa-ji's cold cases.'

'Arrey!'

'What to do, Bhuppi?'

'Well, as of now, Mummy's not going anywhere,' said Bhuppi. 'I've made a curfew.'

'Thank the God,' said Puri.

'By the way, you've reached Rinku, is it?'

'Give me some time, yaar. Just I'll revert.'

Puri, like most of his fellow 1.3 billion Indians, rarely spent much time on his own, and found the absence of anyone else in the office and the accompanying silence unsettling.

It was also downright inconvenient.

Without the help of his staff, he was forced to answer the phones and do such menial tasks as replacing the paper in the printer (prompting the first of several calls to Madam Rani that morning) and fetching his own chai from the market.

Every time the doorbell rang, he also had to stomp downstairs to get the door. And not ten minutes passed without someone turning up.

First came the *kabari wallah* for the recycling (old newspapers and used whisky bottles being of special interest), then the newspaper-magazine vendor asking for settlement of the monthly account, followed by the *nimboo mirchi* woman wanting to hang a fresh bunch of lemon and green chillies over the front door (and wishing to discuss her concerns about her youngest son, who had dropped out of school), and finally the lady who cleaned the office toilets.

Eventually, Puri, who was beginning to feel like the unwitting star of an episode of *Undercover Boss*, stuck a *Closed* notice on the front door.

Not five minutes passed before the bell sounded again.

Puri ignored it at first, but the caller was persistent, alternating between keeping his finger on the buzzer for three or four seconds and then thumping on the door.

'*Salaa*, idiot!' the detective cursed when, eventually, he stomped downstairs again.

He found a skinny young man standing on the doorstep with a disproportionately large, box-shaped rucksack strapped to his back. This was a courier, hardened by long days spent weaving through Delhi traffic. Such types were indifferent to complaints and disdainful of common door-bell-ringing etiquette, no matter the time of day or night. Notices on doors were of no consequence, either. Puri's could have read, *Plague – Keep Out!* and it would not have made the slightest difference.

'One sign,' requested the courier, producing a crumpled delivery form and a pen, to which Puri might have added the signature of Timur the Lame for all he cared, before hurrying off.

Puri returned upstairs and opened the packet to find a DVD inside from Maaya.

Unclear on how to play it on a computer, he had to call Elizabeth Rani again.

After an initial problem – 'The machine is grunting, Madam Rani!' he exclaimed when no image appeared, to which she responded, 'Sir, I do believe you might have inserted the disk upside down' – Puri found himself watching footage shot from a camera mounted in a fixed position of what the index on the DVD sleeve listed as Saanvi's 'first session' with Maaya.

She was in a therapy room lit with flickering candles, lying on a mattress with her eyes closed.

Maaya knelt next to her, dangling a crystal over her face.

Floaty flute spa music played in the background.

'I'm going to count you down from five down to zero,' said the therapist in her dreamy voice. 'Each and every count will take you twenty times deeper into the deepest recesses of your subconscious mind.'

She asked Saanvi to visualize herself standing on top of a staircase with ten steps.

'Descend,' she instructed.

With every step she would fall even deeper into a trance.

At the bottom she would find herself in a corridor.

At the end of the corridor there was a door.

Beyond, lay a garden.

'Describe it for me,' said Maaya, laying the crystal to one side.

'There are trees and grass and white flowers

and butterflies. It's beautiful,' answered Saanvi, her lips barely moving.

'Good. Now I want you to use your mind and project a message into the cosmos. I want you to ask your spirit guide to join you. Our spirit guides are always waiting in the afterlife to help us. They will always come.'

It took a minute or so for the spirit guide to turn up and Saanvi described feeling 'a presence . . . an energy all around me . . . so much light'.

'Good. Ask your spirit guide to take you on a journey back in time to your past lives. You will observe these past lives like you're watching a movie, like a member of the audience. Follow the path in front of you. It will lead you into a mist. Do not be afraid. You will hear my voice at all times.'

Maaya counted down from five to zero again and then asked Saanvi where she was.

'I'm sitting on someone's lap – bouncing up and down.'

'Look down. What are you wearing?'

'A pink suit . . . white socks.'

'You're a child?'

'Maybe three or four.'

'Whose lap are you sitting in? Can you make out their face?'

'My father. He's laughing and smiling. My mother's there, too.'

'Describe your father.'

'He's wearing a blue *pagri*.'

'He's Sikh?'

'Yes.'

'Very good. Now at the count of three I want

you to ask your spirit guide to take you to the next significant event in your past life.'

Saanvi described various rites of passage in any Sikh childhood, her school graduation and then her engagement at twenty-two.

'Can you tell me your name?'

'It's Riya.'

'Is your husband there?'

'Yes.'

'I want you to look into your husband's eyes, directly into his eyes. What's his name?'

'Mantosh. Mantosh Singh.'

Puri paused the video and managed to play this last section again.

As far as he could make out, it had not been edited.

He pressed play again.

'Describe your husband for me,' said Maaya.

'He's young, handsome.'

'Do you love him?'

'No.'

'Do you want to marry him?'

'I'm not sure.'

'Why are you marrying him, then?'

'My parents want me to.'

The next significant event was the birth of a child.

Saanvi was in a hospital bed surrounded by nurses who had her pinned down.

'I can't take the pain. It's agony. Like nothing else I've ever experienced. I want to die,' she said.

Soon, the baby came.

'A boy?'

'No, a girl.'

'Is your husband there?'

'Yes, but he's disappointed. So is my mother-in-law.'

The first session was almost an hour long, but it took much longer to watch as Puri kept going back to check that the video hadn't been edited and often paused to take notes.

Then he proceeded to watch the second session on the DVD.

It began with the same routine: the stairs, the corridor, the arrival of the spirit guide, the mist . . .

This time, Saanvi was a young village girl sold by her parents to another family.

It was a life of bondage to an old man – cooking, cleaning, working in the fields.

When Saanvi described the old man forcing himself on her, she grew highly agitated, her head rocking from side to side. Tears rolled down her cheeks. Her breathing became erratic. She claimed there were rough hands around her throat. She seemed to be struggling for breath.

Maaya tried to sooth her, reminding her that she was an observer of her past lives and that her spirit guide was there to protect her. But Saanvi started to scream and Maaya had to bring her out of her trance.

The transformation was extraordinary to watch. Saanvi opened her eyes, blinked and sat up, unaware of the intense distress she'd been exhibiting just moments earlier. With a smile, she asked for some water.

Puri paused the video and sat staring at

Saanvi's image, trying to process what he'd just seen. He'd expected to find Maaya leading her client on, inducing, coaxing out the so-called 'memories'; instead, Saanvi had spoken without hesitation and he was left in no doubt that her distress had been very real. Presumably this was evidence of her multiple personalities manifesting themselves, but he was going to need some expert advice.

Puri moved on to the third session – in which Saanvi was Riya again.

She described playing with her infant daughter; a visit to Amritsar to worship at the Golden Temple; an unhappy marriage.

'If I disobey him, he locks me in my room for hours on end,' she told Maaya.

Her mother-in-law often berated her as well.

'She's a witch, I hate her. She often threatens to send me back to my parents. I can do nothing right in her eyes.'

Only the cook was kind to her.

'She's got her own key to the room and feeds me secretly when Mantosh and the others are out,' said Saanvi. 'Without her, I don't know what I'd do.'

The next significant events in her life saw her locked in her room, feeling sleepy, lying on her bed. It was dark outside.

'I can hear men shouting, lots of voices nearby. They're angry. I can hear screams as well. I go to the window. Down in the street I can see a group of angry young men. They're coming closer. They're carrying iron bars, knives, cans of kerosene. They're shouting, "Kill the snakes!"

I can see flames coming from the neighbour's house. A Sikh family lives there as well. There's smoke rising into the sky. They're at the gate. It's locked. They're trying to get inside. Oh God. My children! Where are my children?'

'What happens next?'

'I try to get out, but the door's still locked! I can't open it! Oh God! I have to get out! I start shouting for help. Is anyone there? Can anyone hear me?' Saanvi gave a scream. 'Oh God, they're coming!' she shouted.

'Calm yourself, you're just an observer of past events,' said Maaya gently, taking her hand.

But she was inconsolable and the session had to be brought to a sudden end.

There was nothing more on the DVD after that. And for five minutes or so, Puri sat in silence, his forehead crumpled in a deep frown. He could see why Mummy was convinced of the reincarnation claim: Saanvi gave an extremely convincing performance, as presumably only a schizophrenic could. But how had she come to believe she was Riya Kaur? Had Maaya prepped her, seeded the memories, possibly during earlier hypnotism sessions? Had Saanvi been influenced by movies or documentaries about the gruesome events of 1984?

He decided to turn to his old friend, Dr Subhrojit Ghosh, for advice and sent him a message inviting him to lunch at the Gymkhana Club.

While Puri was en route, Flush called.

He'd managed to trace Saanvi's mobile phone.

'She's on a train, boss.'

'Heading to?'

'Looks like she's pulling *into* Delhi.'

'She's come from where exactly?'

'I can find out by downloading her GPS location triangulation logs from her provider,' he said.

'Just reference the train schedule, *yaar*!' growled Puri.

Nine

It was a busy day at the Gymkhana Club and the resplendently moustachioed doorman had his work cut out for him. Four senior bureaucrats' wives fresh from the battlefront that was the bridge room, a couple of retired army officers in shorts and tennis plimsolls with their sports socks pulled up to their grizzled knees, and a freshly pressed young maharaja-cum-politician and his squash partner (accompanied by a peon juggling files and squash rackets) occupied the space beneath the whitewashed portico, waiting for their drivers to collect them.

Puri was obliged to go around the group, slip in between the faux-Ionic columns, and push open the front door himself. Beyond, he found everything in the reception spit-spot, the marble floor polished, the mahogany concierge desk gleaming, the neatly typed lunch menu prominently on display. Today's dessert was Pinky Pinky Pudding, Puri noted with relish, before asking the *incharge* on duty at reception for his

111

messages and correspondence. He turned to the glass case with its institutional-green pinboard upon which the club secretary posted his dictums, each with the ubiquitous subject heading: *Notice. Members playing bridge will have prior right to play. Those desirous to play rummy are requested to observe courtesy and do not deny a table to those waiting to play bridge. Members cooperation is appreciated,* read one.

Another stated simply: *Eatables must be eaten in areas designated only for the purposes of eating. Members found eating eatables in non-designated areas will be referred to the club secretary for infringement of eating regulations.*

With a nod of approval – some of the younger members were guilty of taking snacks into the billiard room and TV room, after all – Puri moved on into the old British ballroom. Here, he made a sharp left so as to avoid passing in front of the office of the battleaxe wife of the club secretary, Mrs Col. P.V.S. Gill (Retd), whom he'd success-fully avoided for weeks.

Keeping within the shadow of the columns that marked the boundary of the dance floor, Puri reached Butler's Alcove[21] where he found Subhrojit ensconced behind the *Indian Express.*

'You've time for a quick game, Chubby?' he asked, lowering his newspaper with a nod in the direction of the chess set on the side table.

---

[21] Named after Spencer Harcourt Butler, the first secretary of what was previously the Imperial Delhi Gymkhana Club.

'If only, *Shubho-dada*.[22] Alas, there is no rest for we wicked. Something is there I wish to discuss. Also, I went without my breakfast and am somewhat famished.'

'Don't tell me you're on a diet,' teased his friend.

'Not today, at any rate.' Puri smiled.

They adjourned to the restaurant, ordered the tandoori pomfret and a couple of cold Kingfishers, and Dr Subhrojit Ghosh was soon fulminating about demonetization, which he considered a 'travesty'.

The news channels were now reporting that there was no cash available at ATMs across the entire country, owing to the fact that there were still no new notes available.

'Can you imagine politicians in any other country treating the population with such wanton disregard?' he said, warming to one of his most familiar themes on the inherent characteristic of the vast majority of Indians to keep their heads down and put up with practically anything that was thrown at them. It took religious or caste sentiments to be tampered with or stoked for the populace to rise up, he contended.

'You're just an old frustrated *Naxal*, Shubho-dada,' joked Puri.

'I mean it, Chubby. If the government imagined for one minute that the common man would not stand in queues for hours on end without riots

[22] *Shubho* is short for Subhrojit; *dada* means 'older brother' in Ghosh's native Bengali.

113

breaking out, they would not risk such a reckless policy.'

'Something has to be done about so much of corruption,' observed Puri. 'Day by day, it is eating away at the very heart and soul of this country.'

'This is not the solution and you know it,' countered Subhrojit. 'Prima facie, the PM's initiative is failing. If there's one thing we Indians excel at, it is getting around the rules. No obstacle can stand in our way. Every *bania* and *crorepati* and *kirana*-store owner will find a means to slip the net. They're out there now, laundering their cash through temples, platinum dealers, getting their domestics to line up at banks, depositing lump sums in their *massi*'s savings accounts. Whatever it takes, they'll find a scam to make it work.'

Puri didn't dare mention how Puran Chandra had paid his debt in cash hours before the prime minister's announcement; it would only prolong the conversation and he wanted to pick his friend's brains about schizophrenia.

However, it wasn't until the fish bones lay bare upon their plates and only foamy residue remained at the bottom of their glasses that Puri was able to turn to the case, providing Subhrojit with a concise briefing and the headlines from Saanvi's sessions.

'What is truly extraordinary is the precise details Saanvi provides,' said Puri. 'She seems to be able to recall smells, conversations, feelings. There is nothing vague or general about any of it. At times her emotions run high, also. During

114

one session, she claimed to recall being married as a young bride and being assaulted by her husband, an old man. She was not acting – of that I am one hundred per cent certain.'

'It's possible that she has experienced such things, but suppressed the memory of it all,' suggested Subhrojit.

'You're suggesting in a past life?' asked Puri, surprised.

'Don't be ridiculous, Chubby. I mean this one, *this* life.' He reflected for a moment, then asked, 'Did you say she's been seeing a psychiatrist?'

'*Was* seeing – a certain Dr Anjali Mittal. You're familiar with her?'

Subhrojit gave a light chuckle. 'We were at Harvard together – she's like a sister to me. Let me have a discreet word with her, find out what I can – off the record, of course. Meantime, don't be deceived: schizophrenics are capable of constructing detailed fictions and fantasies. We are talking about a type of psychosis whereby the patient is unable to distinguish his or her own thoughts and ideas from reality. Hallucination is not uncommon. You have a copy of the sessions?'

Puri handed over the DVD just as his Pinky Pinky Pudding was brought to the table.

Subhrojit sipped his lemon tea and watched him eat the refulgent dessert with an expression of mild bewilderment.

'What is that stuff made of?' he asked.

'Fifty per cent goodness, forty per cent flavour and the rest is . . . well, pink.'

Puri polished it off in seconds and turned to his own cup of chai.

'Thank you for clarifying certain things,' he said. 'For a moment there I was starting to wonder if Mummy might not be right – about Saanvi remembering her past lives and all.'

'That is hardly surprising, Chubby. If you believe in reincarnation then, naturally, you'll be susceptible to this idea that somehow memories of past lives can be conjured up during hypnosis.'

'You're not a believer in reincarnation, I take it?'

'You know me, Chubby – a true agnostic. In my view, reincarnation is just a way to make everyone feel better about death.'

'Not if you face the prospect of being reborn a cockroach, surely?'

'I wonder how many people have undergone this so-called past life regression therapy and been told they were once cockroaches,' said Subhrojit.

Puri returned to Khan Market at a few minutes to three to find half the shops shuttered and the queue for his bank still eye-wateringly long. Many of those standing in line had spent up to seven hours shuffling forward at an agonizingly slow pace and looked tired and weary. He could only imagine that they were staying put in the hope that the bank would remain open beyond the usual customer cut-off time of three twenty.

Puri lingered for a few minutes, watching the entrance to see who was coming and going, and noticed a police officer in uniform jump the queue. This gave him an idea and he hurried back to his office, collected the five lakhs he wanted to deposit and placed the bundle of notes in an official-looking attaché case.

He then went in search of his car and asked Handbrake to drive him to a nearby deserted back lane off Lodhi Gardens. Here, he had the driver affix *On Govt Duty* plates to the front and back of the car, put a fake South Block parking permit inside the front window, and mount a flashing red emergency beacon on the roof.

They then drove back to Khan Market, this time through the main entrance, with the beacon whirring.

Handbrake pulled up in front of the bank and hurried around the back of the car to open the passenger door.

Puri stepped out with his mobile pressed to his ear, speaking loudly into it – 'The investigation should proceed immediately! No delay or heads will roll! This comes directly from the PM's office!' – and marched brazenly up to the bank's entrance.

'Official business,' he told the guard on the door, who, though he knew Puri well, hesitated but only fleetingly before letting him through.

Inside the branch, Puri found little room to manoeuvre with dozens of customers clustered around tellers' windows like iron filings stuck to a magnet. Sharp rebukes flared suddenly above the din of keyboard tapping, phones ringing, and the fizz of counting machines – evidence that the bank's employees had abandoned any pretence to polite customer service, rendering the beaming smiles of the individuals featured in the promotional posters on the walls spurious.

Puri was only able to reach his goal – the little waiting area outside the manager's office reserved for Exclusive Platinum Account members – thanks to his weight, which propelled him slowly but inexorably through the crush.

He found the little cosy red couches all occupied, and all the complimentary chai capsules used up. With a number of others waiting to speak with the receptionist ahead of him, it was a good five minutes before he was able to ask to see the manager.

Unfortunately the receptionist was new and not in the least bit impressed by Puri's assertion that he was a 'long-standing and highly valued customer', nor that he was 'a well-known person' who happened to have played golf with the country director.

On the plus side, however, she didn't challenge him on his assertion that he was an Exclusive Platinum Account member and added him to the list of half-a-dozen genuine Exclusive Platinum Account members waiting to see the manager ahead of him.

'Sir, kindly take a seat,' she added redundantly.

Puri was forced to turn back from the desk. But soon he hit upon a strategy to overcome the last obstacle standing in his way.

It relied upon the manager, who wore distinct footwear, needing to make a call of nature.

Step one involved explaining to the receptionist that he was suffering from 'certain stomach ailments which create so much gas of an unpleasant and, frankly speaking, fragrant nature' and asking for the key to the men's executive toilets.

Puri then took up position in one of the two stalls and, each time someone took up occupancy in the second, neighbouring stall, he peeked under the divide to check their footwear.

The third gentleman to step inside was suffering from genuine tummy issues.

So intense was his onslaught upon the toilet that he came close, albeit unwittingly, to driving Puri from the room altogether. Only by breathing through his handkerchief, which reeked of Sexy Men aftershave, was Puri able to keep his place.

Thankfully, the third man left and was soon replaced by a gentleman who wore *Kolhapuri* chappals and possessed thick ankles and especially hairy toes.

Puri paid the stranger no attention – that is until he answered his phone.

The ensuing conversation was conducted in Dogri – a language spoken by around five million people in northern India, Puri being one of them. And it was about a very large sum of money – some three crore rupees.

Hairy Toes, whose tone was boastful and louche, was acting as a laundering broker for the person on the other end of the line.

He had 'found a route through the bank' thanks to 'a helpful person on the inside'.

The caller need not worry – everything would be taken care of.

'No tension, I've fixed it, the rest is fine,' Hairy Toes added in English.

The call ended with Hairy Toes giving a grunt. He then finished up his business, hummed the chorus to the hit, *Aunty-ji Get Up and Dance*, cleared his nasal passages into the sink and left.

Puri exited his stall with the intention of identifying him.

Unfortunately, just then, the general manager, Mr Dhawan, entered the toilets – the very man Puri had been waiting for. He looked and sounded as sprightly as ever.

'Mr Vish Puri, sir, a very good afternoon to you.' He grinned. 'You're making use of our excellent facilities, I see? Trust you're finding everything to your general satisfaction?'

'Yes, yes, wonderful,' said Puri, trying to manoeuvre around him in the cramped space.

'You've some work for me, sir?' asked the manager.

'I wish to make a deposit,' said Puri.

'My sincerest apologies for any wait you've experienced. I'd be happy to attend to you shortly if you'll allow me one minute or so. A call of nature.'

'You please carry on,' said the detective, managing to get out the door.

There was no sign of Hairy Toes, however. The bank had emptied. Only the staff remained, working feverishly at their desks.

'The last gentleman to exit ahead of me – we got to speaking, one stall to another, yet I failed to get his name. Do you know him by chance?' Puri asked Mr Dhawan after he emerged from the toilets.

'One of our Exclusive Platinum Account members – Mr Hari Dev. Into marble, I believe. Now, if you'll please accompany me, I would be

120

glad to assist you. Our loyal customers remain our top priority, even in these most challenging of times.'

Puri followed the manager into his office, noting that he was wearing his black leather loafers with tassels, a style rarely seen in India. These had been given to Mr Dhawan by his uncle living in Trenton, New Jersey, USA.

Ten

'Chubby, Bhuppi this side. You've heard from Mummy-ji?'

'Why exactly?'

'I can't find her in her room.'

'Don't tell me. You've checked with Jassu?'

'Says she took Mummy some *amla* and ginger tea forty minutes back. She was sitting up in bed and her fever was getting over.'

'Sure she's not taking wash?'

'Her coat is absent from the hook.'

'By God! How she left the house undetected, I ask you?'

'What to do, Chubby? I had some urgent business in the market.'

'You tried calling her?'

'Getting the same message, yaar: "This number is not bloody reachable."'

'It is high time we purchased Mummy a new handset.'

'I've asked her so many of times! She's very

121

much attached to her portable. Old is gold and so on.'

'Where's her car exactly?'

'Lying idle in the street.'

'I've an idea where she's gone to. Must be she's taken an auto. In this weather she'll catch the death of cold.'

'You want I should go after her?'

'No, no, better I go.'

'I tell you, Chubby, she's getting worse. *Waat lag gayi!*[23] By the way, you've reached Rinku, as of yet?'

'Bhuppi, don't do tension, yaar! I'll get hold him tonight, only.'

Puri guessed that Mummy was off searching for the Singh family cook and thought he knew where to find her.

The Ambassador, by now stripped of its fake Government of India accoutrement, had to endure the grind of the rush hour along with the rest of the hoi polloi, moving slowly east. Crossing the Yamuna over the DND Flyway took a good forty minutes; it was almost seven o'clock and dark by the time the car peeled off from the grinding, honking hell of the Gazipur Road and turned into Trilokpuri.

A so-called 'resettlement colony' where slum dwellers were housed in the early Seventies, the area had expanded into a vast sprawl of crudely constructed, teetering buildings, which were suffocating just to look at. Wonky brickwork

---

[23] We're screwed.

oozing dried mortar and iron supports jutting out of roofs in expectation of additional floors yet to be added suggested a dangerous fragility, more given the area was a flood plain lying on a high-risk earthquake zone.

As the Ambassador nudged through the streets, cut off repeatedly by labourers carrying everything from ladders and panes of glass to piles of bricks balanced on their heads, Puri could only thank his lucky stars that his had been a relatively privileged existence. In summer, when temperatures in Delhi settled in the forties for weeks, the buildings, many of which were three or four storeys high, were like ovens. In winter, they were as good as fridges. There was no running water, only communal taps on the odd street corner. Electricity was come and go. Government schools and government hospitals strained to breaking point.

Though extreme poverty bit constantly at the heels of the population, the evening markets were teeming, thousands haggling over cheap clothes, belts, wallets, knockoff Chinese Disney toys all heaped on barrows. Day labourers and rickshaw drivers – many returned from working in affluent, neighbouring Noida – thronged to crude street kitchens where they dined standing up on hot *kachoris* with *sabzii* and aloo *tikki*. Outside a local cinema theatre, where the latest *masala* offering cost just twenty rupees, a scrum of young men pressed in around the ticket window like crazed zombies. Further on, they passed a pavement pitch where a hawker was selling posters of Hindu gods, along with ones of Mother Teresa,

Jesus Christ and Bollywood beauty Aishwarya Rai, and Puri spotted a father with a son, selecting one of the young Hindu cowherd, Krishna.

Though Puri was never one to romanticize poverty – recognizing it as grinding and debilitating – on his travels, it often struck him how much people could make of so little, whereas plenty could often prove a curse. These thoughts led him to consider how, in his experience, the common man wanted to co-exist in peace. It was only ever a small minority that hungered for violence – and more often than not it took politicians to incite them. Take the headline-grabbing troubles here in Trilokpuri a couple of years back, for example. The initial spark had been a drunken brawl between some local Muslim and Hindu boys. It was not until the next day, not until local bigwigs had stoked the coals, however, that the riots began. 1984 was the same. Had the ruling party called for calm and ordered the police on to the streets to protect Delhi's Sikh communities, there would have been little trouble. Instead, the mob, furnished with voter registration lists, was sent out to avenge Indira Gandhi's assassination.

The bloodshed in Trilokpuri was some of the worst. Four hundred Sikhs were murdered. Men were dragged from their homes and burnt alive in the streets. Women and children were not spared, either. In the aftermath, the terrified survivors were herded into camps, to be rehoused later in other areas of the city.

Only a handful of Sikhs remained in Trilokpuri today.

The gurdwara in Block 36 stood as a symbol of the lost community.

It was here, Puri had reasoned, that Mummy would come if she hoped to trace the cook.

By the time the car pulled up in front, however, it was eight o'clock and Puri was worried that Mummy might have come and gone.

He wasted no time in exiting the car, taking off his shoes at the entrance and hurrying inside.

The *langar* hall, which in any other part of Delhi (or indeed any other part of the country) should at this time of the evening been thronging with worshippers, was empty save for a lone cleaner dusting the images of the gurus on the walls and the portraits of some of the victims of 1984.

The sound of a single male unaccompanied voice singing from the *ragas* drew him into the adjacent prayer room, the *darbar*. There he found the Granthi, a large, bearded man in a blue turban, sitting behind a raised platform draped in a blue cloth embroidered with the symbol of a double-edged sword.

He was alone – there was no sign of Mummy.

Puri could hardly interrupt him to ask if his mother had visited earlier, so he decided to pick a spot on the rug upon the floor and managed with some difficulty to sit down.

The hymn spoke of how the exhibition of religiosity – parrot-like repetition of sacred texts, daubing the forehead with saffron – is of little avail if there is no truth in the heart.

'*We come into the world with a clean slate and thereafter gain or lose accordingly as we do good*

125

or evil,' the Granthi sang. '*We return as naked as we arrive.*'

Puri closed his eyes, allowing the sound of the man's voice to flow over him, meditating upon the sentiments.

When he opened his eyes a few minutes later, he found a small figure swaddled in layers of clothes, her head covered by a chunni, sitting quietly next to him. For a split second, Puri didn't recognize her.

'Mummy-ji, what are you doing out and about?' he said with a start.

'I should ask you the same question, na!' she whispered back.

'You should be at home in bed.'

'Don't do lecturing, Chubby, I'm very much fine. Just a little congestion, that is all.'

'Bhuppi told me you were running a fever.'

She gave a tut. 'That one is always doing exaggeration.'

'Dr Chugh said you required bed rest.'

'If Dr Chugh got his way, every which person would be taking bed rest round the clock,' she said dismissively.

'*He alone is truly truthful; who knows the art of living; who prepares his body like a garden bed and plants the seed of the Lord therein.*'

Puri asked, 'You've been here some time, is it?'

'One hour, give or take. Just I was across the road taking some chai when I saw you pull up.'

'You found out what you wanted?'

'Regarding?'

Puri sighed. 'Please, Mummy-ji, no games. I

know why you're here. You're looking for the cook. She was a witness that night and Papa-ji mentioned her to you – and now Saanvi spoke of her also in one of her sessions and you believe it can't be a coincidence.'

Mummy's eyes lit up. 'So you believe me now, regarding Saanvi's past?'

Puri held up a hand, beseeching patience. 'There's something I wish to tell you regarding Saanvi,' he said. 'She's not well. Not well in the head, actually.'

'That I know. So depressed she becomes. For a long time she was on medication.'

'It's more complicated than that, Mummy-ji,' said Puri, not wishing to reveal precisely what Saanvi's father had told him about his daughter's mental state. 'She may be imagining that she's Riya and adding to events with her own ideas. Without doubt, some fiction is there.'

'Then how she knew about the cook, tell me?'

'Which family in Delhi does not employ a cook?'

'And the key?'

'What key, exactly?' he quipped. 'Saanvi describing a key means nothing. She might have mentioned a pot of gold, also, but I'm not about to go looking for it!'

'Then why you came here, Chubby, tell me that?'

'Out of concern for your health,' he said. And then paused, adding in a conciliatory tone, 'And to speak with you about the case, also. I'm concerned for Saanvi's wellbeing and want to get to the bottom of this matter, also.'

Mummy sat in silence, her jaw set hard, eyes blinking slowly as she watched the Granthi.

'*He alone is truthful who accepts the true message; towards the living shows mercy; gives something as alms and in charity.*'

'Mummy-ji, listen, I've no wish to argue,' said Puri. 'Allow me to drive you home and we can discuss this matter further while in the car.'

She rocked her head gently from side to side, indicating she was agreeable to his offer. 'Agreed, two heads can be better than one,' she said.

They did not leave immediately, however. Out of respect, they remained sitting, both humbled by the power of Guru Nanak's message and the arresting quality of the Granthi's voice.

'*Out of the cotton of compassion; Spin the thread of tranquillity; Let continence be the knot; And virtue the twist hereon.*'

At around the same time as Puri and Mummy were leaving the gurdwara, Facecream was wishing she was at home tucked up in bed, watching TV – or just about anywhere else other than the back of Flush's cramped, stuffy Bajaj three-wheeler, which was packed with an array of surveillance gear and monitors, and a collection of old pizza boxes.

The absurd nature of the assignment didn't help. Facecream couldn't have cared less why Vikas Gupta snored so badly or if his spoiled wife was finding it hard to sleep. But she didn't doubt Puri's concern. Ram Bhatt's threat of a lawsuit posed a real threat to the firm. And being fiercely loyal to the boss, Facecream was not about to let him down.

So far everything was going to plan.

The two operatives had arrived in Mayfair Gardens, one of south Delhi's wealthiest colonies, and parked across the road from the Gupta residence at around five in the afternoon. Under cover of darkness, they'd placed a couple of wireless pinhole cameras on the gateposts of the Gupta residence. The first was trained on the front of the house and the garden; the second on the paved area to one side of the building, which was patrolled by a dog with a sharp, ferocious bark.

This second camera also provided a view of the main door and everyone coming and going from the house. Over the course of the past two hours, Facecream had made a note of everyone she'd watched enter inside. The list read:

Vikas Gupta, the arch snorer.

His wife, Tulsi, daughter of Ram Bhatt (Puri's former client).

Vikas Gupta's parents.

Vikas Gupta's sister, Gracy.

Facecream had also spotted Vikas Gupta's elderly grandmother, who emerged from the house on the arm of a servant and took a slow turn around the garden before returning inside.

Soon after, Flush, who was monitoring all phone calls in and out of the house, overheard Vikas Gupta calling Urban Village, a local restaurant, and ordering biryani.

This presented the team with an opportunity and Flush quickly got ready his remote control gecko, who he called Gordon.

'I've run all the diagnostics and he's good to go,' said the young operative.

Facecream, who was wearing black trousers and a black top, put Gordon into her pack, clipped it around her slim waist and slipped out the back door into the street.

Keeping out of the light cast by the streetlight, she crept along the side of the three-wheeler, being careful not to catch her clothes on the rusty exterior that leant the vehicle its authenticity.

Crouched behind the bonnet, she had a clear view of the guard inside his sentry post. He was warming his hands over a burning cooking ring while listening to the cricket on the radio.

Five minutes passed before Flush's voice sounded in her earpiece: 'Bike approaching. Could be the delivery boy.'

In fact, it was a delivery middle-aged man – and he was riding on an old scooter with a number of bulging plastic bags hanging from either side of the handlebar.

Pulling up, the delivery wallah removed the bags and followed the guard through the gate.

Facecream darted across the street, using the shadows for cover.

'Guard's ringing the bell . . . they're both waiting in front of the door for it to be answered,' came Flush's voice.

'And the dog?' she whispered into her communicator.

'Sniffing the biryani.'

Facecream slipped in through the gate and darted across the garden to the front of the house.

With swift efficiency, she climbed up the drain-pipe and reached the first-floor balcony.

'Gupta's answered the door . . . taken the bill . . . now getting his wallet . . . wait, he's going back inside.'

Facecream took her lock-picking kit from her waist pack and was about to get to work on the sliding French doors when the light suddenly went on in the room beyond. She stepped quickly out of sight, peering in past the silk curtains, where Vikas Gupta started to check the pockets of his work trousers lying on the bed.

He tugged a wad of notes from one of the pockets and left the room, leaving the light on.

Though Facecream could easily have been spotted on the balcony by anyone coming in through the gate, she decided to proceed, making short work of the lock and slipping into the bedroom.

Her task took all of half a minute. Standing up on the dresser, all she had to do was activate Flush's ingeniously designed and extraordinarily lifelike animatronic gecko (this was the 2.0 model with night vision) and place it high up on the wall.

'Gordon's transmitting, all systems go,' acknowledged Flush as the gecko scurried up towards the ceiling.

Facecream waved to him.

'Looking good, babe,' said Flush. 'Now get out of there. They're nearly done. Twenty seconds max.'

'Copy that.'

Just as Facecream was getting down off the dresser, however, she noticed an object on top of the split air-conditioner unit, above which she had placed Gordon Gecko.

131

It was a syringe with a small needle attached – and evidently hadn't been there all that long given how little dust had settled on it.

She decided to take it with her, carefully slipping it into her waist bag. Then she climbed down off the dresser, turned off the light and slipped out the French doors.

'Hold there! They're heading back to the gate,' warned Flush.

Facecream watched the guard and the delivery wallah exit the compound.

The dog followed them to the gate, then turned into the garden, sniffed his way to the bottom of the drainpipe, looked up at the balcony and started to snarl and bark.

'Smart dog,' commented Facecream.

She had come prepared and, taking a little cellophane bag containing a few chunks of meat laced with a sedative from her pouch, dropped them down on the grass.

'Just not smart enough,' she said half a minute later as she slipped past the dozing pooch and then climbed nimbly up over the garden wall.

'Good job. We should celebrate,' said Flush once Facecream was back safe inside his three-wheeler. 'I'll do the pick-up. You want pepperoni or peppy paneer?'

On the drive back to Punjabi Bagh, Mummy revealed that she had learned the name of the cook from the guardian at the gurdwara. It was Surjeet and she lived somewhere in Tilak Vihar in west Delhi.

Puri agreed to accompany her there the next day and then dropped her at home.

That left one last task before heading home: dealing with his brother's request of help with arranging the laundering of his small fortune in cash.

The problem had been weighing on Puri's mind all day, one voice arguing against helping Bhuppi on the grounds that the whole thing was illegal and that he had been idiotic to keep so much cash lying around at home, while a second, more equitable voice born of a deep commitment to family, contended that it was his duty to help. Selling a property for black was not in itself a morally repugnant act, after all, another voice in his mind pointed out. Whenever anyone bought or sold a house, bar a newly constructed one, a significant proportion of the value, often as much as 80 per cent, had to be paid under the table. Even (otherwise) law-abiding citizens were often party to such practice, though it robbed the treasury of billions of rupees a year. The fact that everyone was doing it made it somehow accept-able, in the same way that everyone running red lights in Delhi had become customary.

Puri reached for his phone and found Rinku's name on his speed dial and his finger hovered over the number.

Though the two had grown up as best friends, always in and out of trouble, they rarely spoke these days. Rinku, who had followed his drunkard father into the construction business, had gone over to the dark side. Short of murder, kidnap-ping and extortion, there was nothing he wasn't into. The prospect of having to ask for his help in breaking the law bit deep.

The second voice in his mind won the day, however. Family was family. There was nothing for it. Puri pressed call.

Rinku answered after one ring. His voice was raised over the whine of hydraulics and the roar of a jet. 'Kiddan! Long time! Where've you been hiding? Still chasing housewives?'

Puri had to shout back to be heard. 'Where are you, you bugger?'

'Airport!'

'Coming or going?'

'Neither, yaar!'

Rinku broke off the conversation to give someone a dressing-down – something about crates and a flight plan and a good many expletives.

It was almost a minute before he came back on the line. 'Chubby? You're there? Apologies, I've got a shipment going out.'

Puri hated to imagine what the cargo might be. 'You can meet?' he asked.

'Anytime, anywhere! Just name it, man.'

'You're free now, by chance?'

'Better make it tomorrow, Chubby. *Mera teacher mere sir pe betha hai!*[24] Let's RV in the p.m.'

'You're on, you bugger,' said Puri and hung up.

---

[24] Literally 'My teacher is sitting on my head' – a phrase used by schoolchildren to mean they're stressed out by their exams but used here by Rinku to indicate he's stressed out by his work.

Eleven

Puri dreamed again of the angel and the blood bubbling up out of the earth and woke at seven with a start. For a while he lay staring up at the motionless ceiling fan, trying to figure out what it could all mean. Dreams featuring Chanakya had helped him solve several mysteries in the past, acting as kind of premonitions, though this was a closely guarded secret, something he had never admitted to anyone, not even Rumpi. But this one seemed to have no relevance to anything he was working on and he turned his mind to the events of the day before.

It had been busy, though he'd known busier. Juggling multiple cases was par for the course at Most Private Investigators and Puri prided himself on his ability to multitask. 'In India, an investigator must have four hands like Brahma, the creator,' he'd told a visiting Canadian senior detective recently while helping him track down an art smuggler. 'Working in this place is something of a juggling act, we can say.'

For all his impressive juggling abilities, however, Puri had managed to drop one ball: he'd forgotten to call Rumpi to tell her he was going to be late. And arriving home at eleven, he'd found a note on the kitchen table that demanded he make use of the microwave to heat up his dinner instead of waking up the servants

– *It's simple to use if you'll just find the patience.* Rumpi had also asked that he set aside fifteen minutes in the morning – *before you go rushing off* – to discuss an important family matter. *I want your full attention, if that's even remotely possible these days*, she'd written.

Puri had gone to bed grumpy and hungry.

A fitful night's sleep had left him in a more equitable mood, however, and though he was anxious to get to work and start background checks on Maaya and Saanvi, he headed downstairs to try and make the peace.

He found Rumpi standing at the stove with her back to the door.

'Come, Chubby, sit. Breakfast is ready. You must be hungry,' she said, without turning round.

Puri thought it prudent not to comment on his appetite (to acknowledge his hunger would be a tacit admittance that he'd refused to operate the microwave; whereas to claim that he wasn't hungry would lead to the suspicion that he'd taken outside food, which would compound his crime of returning home late without calling first) and wished her a good morning instead.

Rumpi carried on cooking in silence, patting and flipping and buttering a hot paratha on her *tava*.

When it was ready, she served him and returned to the stove to make another.

Puri added some yoghurt and a little garlic pickle to his plate and began to eat in silence.

A cup of mud-coloured chai was set before him, a second paratha followed, and then Rumpi joined him at the table.

'I saw your note, my dear,' he said, his mouth half-full. 'It was my intention to be here in time for dinner, but—'

Rumpi shot up a hand. 'Spare me your excuses, Chubby. Jassu told me everything,' she said.

'Regarding Mummy-ji and all?'

'About her cold, the firing of her driver, her running off to Trilokpuri, the gurdwara, you taking her home, yes everything.' Rumpi sighed. 'All I ask for is that you take a minute to call, Chubby. How many times do I have to ask? Never mind that I've hardly seen you since Diwali.'

Puri stopped eating. 'So many demands are there, my dear,' he said, softening his tone. 'How was I to know the government would introduce this notebandi? It is creating so much of disruption to everyday life.'

'If it wasn't that, it would be something else. You're working too hard, Chubby. You can't keep going on like this. Think of your blood pressure, if nothing else. You promised me we would go away together for a break and now you're busier than ever.'

Puri began to fidget with his cutlery. 'You are right, my dear, a promise is a promise. I gave you my word,' he conceded. 'I'll take you to Udaipur next week come what may. The weather is perfect there this time of year. I could do with some meter down.'

'That would be nice, Chubby, I'd like that. But first I've something to tell you. And I'd ask that you try and keep an open mind. Promise me you'll not fly off the handle? Try to remember

137

this is 2016 and times change.' She paused. 'It's concerning Radhika.'

Radhika was their youngest daughter, now in her mid-twenties. Fiercely independent, she was working in Mumbai as a journalist on a national newspaper.

'She's made a *friend*,' said Rumpi.

'A . . . *boy*?' Puri stopped eating.

'He's twenty-five, Chubby.'

'What all happened to that Bunty fellow?' he asked.

'I told you before, he was a *bhai* friend. It wasn't . . . well, like that . . . not a relationship, per se.'

Puri's knotted eyebrows gathered heavily over his troubled face. He was almost afraid to know more. 'They've been *friends* for how long exactly?' he asked.

'A few months, I think.'

'His name?'

'Bishwanath Ganguly.'

Puri's eyes widened. 'A Bong?' he asked.

'Yes, Chubby, a Bengali – much like your dear friend, Dr Ghosh,' answered Rumpi. 'You wouldn't object to his son marrying your daughter, would you?'

'That is a totally different thing. You know full well that Shom got married two years back.'

'That's not the point.'

'So often I tell my clients, "You would not invite a stranger in your house. Why invite any Tom, Dick or Harry in your family?"'

Rumpi explained calmly that Radhika had

asked that they both meet with 'Bish', whom she seemed keen on marrying.

'What does he do exactly, this boy?' asked Puri with disdain.

Rumpi composed herself. 'He's a TV producer.'

'That is what passes for a job these days?' He pushed away his plate, the second paratha half-eaten. 'At least Bunty was a decent sort.'

'You only liked him because he was Punjabi and he had a moustache.'

'What is wrong with that, my dear? I happen to be Punjabi. I sport a moustache also, and am in favour of others doing so. It denotes a certain masculinity and I'm in favour of our daughter marrying a man not a mouse.'

'Chubby, I'm not going to debate this with you.'

'Mark my words,' he said darkly. 'Should Radhika marry this Bish character it will be fish fry and *pulao* with egg at the wedding. We'll spend the party discussing poetry!'

'That's ridiculous. You know full well that Bengalis don't only eat fish. The important thing here is Radhika and her happiness. She's telling me that she loves him.'

'This is not the proper way. Marriage concerns the entire family,' said Puri.

'Radhika would never do anything to disrespect you, Chubby. Promise me you'll meet him and then you can make up your mind.'

'I'll think on it.'

'Well, don't take too long about it. And don't go snooping around in this boy's life. Radhika would never forgive you.'

* * *

139

Elizabeth Rani was the first to call while Puri was on his way to the office. She'd spent five hours queuing up for the bank yesterday but failed to deposit her old notes or get hold of any usable cash. As of now, she and her husband had only three fifty-rupee notes between them. In short, she needed 'another off'.

She was not the only one.

Mrs Chadha and Door Stop called to say they would be no shows again. And Tubelight informed him that he was away in the Haryana boondocks where one of his relatives worked as the manager of the local branch of a state-owned-bank; though this individual was proving helpful, the work of opening multiple bank accounts on behalf of a number of accommo-dating farmers was taking time and Puri's chief operative anticipated not returning to the city until late in the evening.

However, being out of station had not prevented him from looking into Hari Dev, aka Hairy Toes, as per Puri's request last night.

'Guy's a total goonda, boss,' was how Tubelight summed him up. 'Owns Delightful Marble Emporium in Bhogal and doubles as a money agent for *netas*. They say he's got benami invest-ments in coal and steel. Heavily into real estate in Jalandhar. Was implicated in an illegal rice export deal a few years back. Also, faced charges after the shooting of his partner, but got off after the key witness met with an accident.'

'How?'

'A truck went over him. Twice.'

*　　*　　*

Next, Puri spoke with Facecream. 'How's the snoring?' he asked.

'Deafening! It sounds like a cross between a chainsaw and thunder!' she said. 'When it started, I was wearing a pair of headphones and I nearly fell off my chair. I swear my ears are still ringing.'

'It's possible the microphone exaggerated the sound in some way?'

'When I stepped outside of the van to get some air, I could hear him from down in the street!'

'Tulsi's not exaggerating, in other words.'

'Right, and there's no way he was doing it before the marriage. We would have known. The whole neighbourhood would have known!'

'Meaning the cause is psychological or something is aggravating this extreme snoring,' observed Puri.

This led her to tell him about the syringe. 'Someone either left it there by mistake or it was placed there out of sight.'

Facecream suggested that he send the black residue inside for analysis; she also asked to look over the Vikas Gupta matrimonial file.

'It's possible we missed something. He had a former girlfriend called Ruchi. Perhaps she's taking revenge, trying to break up the marriage,' she speculated.

Back in the office alone and with his *Do Not Disturb* notice hanging back on the front door, Puri found himself preoccupied with his youngest daughter, to whom he had always been closest. After the initial shock, he had calmed down and begun to accept that perhaps he'd overreacted about the boy being a Bong. Rumpi was right: he wouldn't have objected to Subhrojit's son, Shom, marrying his daughter. Quite the reverse, he would have been proud to call the young man his son-in-law.

At the root of his discontent, he now realized, was the prospect of Radhika making up her own mind and presenting the boy as her choice and her choice alone. Things had never been done in such a way, not even with his first two daughters, both of whom had gone into arranged marriages. With good reason. Whirlwind love affairs often ended in tears and parents were generally better judges of a potential spouse's character. Marriage was not just about love, after all, though it was an important component. Any couple would face challenges and turbulent seas and when they did, their family should be there to support them, and vice versa. Never mind Rumpi's warning not to check up on this Bishwanath Ganguly's background; it was his responsibility to ensure that he was trustworthy, respectable and decent. Making enquiries about his family to ensure there were 'no skeletons in any *almirahs*', as Puri put it, was only prudent as well.

For this he had just the man, his counterpart in Kolkata, Saptashwa Bhattacharyya, who was known to everyone as 'Dingo'.

First, however, he needed Bishwanath Ganguly's home address and his father's name.

This took less than an hour. Step one involved searching through Radhika's latest mobile phone bill for the most frequently dialled number. Puri then called it, asked for Ganguly by name and

142

promptly hung up. Finally, Puri asked Flush to get hold of the account holder's details and phone records, and this gave him a residential address in Kolkata.

Typically, Dingo, who had connections running across the City of Joy, knew the family, at least by reputation.

'They're residing in Alipore vicinity since long back,' he said. 'Highly regarded, respectable, intellectual, well-known family. Father is a history professor, daughter is married to Dr Satish Vidyabhusan, eldest son to Dr Jayanti Chaterjee.'

'Intellectual types,' commented Puri, unfavourably.

'No scandal, highly reputable family, squeaky clean.'

Puri wasn't taking any chances, however, and asked Dingo to root around, see what he could dig up.

'Honour! I'll get you the total package!' he promised.

Puri turned his attention to other pressing matters. He arranged another meeting with Inspector Singh, whom he intended to tip off about Hairy Toes and his plans to launder money through the bank. He sent Handbrake to pick up the syringe and deliver it to a private Swiss testing laboratory he used. He divided up the wad of one-hundred-rupee notes he'd been given at the bank yesterday afternoon by Mr Dhawan for his employees.

Finally, he dedicated some time trying to deal with his cash problem without breaking the law. His approach to his landlord to pay the office rent six months in advance failed, however, and his request to the Gymkhana Club accountant to accept the amount in lieu of his future membership fees and bills was politely rebutted as well.

Soon after, Mummy called.

Though Puri had little faith that the new détente between them would last given his mother's impulsive nature (and felt disinclined to fully cooperate with her as a result), he was all sunshine. Her tone was equally engaging and helpful.

'Saanvi called me five minutes back, na,' she said.

'She's where exactly?' asked Puri, though he knew full well that she had spent the night at an address in Hauz Khas.

'Staying with her friend Sheikha. But she intends on meeting with Maaya again at three o'clock.'

'Today only?'

'In SDA.'

It occurred to Puri that perhaps he should tip off Saanvi's father. It might well do her a favour, after all. But he was also curious to see one of the sessions for himself and suggested to Mummy that he attend.

She sounded surprised. 'You, Chubby? Sure?'

'You're worried I'll interfere?'

'No, no, nothing like that.'

He pressed for an answer and she confessed to being concerned about him falling asleep during the session.

'Snoring will disturb the hypnosis,' she added.

'There will be no snoring, of that I can assure you.'

'Chubby, na, such plinky plonky music makes you dozy like when you were a baby. Remember how you used to fall asleep in the dentist reception?'

'Mummy-ji that was when I was six!'

'Some habits never go away. Better I bring my poking stick in case,' she said.

Puri lunched again at the Gymkhana where he could charge the bill to his account and conserve his precious cash.

He was finishing his dessert when Dr Subhrojit Ghosh put his head inside the restaurant, evidently looking for him.

'A private word?' he suggested, eyeing the last of Puri's Pinky Pinky Pudding with misgiving.

They adjourned to Butler's Corner, ordered tea and went into a huddle.

'Regarding your client, Saanvi,' said Subhrojit.

'She's not my client, exactly,' pointed out Puri.

'Be that as it may, I had a word with Anjali – sorry, Dr Mittal. We managed to speak about her patient hypothetically, without naming her. I described a young woman of Saanvi's age, unmarried and living with her father, who had recently undergone past life regression therapy and so forth, and she got me right away.'

Subhrojit leaned in closer, his brow tightly knitted. 'Chubby, listen to me, this is important,' he continued, keeping his voice down. 'It is Dr Mittal's opinion that Saanvi isn't strictly a schizo-phrenic but suffers from Dissociative Identity Disorder, or DID. She manifests at least three personalities.' Subhrojit sank his voice still further. 'Saanvi's condition was almost certainly triggered by sexual abuse during childhood, though she has no conscious memory of the abuse.'

'Her father was the one who abused her, is it?'

'This is something Dr Mittal was trying to get to grips with, but Saanvi discontinued her sessions.'

Puri reflected for a moment, then said, 'If he was the one abusing her, then why send her to a psychiatrist? He would risk getting found out.'

'True. But Dr Mittal said that when asked about her childhood, Saanvi's father said that it had been a happy one, which was clearly a lie. His main concern seemed to be medicating her rather than curing her.'

'Is there a cure?' asked Puri.

'With the right combination of therapy and medication, yes. Conversely, this past life regression therapy is extremely dangerous for someone with DID. It will only serve to confirm in her mind that her "alters", her other personalities, are real.'

'These personalities – where do they come from?'

'Her mind constructs them.'

'So she has *constructed* Riya Kaur in her mind?'

'Perhaps from reading about the Sikh massacres, watching movies and documentaries?'

'Or someone could have fed her the details?' suggested Puri.

'That too.'

Twelve

Saanvi's hair hung down over her face. The infectious smile and youthful enthusiasm she'd exhibited two days ago had been replaced by stark melancholy. She was unresponsive to her name and didn't seem to recognize the detective, either.

'We met just two days back,' Puri reminded her.

'Did we?' she asked, her voice child-like. 'Where?'

'In SDA. You took some ice cream.'

'Me? No, it can't have been. I don't eat ice cream.'

'It was a chocolate sundae.'

'Oh, a chocolate sundae! That must have been Saanvi,' she said. 'I'm always telling her she shouldn't eat stuff like that. At school, Mrs Kapoor told us it's junk food and rots your teeth.'

Puri felt a slight chill run down his spine. He and Mummy exchanged a puzzled look, she apparently just as taken aback as he was. But before either of them could ask Saanvi who she was, or at least who she thought she was, Maaya came sweeping into the room. *She* had not changed, Puri noted with regret – her greeting was all gush and air kisses, even in the face of Saanvi's sleepy detachment and his own stiff reserve.

'How nice! Mr Puri, I wasn't expecting you.' She beamed. 'Did you want to sit in on the session?'

'If that would not be inconvenient, madam,' he answered.

'Personally I have no objection and I'm sure Saanvi doesn't either. But I must admit to being a little surprised. When you came to meet me the other day, you didn't seem at all convinced by my methods.' Still smiling, she searched his face with her keen, sparkling eyes. 'Ahh, I think I understand!' she continued. 'You're here to try and find out how I do it, how I've managed to brainwash Saanvi. That's it, isn't it?'

'It is my job to leave no stone unturned,' he replied, stony-faced.

'Well, I'm afraid you're likely to be quite disappointed, Mr Puri.' Maaya shook out her sleeves. 'No trick cards up here, I can assure you!' she said playfully.

Puri lowered his voice and said, 'It has been brought to my attention that Saanvi was seeing a psychiatrist and believes she is several different people at once.'

Maaya folded her hands in front of her and inclined her head like a schoolteacher explaining basic arithmetic. 'Now, Mr Puri, I think you'll find that we're all many people. Don't you find you have different voices in your head?'

'That is a totally different thing, madam.'

'Is it? I take the view that we form different personalities during our former lives as we're influenced by the times and cultures we're born into. We carry those personalities with us still and often they jostle for position. This is especially the case when someone has suffered a terrible hurt in a past life and the pain remains acute. If we can only understand these past lives, come to terms with the residual emotions, then all our past identities will merge into one. I hope that answers your question?'

Puri was not conscious of having asked one. 'Well, um,' he managed.

She sailed straight across him with a lively, 'Good! Then I think it's time!'

Maaya took 'Saanvi' by the arm and led her slowly upstairs, reassuring her in velvety tones that all would soon be well.

Puri followed them into the small therapy room, where the diyas and incense sticks were already lit and the yogic mantras resonated softly in the background, giving the place a monastic feel. He picked out a spot on a cushion next to Mummy and, with a few moans, lowered himself down on to the floor and leaned back against the wall.

By now Saanvi was lying on the single mattress in the middle of the room with her eyes closed.

It only remained for Maaya to ask Puri and Mummy to switch off their phones and turn on the video camera, which stood on a tripod in one corner of the room, for her to begin.

'I want you to start to take deep breaths, let your lungs fill with air, then exhale slowly,' she said. 'I want you to listen to the rhythm of your breath. In . . . and out. Good. Now I want you to relax your arms, let them sink down into the mattress. Now the back of your neck. Now your legs and feet. Imagine your calves and your heels turning to jelly, melting away. And now I want you to picture yourself sitting in a quiet, peaceful place. It might be a meadow full of wildflowers or a beach with the water lapping on golden shores . . .'

There was nothing to indicate to Puri that Saanvi had entered a hypnotic state, but before long her breathing settled into a gentle rhythm, and Maaya deemed her ready for the next stage.

It was the same routine as before: Saanvi called her spirit guide, who quickly turned up, and asked to be taken back through time to her past life. She was told to follow a path through the mist until she was in front of several closed doors. She entered through one and found herself in a park watching a young girl with ponytails wearing a pretty dress playing catch with friends.

'Who is she?'

'Riya.'

'How old is she now?'

'Seven.'

'Are you happy?'

'It's my birthday. Papa has bought me a bird. A yellow canary.'

Maaya told Saanvi to go to the next 'significant event' in her life, then the next and so on, though none of them were especially significant or revealing as far as Puri was concerned. Riya was a teenager experiencing her first period; next she was in the hills on holiday somewhere in the Himalayas, trying to catch butterflies; finally she was a young woman, celebrating her first child's birthday.

Forty-five minutes passed in this way and

though Puri felt pins and needles creeping into his legs and buttocks and had to shift his weight and stretch out his legs every ten minutes or so, he began to feel drowsy. Soon, he had to right himself, blink hard and rub his eyes before checking, furtively, to see if Mummy had noticed. But it was no use: the soft music, candlelight, and sweet smell of incense proved a fatal combination, and it was only a question of time before he nodded off.

He must have slept for a good ten to fifteen minutes, for when he awoke thanks to a few sharp jabs in his upper arm, he could hardly feel his legs. In moving them, he had to suppress a howl, and the intense pain brought him sharply back to reality just in time.

'I'm back in the house again, locked in my room!'

Saanvi sounded terrified. 'Mantosh left me here. He's left me to die! Oh God, no! Outside – I can hear men shouting. I can smell smoke. Through the window I can see flames. They're coming!'

'Remember that you're just an observer,' said Maaya. 'You can't come to any harm. You're safe with your spirit guide. We need to know what happens next. Can you tell us?'

'I go to the door, but it's locked. I can't get out. I call out for help, but I'm afraid the men will hear.'

Maaya rested a hand on Saanvi's shoulder. 'Tell us what happens next,' she urged.

'OK, I'll try.' Saanvi paused, pursing her lips, and then went on: 'I decide the only thing to do is hide under the bed. I wait there for a while.

Then I hear footsteps. Someone's coming up the steps to the door. There's a scraping sound. Metal on stone. It's a key – someone's pushed it under the door. More footsteps, this time hurrying away. I get out from under the bed and pick up the key. It's for the door! I unlock it.'

'Who brought you the key?' asked Maaya.

'I don't know – there's no one there.'

'What do you do now?'

'I run down the stairs. They lead into a courtyard behind the kitchen. There's a ladder leaning against the wall. Someone must have left it there. I can hear the mob trying to break down the gate. I climb up, get on to the top of the wall and push the ladder away. Then I hang off the back of the wall and let go. It's a high drop. I hit the ground and feel this shooting pain in my ankle. I think it might be broken. Yes, I'm limping. But I've got to get away. I hurry down the alley, propping myself up against the wall. I can see a house on fire up ahead. There are flames shooting out of the roof. I can hear a woman screaming, begging for the life of her husband.'

Saanvi described Riya tripping, falling over, cutting her hand on some broken glass, picking herself up, limping on.

'Wait,' she said. 'My chunni! It's gone. It must have come off! I stop to look back, can see it lying on the ground where I fell. But I can't risk going back. There are voices close by. I've got to hurry.'

Soon, Saanvi spoke of coming to the end of the galli and, under the cover of drifting smoke, reaching a park.

'I'm coughing, my eyes are streaming. I need a minute.' She paused, then: 'The park is empty. There's a path snaking through it, but I stay close to the trees and shrubs. There are a few benches . . . a fountain made of lots of rocks piled up. I reach the end of the park. There's a gate. It opens on to the main road. It's wide the road, three lanes on both sides. I can see a few cars burning . . . there are people running back and forth . . . and there's a group of men coming towards me. They're armed with clubs and bars . . . carrying cans of kerosene. They're shouting. "Blood for blood!" Oh God, they're getting closer. I've got to hide. There are some bushes. I get behind them and wait.'

'Ask your spirit guide to take you forward to the next significant event,' said Maaya.

Puri waited in rapt attention, ignoring the pain in his legs.

'I'm in a room, but I can't move. My arms are tied up, I'm lying down . . . on a *charpai*, I think, face down. The string is rough on my skin. A door opens behind me. Someone comes in, closes the door. A man, I think. I try to turn my head to see his face, but I can't.'

Saanvi gave a sudden gasp. 'No, stop, please! Oh God, no!' she whimpered.

'Calm yourself. Remember you're an observer. Stay close to your spirit guide,' Maaya reminded her. 'Tell us what's happening.'

But Saanvi started to scream.

The sound of her suffering penetrated deep into Puri's core. 'Enough!' he bellowed. 'Stop this!'

And the room crashed into silence.

*   *   *

Puri left Maaya's house puzzled and angry. Puzzled because Saanvi's 'performance', for want of a better word, had been so convincing and he failed to understand how her description of events could be so detailed; angry because she'd made him doubt himself, made him wonder if there wasn't the slightest possibility that perhaps she might be the reincarnation of Riya Kaur after all, and he had got the whole thing wrong.

Back in the Ambassador without Mummy, whom he urged to remain with Saanvi (though she'd come out of her trance with a smile, back to her former, *former* self, and oblivious of the distress she'd exhibited only moments before), these emotions quickly culminated in a sense of purpose. Everything else Puri was dealing with faded into the background and he resolved to apply himself to the case wholeheartedly. His priority now was to see the house for himself and get to grips with the geography of the place, something he would have done right at the beginning of any conventional investigation.

The route to Rajouri Garden led first through Delhi's spacious diplomatic area with its broad, tree-lined avenues, high perimeter walls with national flags fluttering beyond, and the odd line of weary visa applicants waiting on pavements. Then through the concrete knot of overpasses at Dhaula Khan that delivered them to Delhi Cantt,[25] the city's expansive army base. Here bored-looking *sepoys* in sandbagged positions guarded

[25] Cantonment.

a realm of martial order where neat barracks abutted well-swept parade grounds, though the sight of undershirts and *chuddies* drying on tree branches suggested that the Indian Army laundry facilities were somewhat rudimentary.

Soon, the acres so carefully preserved by the top brass fell behind and the city began to press in once more as if threatening to crush the vehicles travelling between its concrete palisades. Man had stamped his brutal mark on every inch of space here. Tight formations of cars lined the side of the road as if arranged for a daredevil motorbike rider planning a death-defying stunt. Long columns of shops, offering a random selection of merchandise – luxurious silk saris in one, giant spools of electric cabling in the next – were interrupted by malls with reflective glass facades.

A couple of turns off the main road, Mahatma Gandhi Marg, and the Ambassador reached Rajouri Garden with its large villas and apartment blocks housing burgeoning Punjabi families.

Puri knew the area well. It lay just a couple of miles from where he had grown up, and he couldn't turn a corner here without remembering some episode from his past – a Diwali party involving a dodgy rocket that shot into a neighbour's living room; a confrontation with a bully; a prank he and Rinku carried out on their friend, Chetan Bhatia; an incident with a monkey that snatched his friend Mintu's kulfi out of his hand.

He directed Handbrake to F Block and they drove slowly past Mantosh Singh's residence before parking up the street.

Puri then made his way back to Number 92 on foot and found an inconspicuous spot in the shade of a mature *peelu* tree from where he could look over the house.

The original building that Riya had lived in was gone, torn down and replaced with an American-style McMansion that was like a cross between the Parthenon and a Wendy house, all clad in crazy paving.

There were no features identifying it as a Sikh household, on the outside at least. Puri assumed this was deliberate, for though the political tensions between Sikhs and Hindus had long abated, the murderous events of 1984 were by no means forgotten. Indeed, the family took its security seriously. There were a couple of cameras on the gatepost, another visible up on the side of the house trained on the entrance, a sign warning that the property was alarmed, and a state-of-the-art video door-entry system mounted on the gatepost.

Voices approaching from down the street drew Puri's attention.

Two tall, confident-looking Sikh men, both in their early sixties and dressed in T-shirts and shorts for exercise, were brisk walking in his direction.

Certain that he would be spotted loitering and concerned that one of these gentlemen might just be Mantosh Singh, Puri stepped out into the road and walked in their direction.

The man on the left, whose turban was blue, fixed hard, suspicious eyes upon the detective.

Puri avoided eye contact as he passed by.

Once he'd reached a safe distance, he stepped behind a parked car and looked back.

The two men were standing to one side of the peelu tree. They remained there for a couple of minutes, chatting amiably, their body language and mannerisms indicative of old friendship, Blue Turban throwing the occasional glance down the street in Puri's direction.

A couple of minutes later, the two men parted company and Blue Turban took one last look down the street before heading through the gates of Number 92.

This, surely, was Mantosh Singh himself – not exactly the most sensitive-looking individual, with his great greying beard and vinegary mien, it had to be said. But that didn't make him a murderer, and, determined to concentrate on the task at hand, Puri put him out of his mind and continued down the road a short distance, turning left down the next side street.

After a block, it was intersected by a galli that ran north past the back of the Kaur property and south to the nearest market.

Puri recognized it now, having biked along it many times as a boy with the other members of the notorious Yo-yo Gang. Free of traffic and obstruction, this had been their short cut to the old Imperial Theatre, which burned down in the Nineties.

On the afternoon of 1 November 1984, it had provided safe passage for the Singh family. And he had no difficulty picturing a younger Mantosh Singh carrying his children in his arms, pausing on the corner of the side streets that intersected the galli, looking left and right to make sure the coast was clear, then herding his parents and other members of the household down the next section until they reached the back door of the cinema.

He was loath to imagine Riya making her escape based purely on hearsay. There was no hard evidence to suggest that she had done so. Quite the reverse, the blood found in the back of Mantosh Singh's car along with a shovel and dirt indicated that the husband did away with his wife himself, just as Riya's father had contended. And it was Bobby's theory that she had been killed during the riots, Puri reminded himself. In his view, Mantosh Singh had returned to the house on the night of 1 November and disposed of the body among the other victims of the mob.

The fact that Saanvi knew of the galli and could describe the geography so precisely proved nothing. She could have visited the area recently, chaperoned or otherwise. Or she had picked up the detail from a newspaper cutting or perhaps, somehow, read the pages from the missing case file.

Puri only felt compelled to retrace the route Saanvi had described on the grounds of trying to identify some detail she had provided that Riya could not possibly have seen in 1984 – and in this way disprove once and for all the reincarnation theory. He would then confront Saanvi and Maaya and try to get to the bottom of what her or their game was.

Turning north into the galli, which was about seven feet wide and hemmed in by high graffiti-besmirched walls and rusting back gates that showed no sign of use, Puri picked his way through a detritus of broken bricks, tufts of grass and weeds, and the occasional dog turd.

A wind was blowing up the galli behind him and caught hold of the odd bit of rubbish, a cigarette packet here, a plastic bottle there, and sent it rattling along the concrete. A stray dog appeared around a slight bend and started snarling and barking. Puri reached down for a stone to lob at him, but just the action was enough to send the cur tearing away.

A moment later – too late – Puri spotted two surveillance cameras positioned up on the wall at the back of the Kaur McMansion, both pointing down into the galli in opposite directions.

His initial reaction was to curse under his breath, furious with himself for blundering into their line of sight. His objective had been to take a discreet look at the house and its surroundings; instead he'd been spotted by Mantosh Singh and, worse, caught on film. 'Smoothly done, sir-ji,' he mumbled to himself. But then he began to reconsider. Perhaps it was for the best. There were cases, and this was one of them, surely, when the best (perhaps only) hope of success was to beat the undergrowth and see what came flapping out.

Either way he had nothing to lose in spending a few minutes in full view of the cameras, going through the motions of examining the Singh's back wall and taking photographs of it with his phone.

When he carried on along the galli, he did so

with head bent down like a tracker who'd spotted fresh tracks.

Only when he was out of sight and could drop the act did he stop to think back on Saanvi's session and allowed her words to play back in his head.

'I've got to get away. I hurry down the alley, propping myself up against the wall. I can see a house on fire up ahead. There are flames shooting out of the roof. I can hear a woman screaming, begging for the life of her husband,' she'd said.

For a moment, Puri thought he could hear them too, could smell the smoke, taste burnt kerosene fumes on his tongue, and though he resisted the temptation to enter into Saanvi's fiction, pictured a young woman hobbling past him, escaping up the galli.

He followed, watching her stumble, trip, cut her hand on some glass. Her hand was bleeding now, but she picked herself up and carried on.

Then she turned and looked back, searching for her chunni.

'I can't risk going back. There are voices close by. I've got to hurry.'

Puri stopped and took out his notebook, referring back to his conversation with Bobby.

Riya's father had found the chunni *in front* of the house, he'd said. And Bobby was rarely wrong on the details.

This, then, suggested a hole in Saanvi's story. For the chunni to have got into the street someone would have to place it there – hardly likely in the middle of a pogrom.

Eager to identify more holes, Puri pressed on.

Soon reaching the end of the galli, he crossed the road into the park.

'There's a path snaking through it, but I stay close to the trees and shrubs.'

Puri kept to the path, but pictured Riya off close to the trees, frightened, out of breath.

'I pass a few benches . . . a fountain . . . it's made of lots of rocks.'

At the far side of the park, which covered a few acres at most, Puri came across a fountain that matched her description – a heap of boulders concreted together.

Water dribbled down one side into a murky pool in which soggy sweet wrappers and a Coke tin floated around. This, surely, had been constructed after 1984, Puri told himself with expectation. But a plaque on the railing around the fountain, placed there by the local residents' association, dated the fountain to 1983.

Disappointed, he stepped over to the gate at the end of the park where he pictured Riya standing, catching her breath, surveying the road. It was busier than it had been in her day, a barrage of noisy traffic running in either direction.

The police station opposite was the same building as it had been in 1984 with the red and blue colouring of the sign, the official colours of the force, marking it out.

There were a couple of Mahindra jeeps parked in front. A *jawan* and an officer emerged from the entrance, climbed into one and drove off with the siren wailing.

Puri went and found an empty bench and began to jot down everything that had happened in

161

connection to the case in the past few hours – the details of Saanvi's session, the McMansion, his impression of Mantosh Singh.

He sketched a rudimentary map of the area, indicating the house, the galli, the old cinema and the park, and returned his notebook to its rightful place. Then he considered what to do next. Mummy was right to be looking for the cook, he could see that now, and he decided to definitely collaborate with her on that score. Tomorrow, he would also try getting to the bottom of how Saanvi knew the geography of Rajouri Garden so intimately and try to exploit the detail about the chunni being dropped in the galli when in fact Riya's father found it bloodied in the street in front of the Singh residence.

By the time he recrossed the park again, the wind had picked up and was blowing hard down the galli, driving random bits of garbage towards him.

Pages of a newspaper whirled in an invisible eddy. A soft drinks tin rattled over the pavement. And then a light blue plastic bag took to the air like a bird.

Puri watched as it sailed higher and higher, drifting over the rooftops of F Block.

He hurried along the pavement, captivated by its progress – and as it began to lose height, floating down into Mantosh Singh's street, he could not help but picture it as a light yellow chunni.

Thirteen

Facecream and Flush were waiting outside the laboratory where Vikas Gupta's ex-girlfriend, Ruchi, worked. Thanks to certain technical know-how (in other words, malware uploaded to her smartphone that allowed them to listen in on her calls), they knew that she was due to attend a wedding in the evening and planned to visit a 'Shanaz' beauty parlour beforehand to get her nails done and eyebrows threaded. Which of the four or five Shanaz Hussein beauty parlours in Delhi she intended to head to wasn't clear from the conversation she'd had with her mother, however – thus the need to tail her.

For this purpose, Flush's battered and lopsided Bajaj three-wheeler had the advantage of appearing inconspicuous. Indeed, for the first half of the journey, which led through the congested streets of Dakshinpuri, the team were able to maintain a position directly behind Ruchi's car without fear of raising suspicion. Once they reached the ring road, where the traffic was comparatively light by today's standards, however, the vehicle was less than ideal. Ruchi, who drove a nippy little red Maruti hatchback and might well have considered a second career as a racing driver, slalomed between the assortment of other cars, autos, scooters, tempos, buses, bicycles and the odd animal and random obstacle (including a couple of men on a bamboo ladder attempting to fix a traffic light at a chaotic interchange) with gay abandon, forcing Flush to accelerate his old four-stroke engine to its maximum speed of forty-four miles per hour. The Bajaj strained and shook so violently that Facecream had to clench her teeth to prevent herself from biting her tongue and Flush's prized dashboard hula doll jiggled so wildly that she looked like she might lose her grass skirt. The three-wheeler had a steering issue as well – namely it didn't respond as quickly as was ideal.

Soon, Ruchi's car was out of sight.

But all was not lost: Flush was able to trace Ruchi's mobile signal to GK2 Main Market and Facecream caught up with her in the Shanaz parlour around twenty minutes later where she was already having a facial.

Puri's operative was shown to one of the adjacent treatment chairs and put in the care of a keen, sparky young beautician called Naaz, who was full of gossip and scandal and for whom no subject seemed taboo. While she was being given a pedicure, Facecream, who posed as a student at Delhi University, learned that the wife of a big Bollywood star was a regular, but didn't tip; a certain Mrs Sadani had backed her brand-new Mercedes into a drain; and the daughter of another customer had developed terrible acne and was finding it impossible to find a groom.

Ruchi couldn't have missed any of this, though unlike the other customers and beauticians dotted around the parlour, she refrained from being drawn into the tittle-tattle and sat reading a glossy magazine. When Facecream attempted to strike up a conversation with her, it failed to spark. But in Facecream's experience there were two things people could not resist: a love story and the urge to give advice (and in doing so share their own experiences), and so Puri's operative began to confide in her beautician about her (fictional) man troubles.

Karan was his name and he was dreamy looking – green eyes and dark wavy hair. An airline pilot based in Mumbai, who flew around the world and came to Delhi twice a month, he'd lavished her with perfumes and chocolates, and taken her to fancy restaurants.

Naaz lapped it up. 'Do your parents know?' she asked, all eagerness and anticipation.

'Not yet. I'm worried they'll tell me to leave him.'

'Has he said he wants to marry you?'

'Yes . . . just after he's got this new job with another airline. Then he says we'll live in Singapore.'

'Wow! My friend went to Singapore and said it's amazing!'

'Right. But what if all he's after is . . . You know, he just wants to get me into bed.'

'You mean you haven't slept with him yet?' hissed Naaz, though the entire parlour heard her.

Facecream feigned embarrassment, letting her large brown eyes fall to the floor. 'I haven't been ready,' she said shyly.

This was the beautician's cue to give of all her wisdom on matters of the heart. Times were changing, she said. Women were getting

165

liberated. What was wrong with sleeping with a man before marriage? Men could get away with it, why not women? It wasn't a moral issue; it was a question of ensuring that two people were compatible. Besides, a friend of hers had become an air hostess and married a pilot and she now lived in Dubai.

'They've got this villa with a *private* swimming pool!'

Throughout Naaz's discourse, Ruchi remained absorbed in her magazine, her expression impassive.

After her treatments came to an end and she sat drinking a cup of complimentary chai, however, she spoke up suddenly. 'That pilot of yours is after only one thing,' she told Facecream darkly. 'Believe me, he'll break your heart.'

'Karan? Why do you say that?'

Ruchi's eyes burned with resentment born of betrayal. Facecream recognized it only too well; in her early twenties she, too, had been the victim of a shattering disloyalty.

'Men will say anything to get what they want. And after they've had their fun, then it's all duty to parents and family,' she said bitterly.

'Why do you say that?' asked Facecream, playing dumb. 'Did that happen to you?'

'He said he loved me, said he'd do anything for me,' said Ruchi, with a cold, distant look. 'I gave myself to him, body and soul, and then he turned around and married the girl his parents wanted him to. Didn't even put up a fight.'

'That's terrible. I feel so sorry for you.'

Ruchi's eyes glinted like steel. 'I don't need

pity. I was stupid. And believe me, Vikas is paying a price. Yes, he's getting exactly what he deserves.'

Facecream called Puri to share what she'd learned – that Ruchi and Vikas Gupta's relationship had been far more involved than either of them had admitted to their families.

'Somehow we managed to overlook the fact that Ruchi was in love with him,' said Facecream.

'That is not strictly true,' Puri corrected her. 'In actual fact, I did not neglect to flag the fact that Vikas Gupta had kept a girlfriend and that we could not rule out sexual relations between the two, young people engaging in such activities these days before marriage. But Ram Bhatt was not in the least concerned. Brushed it aside, in fact. Said something about there being no harm in young men enjoying a bit of sport before settling down and tying the knot.'

'Well, Vikas seems to have broken Ruchi's heart, boss. I can only imagine she kept quiet because she does not want the facts known either.'

'You think that in some way she's causing the snoring, is it?' asked Puri.

'She's got the motive and works in a laboratory where they do research into allergies. Also, it says in the file that Ruchi and Vikas's sister, Gracy, are close friends, so it's entirely plausible that Ruchi has visited the house since the wedding and got up into the bedroom.'

They agreed that once the report came back from the lab, they would speak again, the expectation being that if the syringe was found to contain a potential irritant, then Facecream would endeavour to trace it to Ruchi's lab and figure out how it was inducing the snoring.

'Tip top, very good,' said Puri and hung up.

'Working another case, is it, Chubby?' Mummy asked with a motherly undertone that hinted of disapproval.

Puri had picked her up a few minutes earlier and they were driving to Tilak Vihar to try and find the cook.

'A small matter only,' said Puri before quickly changing the subject. 'Now what were you telling me, exactly? Saanvi went home to her father, is it?'

'Correct. And like I was telling you, na, she did so willingly. No anxiety was there. Any memory of the other day when her father dragged her away was totally absent,' said Mummy. 'Seems her character changes from day to day.'

Puri was not about to let on regarding Suro having spoken on his behalf to the psychiatrist, but told her instead that he had consulted with an expert and in his opinion Saanvi suffered from multiple personality disorder.

Mummy took in this information with a series of nods and an intense frown and then declared, as if it would come as some great revelation to her son, 'You know, Chubby, just some doubt is forming in my head. Maybe Saanvi is not the reincarnation of Riya after all. Could be the whole thing is a sham, na.'

Puri's eyes widened to almost comic proportions. 'Come again, Mummy-ji?'

'Personally I had some doubts from the start,'

she continued, nonchalant. 'Two and two did not add up to four. But Saanvi was convincing. So much detail she described. How else she could know such things?'

Puri sank his chin to his chest. He felt a strong urge to drive home, pour himself a large Royal Challenge and get into bed with his hot water bottle.

'See, after the session was getting over and you rushed off leaving me there with Saanvi and Maaya on my own . . . well, I required the bath-room,' she went on. 'It is located down the corridor. But some confusion was there, na, and I entered through a wrong door. Thus I found myself standing in the doorway of Maaya's study. What I came across was as a shock, that is for sure. One wall was covered in newspaper clip-pings relating to Riya Kaur. So many there were. And photos, also.'

Puri's head sprang up. 'What kind of photos exactly?' he asked.

'A large print of Mantosh Singh, taken recently with a telephoto lens, looked like,' she answered. 'There was one taken of Saanvi, also. And one more thing: there was a file on the desk marked *Unsolved Murders, 1984.*'

'You got a look inside?' asked Puri with eager expectation.

'That was my intention, naturally, Chubby. But before I could proceed, I heard Maaya coming out of her therapy room.'

'She realized you'd seen inside her study?'

'I closed the door in time and pretended to do confusion. There was no suspicion on her part.'

Puri clapped his hands together, part with relief, part in muted triumph. 'As I suspected, Maaya has in some way brainwashed Saanvi,' he said.

'But why, Chubby?'

'Rest assured, Mummy-ji, that much we must and will find out.'

'And the Riya case. We will solve it also, na?'

There was a pause and Puri breathed a sigh into it. 'Mummy-ji, I would love to get to the bottom of what all happened, truly I would,' he said. 'But Papa-ji tried to solve the case all those years ago and came up empty-handed, and since that time, no new witness has come forward. Not one piece of fresh evidence has come to the light, either. *And* all the notes and statements have vanished. We are still at square one.'

Puri considered stopping and turning the car around rather than carrying on to try and find the cook. But given that she was the only living witness in the Riya Kaur case and the fact that by now they were nearing Tilak Vihar, it seemed remiss not to speak with her. Then he could formulate a plan for exposing Maaya and perhaps find a way of getting Saanvi out of her clutches and back into professional care.

'We need C Block,' he told Handbrake. 'The widow colony.'

The Sikh in the blue turban with pitted cheeks idling in the street outside the gurdwara looked Puri up and down with something approaching scorn.

'You're with the media?' he asked after the detective approached him, asking if he was local.

170

'No, no, not at all,' said Puri.

'Because we've had enough of journalists coming here speaking to our mothers and taking advantage of them,' the man went on, regardless. 'Every year on the anniversary of the tragedy, it's the same thing. Our mothers cry for the cameras, tell their stories about how our fathers were burned alive or beaten to death . . . how they cut their boys' hair and dressed them as girls and stuffed handkerchiefs into our mouths to stop us from crying. They speak about how they're tortured by the memories. But what good has it done? Where has any of it got any of us? Have any of the murderers faced justice? No, and our mothers will take their pain with them to the grave.'

'I'm not a media person,' reiterated Puri.

'A lawyer, then?' By the sound of it, the young man, who Puri judged to be in his mid-thirties, had little regard for their kind, either.

'We're investigators, doing investigation, na,' piped up Mummy.

'You're with the police?'

'Working in a private capacity, only,' said Puri and produced a copy of his card. 'My name is Vish Puri, Most Private Investigators. Some time back I was featured on the cover of *India Today*.'

The young man stared blankly at the card.

'And *she*?' he asked, gesturing to Mummy.

'My mother. We're working together,' said Puri, though it pained him to say it.

'We're looking for someone. Perhaps you know her,' said Mummy.

'I know a lot of people,' he answered.

171

Fortunately, this included Mantosh Singh's former cook, Surjeet, or Surjeet Auntie as he referred to her. She was his neighbour and had practically raised him.

Before taking them to her, however, the young man, whose name was Balwant, wanted to know why they wished to speak with her, and Puri was left with little choice but to outline the basics of the case and how they needed to go over Surjeet's statement.

'So this is one of those cold cases that retired cops work on when they're old and then come across some new piece of evidence, like on the TV?' asked Balwant with a glint in his eye.

'It's all very hush-hush. Might be we are looking at murder after all,' said Puri with a wink.

'Sure thing,' said Balwant, though he proceeded to shout across the road to his friend at the cigarette and *paan* stand that he was taking 'them' to Surjeet Auntie and would be back later.

They set off on foot down lanes as narrow as those of a medieval city with balconies almost touching overhead, each hung with laundry. Rows of small doors with boxy, sparsely furnished rooms beyond lent the place a monastic feel. But this was no ancient medina or citadel; none of the buildings dated back more than twenty-five years, and the red brick walls were as wonky and uneven as teetering Jenga towers. Extensions had been added to extensions, floors upon floors, with flat roofs staggered at different levels, each crowned with ugly black Sintex water tanks and grey steel pipes poking out like bent periscopes.

172

'See how we have to live?' said Balwant over his shoulder, pointing to the open drains. 'During elections, politicians promise to help us, say they'll make improvements, but nothing changes.'

The sight of rows of large plastic containers for collecting water at communal taps lined up outside homes and the odd diesel generator puttering away in the absence of electricity further emphasized his point.

'Growing up here was tough for other reasons, as well. Our fathers were gone and our mothers had to work during the day, so plenty of my friends got hooked on alcohol and drugs and got into crime. Things are getting better now, but it's hard to find a wife. Families from other areas don't want their daughters marrying a boy from here. I myself remain unmarried.'

The entrance to Surjeet's home would have been near impossible to find without him – an alley wet with water dripping from an overhead pipe led to a steep, echoing flight of bare concrete stairs with walls streaked with paan stains, then finally a steel door painted dung brown.

Balwant was about to knock on the door but stopped short. 'By the way, Auntie-ji's not been keeping well recently. She was in hospital for some days but hasn't got the tests back yet. It might be she's resting,' he warned.

Indeed, the face that appeared after a couple of bangs on the door looked tired and frail.

'Oh, it's you,' she said, recognizing Balwant. 'I was sleeping.'

'Auntie-ji, I've brought some people to meet

you. They're private detectives; they want to ask you some questions,' he explained.

'Now?' she said. 'What's it about?'

Puri introduced himself and explained that he'd reopened the Riya Kaur case.

'After all these years?'

'We've come across some new evidence,' Puri lied.

Surjeet was quiet for a moment, then said with a pleading expression, 'Go and speak with Mantosh-sir. He can tell you what happened better than me. It was all so long ago.'

'Auntie-ji, we spoke with him and he sent us here,' Puri lied again.

'Just a few minutes of time is required,' reiterated Mummy.

Surjeet blinked a few times, then said with reluctance, 'I told the police everything I knew. For my part, I did nothing wrong.'

Puri had been ready to give up; the prospect of trying to get anything out of this ailing, elderly cook seemed hopeless. But her words struck upon him. *For my part, I did nothing wrong.* What did that mean?

'Auntie-ji, I assure you we don't wish to keep you more than a few minutes,' he said, and before she could raise any further objection, took off his shoes on the doorstep.

Balwant took Surjeet by the arm, led her back inside and switched on a single light bulb hanging bare from the ceiling. The room was revealed to be small, the furnishing frugal with a charpai in one corner that served as a bed. The blanket was pulled back, the pillow cratered. The only other furniture was a dented almirah, a set of moulded plastic garden table and chairs, and a TV on a stand draped in a knitted throw. Above this, high up on the wall, hung a framed, black-and-white portrait of a young Sikh man, evidently Surjeet's late husband.

'You mind me asking what is that, exactly?' asked Puri after he and Mummy and Balwant had pulled up the chair in front of the charpai where Surjeet now sat with her back against the wall and the blanket drawn over her. He was pointing at what appeared to be a framed, grubby ten-rupee note up on the wall.

'The money Auntie-ji's husband earned the day before he died,' said Balwant.

'It was the last thing he ever gave me,' said Surjeet sadly.

'I'm told you were working in Rajouri Garden in Mantosh Singh's house during the danga and managed to escape with the family? We understand Mantosh Singh led you to the cinema?'

'I owe my life to him.'

'Sounds like nothing short of a miracle. God only knows how you weren't spotted,' said Mummy.

'You went out the back gate, didn't you, Auntie-ji?' prompted Balwant.

'A galli ran behind the house,' confirmed Surjeet. 'Had we been spotted, we would have been killed for sure.'

The conversation continued in this way for the next twenty minutes or so, and Puri and Mummy were able to stitch together the order of events.

On 31 October, Mantosh Singh and his father returned home with the shocking news that Indira

175

Gandhi had been assassinated. Their car had been pelted with stones en route and, near Connaught Place, they'd seen a fellow Sikh man dragged from a bus and beaten.

By evening, reports of further violence reached the house, and Surjeet was advised not to return home to Trilokpuri. Subsequently, she spent the night on the kitchen floor, worried sick for the safety of her husband and children.

The next morning brought news of widespread violence and killings and both Mantosh Singh and his father decided to cut their hair and shave their beards. Surjeet made breakfast and lunch, ignorant of the fact that by then her husband and son were already dead.

By eight o'clock in the evening, with the mob at the gates of the house, the family and servant made their escape to the cinema.

'You told the police that Mantosh Singh was absent for around an hour in the middle of the night,' said Puri.

The question made her visibly uncomfortable. 'That's right. That's what I told the police.'

'What time was this?'

'The middle of the night, maybe three, four.'

'You were awake?'

'I couldn't sleep.'

'Did Mantosh Singh know you were awake?'

She hesitated. 'I'm not sure. We were all lying on the floor – the cinema owners had given us some blankets. It was dark.'

Puri paused. 'What happened to Riya? How was it you all escaped from the house but she didn't?'

'Before we all escaped down the galli, sir went to fetch her, but the mob entered the compound and he barely escaped with his life.'

'Where was she?'

'In her room?'

'How do you know? You'd seen her?'

'I'd taken up food.'

'But had you seen her for yourself? Are you sure she was there?'

Another hesitation. 'She was lying in bed; they had medicated her after she gave birth. Sir told us she was very weak. There had been a lot of blood loss.'

Puri pushed on. 'We heard that Mantosh Singh and Riya had marital problems,' he said.

'I was not aware of anything like that,' Surjeet answered, dismissively. 'Mantosh-sir was always good to me.'

'And Riya, she was kind to you, also, na?' asked Mummy.

'Yes, very kind.'

'So beautiful, she was,' said Mummy.

'Always thinking of others.' Tears pooled in Surjeet's eyes.

'You used to talk, the two of you?'

'Sometimes. When we were alone in the house.'

Mummy reached out and took her hand. 'Auntie-ji, we understand your loyalty to Mantosh Singh, but an injustice should not go unpunished,' she said tenderly. 'You of all people should understand that. Your husband was murdered and to date those responsible are walking free. Help us understand what happened to Riya once and for all. If there is anything more you can tell us, do so.'

177

Tears trickled down Surjeet's cheeks and she began to rock back and forth gently as if deliberating. For a tantalizing moment it seemed like she would reveal a truth that remained buried deep inside. But something – fear perhaps – trumped and she gave a sudden obstinate shake of the head, seeing off all dissent.

'I've told you everything,' she said. 'Please go now and let me rest.'

'Did you have a key to Riya's room?' asked Mummy.

The question was met with silence.

'If you helped Riya then you did nothing wrong,' said Mummy.

But Surjeet would say nothing more and Puri and Mummy thanked her for her time and left.

Puri did not speak until they were back down in the alley. He stared back up at the door, his forehead crumpled with regret.

'A pity she wouldn't confide in us,' he said. 'I believe that woman knows the truth.'

'She may yet tell us what we want to know,' said Mummy.

'Why do you say that?' asked Puri.

'Loyalty can only stretch so far. Eventually it reaches a snapping point.'

Fourteen

It had been a long, taxing day. First came the revelation about Radhika wanting to marry some

TV producer. Then Puri had had to endure more of Saanvi and Maaya's theatrics. This in turn had taken him to Rajouri Garden, from where he'd come away with more questions than answers, and finally there'd been the visit to Tilak Vihar and the frustrating interview with Surjeet.

To top it all, Mummy, without a hint of regret or irony (forget apology), had performed a complete U-turn regarding her entire hypothesis about Saanvi being the reincarnation of Riya Kaur and suggested that the great and wise Maaya was a total fraud.

As a result, his other work had gone by the wayside, including meeting Inspector Singh and briefing him on Hairy Toes and the suspected fraud at the bank.

And tomorrow was looking no better. He was left with no choice but to collaborate with Mummy again, the tentative plan being to attend Saanvi's next session and for one of them to sneak into Maaya's study and get a proper look at her file.

All he wanted to do now was to go home, take off his shoes, pour himself a couple of pegs, enjoy a nice home-cooked meal, do some time-pass in front of the TV and make it an early night.

Naturally, this was the moment that Rinku called – and Puri let out a long, disgruntled groan.

Seeing his friend was taxing at the best of times; the prospect of having to ask him for help, albeit on his brother's behalf, especially at night when he drank, was deeply unappealing.

But the urge to answer proved irresistible. Rinku,

his old friend, regarded telephoning someone on a mobile as no different to calling to them from the next room. Indeed, he seemed to measure the length of time it took anyone to answer as some kind of barometer of friendship and allegiance. A delay or even worse a failure to answer would be deemed a slight and, at the very least, invite ridicule.

Puri might have been in the middle of defusing a bomb, sharing intimacy with his wife, or devouring a plate of butter chicken for all Rinku cared.

'Chubby? I'm at the Novotel, come join me,' said Rinku without so much as a 'Is this a good time?'

Had it been anyone else, Puri would have pleaded exhaustion and the wish to return home to his loving wife; instead he heard himself answer, almost gamely, that he was just leaving the office.

Half an hour later, furious at himself for not sticking to his guns, he stepped into the swish lobby of the Novotel, one of a cluster of new uber-modern hotels in Aerocity, a newly constructed 'mixed realty' hub near the airport.

Rinku was on his own near the bar, reclined in a leather armchair, one phone to his ear and a half-empty tumbler of Scotch on the table in front of him.

He'd aged visibly since they'd last met six months ago, his tussled mane and the chest hairs that sprouted between his unbuttoned, tropical-palm-print shirt now mostly white.

Like a bloated, ageing roadie for whom years

of booze and debauchery were finally taking their toll, he wore tight jeans that looked like they risked cutting off the circulation to his feet, and wraparound shades that, rather than oozing cool, suggested the possibility of the need of a seeing-eye dog.

'Chubby, how's the diet coming along?' he asked with mocking eyes after the two had greeted one another with a strong embrace and a couple of matey backslaps.

'Splendid! How's the mid-life crisis?'

'Never better, you bastard!' guffawed Rinku, causing heads to turn elsewhere in the bar. 'I tell you it comes with great perks! The latest is called Katarina! Legs like a racehorse. Goes like the clappers! You should try her friend, Anastasia! You want nirvana? I tell you she's giving one-way tickets.'

'I'm not one to stray off the reservation,' said Puri plainly, and sat down.

'Same old Chubby. One of these days they'll make you patron saint of Punjab and put up a shrine.'

The detective pulled a small, cold smile, uncomfortable with the tenor of the banter. 'How about a drink, you bugger?' he said.

'You tell me, Chubby, seems to be self-service in this place!'

Rinku snapped his fingers to get the attention of the bartender. '*Oye*, boss!' he called, pronouncing it 'baaass'. 'We're dying of thirst over here!'

A young, nervous waiter was summarily despatched to their table.

'Give me another Johnny Walker Red, double,'

said Rinku. 'For the great hero here, better make it that *desi* shit, Royal Challenge – large one. Don't forget soda and ice, yaar. And give us one plate *chaat* masala, one plate peanut masala and two *seekh* kebab, also.'

'May I repeat your order, sir?' asked the waiter.

'You're a bloody parrot or what?'

'Sir?'

Rinku rattled off the items again and dismissed the young man with a contemptuous sweep of his hand. Then he checked his phone for the third time in as many minutes and started to brag about all the illegal money he was making.

'I tell you, Chubby, the last few days . . . *insane.* I'm dealing with HNI[26] clients with lakhs and lakhs in notes. This one bookie from Faridabad, a bad-ass *badmaash* . . . he turns up at my place the morning after the PM's announcement with six garbage bags. Each one's stuffed with one thousand bucks like stuffing in some bloody Christmas turkey. He dumps the lot on my floor, says he'd rather have a bonfire than go to a bank. Turns out he's got two more bags in his Beamer!'

Puri didn't ask him how the cash was being laundered; he didn't need to. Rinku took a perverse pleasure in trying to shock the detective by describing his nefarious activities in unflinching detail.

'I've chartered a plane, flying it up to the Northeast, landing on a private airstrip,' he said. 'So far, I've cleared thirty *khokha* and I'm getting forty per cent.'

[26] High-net-worth individuals.

Puri gave a low whistle. 'What's so special about the Northeast?' he asked.

'Those junglies are all exempt from income tax,' explained Rinku, using a derogatory stereotype for the population of India's northeast states. 'It's got to do with concessions for backward areas or some such technical crap. I've got a contact up there doing the needful, spreading the moola across multiple accounts.'

'A loophole, we can say,' said Puri.

'More like a black hole, yaar!' laughed Rinku, who looked especially pleased with himself.

He went on, scoffing at the government's attempts to undermine the country's black economy. 'Sure a few dudes have been caught with their pants down, but this is India, not bloody Sweden. We people can manage anything. *Chalta hai*, no issues.'

'Of that I am in no doubt at all,' said Puri. 'Yesterday only I heard one of your competitors speaking the exact same thing. Name of Hari Dev. You're familiar with him, by chance?'

Rinku smiled over the top of his glass. 'Still working, Chubby?' he asked.

'*Always.*'

Rinku mulled over the name. 'Hari Dev. I take it he's one of the bad guys like me?'

'Into marble. But he's got none of your flair. No way he could carry off that shirt for instance.'

Rinku gave a mirthless chuckle. 'Flattery will get you everywhere, Chubby,' he said. 'I'll see what I can find out, though no guarantee.'

* * *

183

The first round of drinks didn't last long and Rinku ordered a second, then a third, before insisting that the bottle of Johnny Walker be brought to the table. Though this caused an argument with the bartender who claimed it 'went against hotel policy' for guests to serve themselves – and so the poor man was duly threatened ('I'll bash you up good and proper!') and insulted ('bloody *gaandu*!') – Rinku soon grew nostalgic for the past and lost youth that he and Puri shared, and began to remind him of instances from their childhood, most involving the two of them ending up in a good deal of trouble.

'Bloody good to see you, *braah*!' he bawled several times, reverting to a term of affection neither of them had used in years.

But Rinku was a volatile drunk, as Puri well knew, and by number six his tone turned sour.

'What happened to we two, ha? We used to be like this.' He linked his fingers tightly together and tugged on them. 'The Yo-yo Gang! Remember? We were like this.'

'We were kids, yaar,' said Puri stoically.

By now, Rinku was swaying from side to side in his chair.

'This past Diwali, you didn't so much as set foot in my house,' he said, his words slurred. 'What was that you said to me on the phone? "I've a family commitment" or some such bullshit. *Family?* I'm family, braah, or have you forgotten?'

'No disrespect was intended,' said Puri.

'Sure, the great saint of the Punjab can do no wrong.' Rinku slugged back another peg. 'Who

184

do you think you're fooling, ha? Think I'm not aware of the real reason why you called me up? Bhuppi is screwed and wants my help, so he's getting you to do his dirty work.'

'I won't deny he asked me to speak with you.'

'Ladies and gentleman, the great jasoos has agreed to climb down in the gutter and get his hands dirty!' announced Rinku to the entire bar, before addressing Puri directly again. 'Think such favours are given so freely, Chubby? Why Bhuppi should get special consideration?'

Puri's face was a tableau of forced calm. 'You owe it to him, actually. It was he who saved your life that time – found you lying face down in the gutter, drowning in your own vomit all those years back. He took you to hospital, paid for emergency care, stayed by your bedside. You recall?'

'And you, Chubby? You would have done the same for me?'

Puri shot him a baleful look. 'How dare you ask such a question?' he shouted. 'Alcohol has poisoned your brain – and your spirit. You wish to know what happened to us two? Go ahead and take a hard look in the mirror!'

He pushed his chair backwards and stood, feeling the effect of the whisky suddenly.

Puri had tried to avoid this moment for years, done everything he could despite their differences to preserve their friendship, but enough was enough.

'I'm going home to my wife. If you had sense, you would do the same.'

Rinku stared silently into his drink. 'Simi left

me,' he said. 'She's gone to her sister's, wants a divorce.'

Puri tottered, his face showing startled dismay. 'By God,' he said. 'I'm . . . sorry.'

Rinku removed his shades and rubbed blood-shot eyes. 'Why sorry? I was a bastard to her. The shit I put her through, I tell you. She's better off without me.'

'How long has it been?' was all Puri could think to ask.

'Two months.'

'And the children?'

'She's taken them. I get them on weekends if I'm on good behaviour.'

Whatever Rinku's faults, he loved his kids. The thought of them having been taken away from him tugged at Puri's emotions.

He started to sit down to finish his drink, but Rinku wasn't having it.

'Listen, yaar, I don't want your sympathy. I brought this upon myself. You should go. Get home to Rumpi. She's a good woman. Send her my love, ha. And not to worry about Bhuppi. I'll take care of it. On the house, no charge.'

'Most decent of you,' intoned Puri.

'Tell him to call me up tomorrow. Not too early! And one more thing. Regarding that Hari Dev. Watch your back. The guy has muscle – and connections.'

'So he's known to you after all?' said Puri.

'Right, it just came to me. A funny thing, memory. It's like a broken soda machine: some-times it needs a jolt.'

* * *

186

Puri woke the next morning in a sombre mood, snatches of his conversation with Rinku still echoing in his mind. Though they'd drifted apart years ago, the charge of callousness had left him bruised; and while he washed and dressed, he reflected on how only family and childhood friends stirred such deep feelings, tugging on emotional levers that no one else could reach.

The sight of his wife in the kitchen, smiling, as beautiful as ever – his anchor – was a welcome reminder of how lucky he'd been in his family life and how at times, with all the stress of his working life, he was guilty of taking his good fortune for granted.

Breakfast proved an altogether more enjoyable experience than the day before and husband and wife had an amicable, constructive discussion about their youngest daughter's hopes and wishes. Puri agreed to meet Bish (without daring to mention the background check he'd commissioned) and though he didn't offer an out-and-out apology for his initial reaction, suggested that 'perhaps' he had been 'a little hasty in articulating his opinion yesterday, only'.

A plate of rumble-tumble eggs, an extremely generous helping of mango pickle, a home-grown and especially potent naga chilli dipped in salt and three cups of chai later, he left the house feeling refreshed and in good humour, and ready to face the day in spite of the fact that he suspected it would be another long and taxing one.

Indeed, when his phone rang, displaying

187

Unknown Number, he threw caution to the wind and answered with a genial, 'Puri, this side.'

The male voice on the other end sounded serious, but the detective couldn't make out what he was saying.

'Pardon?' he repeated several times, before encouraging the mystery caller to 'revert', or call back.

When the caller did so his voice was crystal clear – as was his intention.

'Achcha, so you're calling to threaten me, is it?' said Puri. 'Kindly proceed.'

Having received thirty-three direct and unequivocal death threats over the span of his long and illustrious career (this one would make thirty-four), he readied himself for the usual clichéd movie lines inspired by classic Bollywood villains like Gabbar Singh.[27]

'There are no more heroes left in the world,' was a favourite.

'Dogs should learn to lie down,' was another.

On several occasions he'd been advised to, 'Start collecting wood for your funeral pyre.'

Promises of a grisly end invariably followed. In the past, one goonda had threatened to cut off Puri's testes, 'sugarcoat them and feed them to you like *barfi*.'

'You'll be sucking your khanna through a straw,' was another unappealing threat that stuck in Puri's mind.

Today's warning was more nuanced, however. The gentleman sounded calm, menacingly so.

[27] *Sholay*, 1975.

'Play the joker all you like, but I'm warning you to keep your nose out of other people's business or we'll kill you,' he said.

'Which business you're referring to, exactly?' asked the detective. 'I've got my nose stuck in plenty of other people's business just now.'

'We know where you live, we know your movements. Don't test us. Getting to you would be child's play.'

'Listen, I'm not one to respond to threats, believe me.'

'Then you just signed your own death warrant.'

The line went dead and Puri was left frowning at a blank screen.

'By God, why can't these people provide more of details?' He sighed and began to run through a list of possible suspects in his head.

The most obvious one was Mantosh Singh. But the caller sounded like someone experienced in threatening people.

He considered a few other individuals, including a few facing trial, but found himself wondering about Hari Dev aka Hairy Toes.

Puri had asked Mr Dhawan the bank manager about him and it was possible the squeaky clean young man had, innocently no doubt, mentioned his interest to his client.

Whatever the case, Puri didn't take any death threat (clichéd or otherwise) lightly.

Extra vigilance would be required and he called Tubelight, who was back in Delhi, and appraised him of the situation.

'Keep all eyes and ears peeled round the clock,' he said.

Fifteen

Inspector Singh's uncle was watching cricket as usual in the front room of the safe house and the drone of commentary, punctuated by the odd clunk of the ball and the roar of a crowd, filtered gently into the kitchen.

'I'm not following the sequence of events, sir,' said the Sikh inspector, his fierce eyebrows knotted together. 'Why were you hiding in the toilets again?'

'I wasn't hiding, I was waiting,' said Puri, impatient at how slowly Inspector Singh was grasping the facts. 'As I intimated, the bank was due to close and I took the chance that Mr Dhawan, the manager, who'd been inside his office dealing with customers for so many of hours, would require urgent relief, so to speak. I happen to know that he's in possession of a small bladder and is fond of using the toilets reserved for the Exclusive Platinum Account members.'

'And you expected to be able to identify him by his shoes by looking under the toilet partition?'

'The shoes were gifted to him by his uncle in New Jersey. I was admiring them some weeks back in his office. They're distinct with leather tassels on top.'

'But instead of Mr Dhawan, this other individual—'

190

'Hari Dev.'

'—entered the adjacent toilet and you got a good look at his toes. And they were . . . *hairy*.'

'Very much so. He was wearing chappals.'

Singh seemed to suppress a smile. 'I think I follow you now, sir,' he said. 'Please continue.'

Puri went on to describe the conversation he'd overheard in Dogri. A massive fraud was being perpetrated with the connivance of the bank, Puri concluded. If proven, the story would make head-lines across India, 'drawing eyeballs' on national TV. The police officer responsible for catching the crooks would win huge cachet in the current political climate, 'not to mention plaudits.'

Inspector Singh digested this information and mingled caution and scepticism in a prolonged frown.

'Going back to what transpired in the toilets for a moment, sir,' he said. 'How was it you identified Hari Dev if you only got a look at his toes?'

It was Mr Dhawan, the manager, who identified him, Puri explained.

'But rest assured, Inspector-sahib, I would recognize those hairy toes anywhere. Furthermore, I would face no difficulty in identifying his voice, also. As you're no doubt aware, my ear is second to none,' he said.

'I don't doubt it, sir,' replied Inspector Singh judiciously, 'and you have never steered me wrong in the past.' He reflected for a moment, deciding on the best course of action. 'Leave it with me, sir, and I will look into this Hari Dev and get a handle on what his game is.'

'Very good, Inspector. One word of caution, only. I have it on good authority that Dev is well connected. The death threat I received this morning probably came from his camp.'

'Death threat?'

Puri described the call and suggested the possibility that Dev had got wind of his interest in him.

With this duly noted, they turned to other business.

Inspector Singh had completed his check into Saanvi's father, Dr Srivastava, and he was clean – no criminal charges or convictions.

'Any complaints made against him?'

'Not one. Seems to be a pillar of society – has worked for various NGOs and served as an adviser on rural development to the former prime minister.'

'That much I know,' said Puri.

'You sound disappointed.'

'Frustrated, more like. At every turn with this case I run into a dead end.'

'Well, there was one other thing, sir. I wasn't sure if it was relevant . . .'

'Tell me.'

'You mentioned an interest in the daughter? First name, Saanvi?'

Puri's nod was encouragement to go on.

'When I ran Dr Srivastava's name through the computer a reference came up for a court appearance in April 1995. So I got hold of the court record. It relates to a petition he and his wife made for adoption.'

'For Saanvi?' Only Puri's weight prevented him from jumping up out of his chair.

'Yes, sir. The court record further shows the adoption hearing was held four months later and approved by the judge.'

'Saanvi was adopted,' mused Puri, and suddenly everything swung into focus.

Dr Srivastava didn't want the fact that she wasn't his birth daughter revealed, which was why he'd warned Puri not to dig into her past, the detective now realized.

It was entirely possible that the father had hid the truth from Saanvi and she was unaware that she was not his biological child.

Most probably she was abused before she was adopted.

'I'll be needing Saanvi's adoption papers,' said Puri.

But Inspector Singh warned that this might take a few days as the adoption was made in Vrindavan.

Vrindavan, Puri recalled, was where Saanvi had told him her mother – her *adopted* mother as it turned out – had died in a road accident. It was also where she'd travelled on Wednesday and spent the night – that is according to Flush, who'd traced Saanvi's phone after her father grabbed her off the road in front of Maaya's house.

On a hunch, Puri asked Inspector Singh whether the court papers had listed Dr Srivastava's late wife's name.

'Her last name was D'Silva,' he said.

This meant she was a Christian of Goan origin, and her grave was probably in Vrindavan or nearby.

*　　*　　*

193

It was five days since the prime minister's note-bandi announcement and 86 per cent of India's currency was taken out of circulation. The lines at the banks were as long as ever, while the ATM machines, which were yet to be calibrated for the new notes, sat idle. Puri's newspaper that morning carried reports of people across the country struggling to pay essential bills, of farmers having to borrow at extortionate rates to buy seed, of tens of thousands of trucks stranded on highways across the country, of the father of a groom who feared his son's wedding would have to be postponed.

For Elizabeth Rani, though, the nightmare was over. Yesterday afternoon, after a total of fourteen hours spent lining up at her bank, she had managed to deposit her annulled old notes and been able to withdraw four thousand rupees of new money.

Puri had never been quite so happy to see her and, after listening to her tale of woe, got back to work without facing further interruption.

There was plenty to get on with before he picked up Mummy and attended Saanvi's next – and with any luck, last – session. He checked in with Dingo to ask how he was getting on with the background check on Bishwanath Ganguly's family, and was told to expect a full report by tomorrow. He called Bhuppi to let him know that he'd met with Rinku and that he should call him to make the necessary arrangements for laundering his black money. And he went to see his accountant to ask whether he had any bright ideas for dealing with his seven lakhs in cash, only to be told that his best option was to find a black money broker to take the money off his hands in exchange for the new denominations.

At around eleven he got a call from Bobby, who said that he'd remembered a small detail about the Riya Kaur case. It had to do with Mantosh Singh's car.

'Along with the blood and the shovel, I also found a flat tyre,' said Bobby. 'It was punctured by a sweet thorn from an acacia tree.'

Puri thanked him for the information and brought Bobby up to date with the latest developments. Then he went for lunch nearby – the canteen inside Andhra Bhavan, the legation building for the state government of Andhra Pradesh, where the service was no-nonsense, the food 'unlimited' and the cost a matter of one hundred rupees all in.

Moments after he took his seat, a *thali* was placed before him, each section filled with an enticing selection of South Indian fare, including spicy *akakura pappu* (lentils with fenugreek leaves and tamarind) and *dondakaya veyimpudu* (stir-fried Indian ivy gourd), *sambhar* (lentil-based veg stew) and some fiery tomato chutney, followed by kheer with cashews.

In short, Puri was in heaven.

Little did he know it almost proved to be his last meal.

When Puri spotted the black SUV speeding recklessly towards him, it crossed his mind that the driver might be an ordinary, everyday citizen with no malicious intent, as opposed to a hit-and-run driver out to flatten him.

195

It was, after all, notoriously difficult to tell apart the driving habits of the average Delhi wallah and a hired killer.

The vehicle showed no sign of slowing down, however, making any further deliberation inadvisable. And Puri, with only a few seconds to spare, took a couple of hasty steps to his left, got his feet tangled up and lost his balance.

Mummy and Saanvi were standing next to him, haggling with the taxi driver who had brought them to the address, and the combination of his weight and flailing arms ensured that he took both of them and the taxi driver down with him; the four of them ending up in an untidy heap in front of Maaya's gate.

Puri's inelegant reflexes were not what saved him or the others, however. Fate also intervened in the shape of a holy man leading a beautiful horned cow with five legs bedecked in bells, silver spangles and a silk blanket with a slit from which the animal's magnificent hump and fifth limb protruded. This duo had, only a few minutes earlier, departed from the lucrative pitch outside the nearby temple. And it just so happened that they reached the front of Maaya's house as Puri and the others went toppling over.

The holy man, being engaged in the business of rattling his tin and crying out for donations in return for blessings, didn't spot the oncoming vehicle, and unwittingly placed himself and his partner in the way of danger. And given that there is surely nothing in India deemed more likely to ensure bad luck than hitting a cow, let alone a five-legged one dressed in holy saffron-coloured silk, this caused the SUV to swerve suddenly to the left.

Puri, Mummy, Saanvi, the taxi driver, and indeed the cow and its keeper were saved. The Ambassador, however, was not.

Smash went a fender.

A passenger door was cleaved off.

Handbrake went diving for cover.

Shattered red and yellow plastic from the brake lights showered the street as the driver overcompensated and veered to the right.

The SUV took out a long row of carefully arranged clay pots containing marigolds grown by one of Maaya's neighbours, and then the side of a Mercedes-Benz, before slamming into the trunk of a mango tree below a sign on a wall that warned, *No Parking. Otherwise tyre will be deflated.*

The shattering of glass and crumpling of metal were punctuated by the howling of the vehicle's alarm.

Puri sat up, dizzy, with the cow peering down at him, chewing on some sugar cane, and pulled focus to his beloved car.

Its fender was peeled back into a jagged, ugly sneer. The downward angle of the twisted bumper gave the impression of prolonged suffering. The door lay in the middle of the road, bent and battered. Thankfully Handbrake was now back on his feet, looking dazed but uninjured.

Puri turned to check on Mummy and found that she was unhurt, although Saanvi appeared to be in shock.

Just then Tubelight, who'd been shadowing Puri

197

since the death threat this morning, went sprinting past, shouting and pointing, 'Oye! Stop that driver! There he is! Grab him!'

Puri got back up on to his feet with a helping hand from the holy man in time to see the back of a sprightly young man making his getaway on foot down the road away from them with Tubelight and a hobbling Handbrake in pursuit.

'Better get her inside and give her a glass of water,' he called over his shoulder to Mummy, who was ushering Saanvi away from the scene. With a heavy heart, he approached his beloved Amby.

It was bleeding oil on to the road. The engine looked smashed. Puri wondered if it would ever drive again. Hindustan Motors had discontinued manufacturing the Ambassador a few years earlier and, from what he understood, spare parts were now hard to come by.

The thought almost brought a tear to his eye. But this was no time to mourn. The police would be along soon (this was a posh neighbourhood, after all) and he wanted to get a quick look inside the SUV.

The ignition had been forced, he discovered, proof enough that the vehicle had been stolen by an autolifter.

Only at that moment did he know for sure that the incident had been a hit-and-run. Someone had just tried to kill him – assuming, that is, that someone didn't have it in for the taxi driver.

Puri tried to impress upon the two traffic cops who turned up on the necessity of declaring a crime scene. The area required cordoning off in the hope of retrieving fingerprints from the steering wheel and dashboard of the SUV, he pointed out.

Unfortunately, the incandescent owner of the marigold pots, Mercedes-Benz and mango tree dominated the scene. Quick to apportion blame, he accused the drivers of the taxi and the Ambassador of blocking the road and causing the SUV to crash. He demanded that both men be arrested.

The taxi driver was intimidated by the man's wealth and bearing (and by default connections and clout), but Puri put up a fight. For this he was maligned as a 'bloody rascal fellow', and Handbrake, whom the resident accused of fleeing the scene, was cursed as a *salaa kutta*.

'For causing obstruction before absconding the scene he should face stiffest penalties under law!' the resident shouted before delivering his coup de grâce. 'I've the CM[28] on speed dial!'

The traffic cops, who had little appetite for extra work at the best of times and certainly had no argument with such an evidently well-connected individual, duly declared that, in their view, both drivers were responsible for what was clearly an accident and would face charges.

One of the cops searched the SUV and, finding the owner's details in the glove compartment, radioed in his name as a 'possible accused'; while his partner ordered a 'traffic crane' to the scene in order to remove the vehicles.

Though Puri protested, the resident demanded

[28] Chief Minister (of Delhi).

that he be arrested as well and he was duly cautioned.

This resulted in Puri having to call a senior officer in the department to lodge a complaint against the traffic cops. He also arranged for a freelance photographer he often used to document crime scenes (the Delhi force didn't employ one) to join him. And he called for his own tow vehicle.

Puri then went in search of Mummy and Saanvi, but was unable to locate either of them. Maaya said she hadn't seen them. And Mummy's phone was 'not reachable at the present time', according to the usual, all-too-familiar message.

The absconding driver was in his late twenties, fit and nimble. Handbrake, who'd banged his knee when he'd dived out of the path of the SUV, soon dropped out of the chase, while Tubelight, a long-time smoker in his mid-forties, whose rubber chappals were wholly inappropriate for such a chase, struggled to keep up.

Puri's operative was already a good fifty metres behind the driver as he entered Kailash Pati Mandir Park at the end of Maaya's road, and with little prospect of closing the gap and no shortcuts available to him, he continued to appeal to people on the path up ahead – a couple of middle-aged men doing brisk walking, a group of *mazdoors* repairing a path – to intervene and stop him.

Tubelight's pleas went unheeded and he himself was set upon by a couple of the park's stray dogs, who, excited by the commotion, came

200

running towards him, snarling and barking. He was forced to stop and pick up a big stick and see them off. This lost him valuable time, as did the two large aunties with their shopping coming through the gate at the far side of the park; and by the time he clambered over the railings and down into the residential street on the other side, his quarry had gained another thirty metres or so.

Tubelight put everything he had left into trying to close the gap, ensuring that he had eyes on the driver when his target crossed the main road, climbed up the brick *dhalao* where the kabari wallahs sorted the neighbourhood trash, and jumped over the fence into the forested area that abutted Hauz Khas Village.

Tubelight reached the fence as the driver vanished between the eucalyptus trees.

There was no way he could make the same jump. But all was not lost. There were only two ways out of the forested area: the gate next to the Rose Garden, on the Outer Ring Road; and the exit by Hauz Khas Village on the far side of the reserve. Tubelight headed for the Rose Garden exit, which was closest, covering the distance on foot, and en route he called an auto driver called Pawan who operated from a popular spot on the edge of the village and had worked for him in the past. By a stroke of good luck, Pawan was having some meter down and smoking a beedi in the back of his vehicle. Tubelight, though out of breath, provided him with a description of the driver – 'blue jean, T-shirt, buzzcut' – and asked Pawan to tail him should he appear.

'*Thik hai*, bhai! *Chalega.* No issue. I'm here, *bindaas*!'[29]

By now, Mummy was twenty-nine metres underground travelling on the Delhi Metro Yellow Line from Hauz Khas station.

Saanvi was seated in the same carriage, but in an adjacent section.

She was not herself, having switched into an alternate persona altogether.

Withdrawn, vulnerable and child-like, she sat sucking on a thumb and twirling her hair.

The change had been triggered by the close encounter with the SUV and the subsequent crash.

Visibly shaken, Saanvi had fled the scene and hurried off down the road in the direction of the nearest Metro station.

Mummy had managed to catch up with her, but Saanvi didn't respond to her name or seem to recognize her.

Where she was going now was a mystery. But Mummy was determined not to let her out of her sight.

Pawan called Tubelight twenty minutes later. By the sound of it he was driving.

'*Oye*, bhai! Meet me in thirty!' he said, his voice loud and strangely exaggerated.

---

[29] *Thik hai* means literally 'is fine'; *bhai* is 'brother'; *chalega* means literally 'will move'; and *bindaas*, which is Mumbai street slang, is used here to mean 'not to worry, it's cool'.

'Where are you going? I told you to keep watch?'
'I picked up a fare.'
'You couldn't do one thing for me?'
'I couldn't refuse – this guy, he's in a big hurry!'
Tubelight got his drift. 'This guy – blue jean, T-shirt?' he asked.
'Right!'
'Where are you taking him?'
'Gamri Village.'
East Delhi.
'On my way!' said Tubelight.

'Everything OK, boss?' Facecream asked Puri, reading the stress in his voice when he answered his phone.

He told her about the tragedy that had occurred. His Ambassador had 'fallen in the line of duty' and it looked likely that it would 'undergo an early retirement'.

She commiserated. 'I know how much you love that car,' she said.

'It is like losing an old friend,' he bemoaned. 'One who has given so much comfort for many years. We two were inseparable.'

'In time I'm sure you'll get used to another car,' she said.

'It will take something of an adjustment to come round to the idea of one of these new models. Call me old fashioned if you like.'

She'd heard enough.

'About the lab test,' she said. 'The syringe contained cat dander – and as you know Vikas Gupta is highly allergic to cats.'

'You're thinking the former girlfriend brought

203

some samples from the laboratory and administered it in some way to induce the snoring?' asked Puri.

'Right. The question is how it's being distributed in the bedroom. The air-conditioned unit would be the obvious choice, but when we were monitoring the snoring the other night, it was switched off,' said Facecream.

'Better you have another look around,' suggested Puri.

'I'm planning to go back tonight,' said Facecream.

Saanvi exited the Metro train at New Delhi station and headed up to street level. It was a short walk to the mainline station along pavements crowded with hawkers and vendors and food stands that mixed smells of frying kachoris and aloo chaat with the diesel and two-stroke petrol fumes drifting over the feverish traffic.

Mummy remained in Saanvi's shadow, following her into the terminal building and then standing directly behind her in the queue at the ticket counter.

When it came for Saanvi to purchase her ticket, however, the background hubbub of the station and the constant announcements blaring over the tannoy system drowned out her conversation with the vendor. And although this didn't present an immediate problem as Mummy expected to be able to get the information from the vendor when she stepped up to buy her own ticket, a man with considerably thicker forearms than she pushed unapologetically to the front.

Ordinarily, the man would have found himself on the receiving end of a proper scolding. But to take the brute to task would be to risk losing Saanvi and Mummy made the snap decision to travel without a ticket and caught up with her at the A.H. Wheeler book kiosk.

Saanvi came away with a comic book suitable for a ten-year-old and then mounted the stairs to the long bridge that took them over the tops of trains waiting at the platforms. A veritable tsunami of passengers and coolies with piles of bags balanced on their heads came surging towards them, and they narrowly avoided impact by taking the stairs down to Platform 4.

Saanvi led the way to the middle of the platform, weaving past stalls offering snacks and pulp-fiction Hindi books, heaps of cargo sewn in hemp cloth waiting to be loaded on to carriages, and groups of passengers. A large party of Muslim pilgrims here, a family four generations strong fresh from a wedding party there, all sitting on lengths of cloth or bamboo mats spread out on the platform.

At half past five, the Agra Express eased on to the platform, and many of these same passengers, who until then had appeared content to wait patiently, made a rush for the doors, as if the train was due to set off straight away, with toddlers and bags being unceremoniously lifted over the bottlenecks.

In fact, there was a good twenty minutes until the train's scheduled departure, allowing Saanvi to find her seat in an air-conditioned chair-car carriage and for Mummy to settle down a few rows behind her, pondering over their destination.

When she tried to call Puri, Mummy discovered that the screen of her phone had shattered during the incident earlier outside Maaya's house, rendering it useless.

The auntie sitting next to her was kind enough to offer Mummy the use of her phone, but then Chubby's number was engaged.

'Such a *gappu*!' she cursed under her breath after her fifth attempt. 'Who he's speaking to all this time? Doing idle chitchat, no doubt.'

'I was facing a similar issue until I insisted my son put his phone in caller-waiting mode,' said the auntie. 'Now I can reach him night or day, wherever he is, whatever he is doing, no excuse, twenty-four and seven.'

'That is only right,' said Mummy approvingly as the train gave a sudden shudder and the horn lowed. 'We remain at their beck and call throughout childhood – why they shouldn't do pay back, I ask you?'

Sixteen

Mummy was highly susceptible to falling asleep in moving vehicles and had something of a reputation in the family for doing so. She was also tired, what with almost getting run over and having followed Saanvi though the Metro, never mind all the work and thinking and worry she had put into the case in the last couple of days. For the past hour and a half, she had occupied herself by watching out the window, sobered by the sight of the Delhi slums abutting the tracks and, beyond, the unprepossessing tower blocks of the vast, new suburbs marching unchecked into the surrounding countryside. She had taken a cup of strong sweet tea when the chai wallah had come noisily through the carriage – 'Chai, coffee, chai!' – with his thermos and plastic cups. She had got up out of her seat a couple of times to walk around. And when Saanvi had gone to the toilet, Mummy had followed on, anxious not to allow her out of her sight.

But now it was dark and the sound of her neighbour talking incessantly about her son – 'I never eat before him,' she'd declared imperiously earlier – and her daughter-in-law, whose chief crime seemed to be putting too much ghee in the daal – was conspiring with the train's motion to sabotage Mummy's mission.

Had it not been for the train conductor, she would have almost certainly slept through to Agra, the train's last stop.

His loud, commanding voice acted like shock therapy – *'Ti-cke-ttt!'* – and Mummy gave a start.

Her excuse for travelling without a ticket – 'Just I reached the station late, na' – was met with a weary, placid expression born of apathy and a mild rebuke. Mummy, though still not sure of her destination, purchased a single ticket to Agra.

The return of the chai wallah again precipitated a badly needed second cup of chai, and the auntie neighbour ordered one, too, bringing a welcome pause to her monologue, and presented an opportunity for Mummy to ask to borrow her phone again.

This time Chubby answered.

Though relieved to hear from her, he didn't make a very good job of it.

'By God, Mummy, where did you get to? Your mobile has been unreachable, I've tried so many times,' he said.

'I've been calling you also and your number is constantly coming engaged,' she said, after explaining that her phone had broken when he'd landed on her.

An announcement came over the speaker, something about not littering and watching out for thieves.

'You're on a train?' asked Puri, with alarm.

Mummy explained how Saanvi seemed to have reverted to being a child and no longer recognized her, and how she had hurried away from the scene of the crash to New Delhi railway station and boarded a train.

'She's on her way to Vrindavan again,' mused Puri.

'How do you know that?' asked Mummy.

He didn't want to reveal that he'd been secretly spying on Saanvi, nor that she'd been adopted, and had to think fast. 'Simple, na,' he said, unintentionally copying her idiom, 'she told us some days back that her mother was killed in a road accident near the town. Perhaps she's visiting the spot.'

'No, Chubby, you said visiting Vrindavan *again*,' his mother pointed out, suspicious.

Puri cursed silently to himself, reminded of one

of the main reasons why he refused to allow his mother anywhere near one of his investigations: she had this infuriating way of knowing when he was holding something back and it was impossible for him to control information in the way he saw fit.

'Better if I bring you up to date one to one, in person, Mummy-ji,' he said. 'Let me know where you're putting up once you reach Vrindavan. I'll be with you in two hours maximum.' He paused. 'No, wait . . . seems I'm without a car. Better make that three hours, give or take.'

Chubby's prediction proved prescient and Saanvi got off the train at Mathura Junction, the closest station to Vrindavan.

Outside the station, hundreds of pilgrims, anxious to reach the holy city associated with the deities and lovers, Krishna and Radha, jostled for seats on shared autos.

Saanvi found a space among a group of foreign Hare Krishna devotees festooned in saffron *harinam chadars*, singing their usual mantra and fiddling with their *japa* beads.

Mummy had to wait five minutes until she was able to hire a private auto of her own.

It took a good ten minutes more (and an extra cash incentive for her driver) to make up the lost time. And thanks to the Hare Krishna singing, she was able to positively identify Saanvi's vehicle from among the dozens of others speeding down National Highway 19.

Huddled on the back seat with only her shawl to protect her against the biting cold blasting in through the open side of the three-wheeler, Mummy endured another quarter of an hour of pursuit through heavy, noisy evening traffic.

The sight of the ivory-white pyramid domes of the city's hundreds of temples, floodlit in the darkness and rising like snow-capped mountain peaks, cheered her a little, however. She had fond memories of visiting Vrindavan with her husband and in-laws a few years after her marriage. They had come during Holi, the spring festival celebrated in much of northern India as a commemoration of the divine love between Krishna and Radha. The city had thronged with worshippers, dancing and singing, throwing colours and making offerings at the many temples. Early one morning, they visited the *ghats* and bathed in the Yamuna River. She remembered one afternoon vividly: walking through dappled sunshine, exploring the forests where, legend had it, the mischievous young cowherd, Krishna, enchanted the *gopis*.

Vrindavan had been transformed from a village to a large town since then, of course, with the Curse of Concrete marring the road that led through choked outskirts. The procession of brick blocks, unkempt markets and neon-lit roadside dhabas spoke of a depressing inevitability. But there was much that was familiar to Mummy as the vehicles weaved in convoy into the ancient heart of Vrindavan. The narrow, twisting lanes with their long, crumbling, pastel-coloured walls thronged with pilgrims. Bells rang out from temples and the sounds of devotion, of *pandits'* sonorous voices rising above their congregations,

210

mingled stirringly in the night air. They passed great stone archways and the grand entrances to old stone *havelis* with carved rosewood doors that spoke of the promise of fairy-tale gardens beyond. And Mummy caught sight of the Yamuna with hundreds of devotees gathered on the banks offering prayers and floating twinkling diyas upon the water.

But there was one aspect to Vrindavan that had disturbed Mummy all those decades ago and she could see evidence of it now, passing through the lanes: the sight of old women begging. These were widows cast out of their homes after their husbands' deaths.[30] In the absence of adequate state aid for the elderly in India, thousands had been drawn to the holy city where they relied on charity, many living far below the poverty line.

It was in front of an ashram populated by widows that Saanvi's auto finally stopped.

Having paid her fare, she walked straight up to the guard, who evidently knew her, and went through the door.

Mummy let her driver go and tried to follow Saanvi inside, but was stopped.

'No visitors without prior arrangement,' said

[30] The elderly in India are mostly cared for within their families. But in some sections of society, the belief persists that a widow is cursed and women who lose their husbands can be left financially vulnerable. A recent survey revealed that among the 40 million widows in India, death from malnutrition is 85 per cent higher than among married women. Source: Global Ministries Foundation.

the guard brusquely. He pointed to a sign on the wall that spelled out the rules.

'I'm with her, with Saanvi,' explained Mummy.

The guard made a face. 'Who?'

'Her – the young lady who just entered.'

'What did you call her?'

'Saanvi.'

'That's Jyoti.'

'Jyoti, then. Listen, I'm trying to help her.'

The guard started to close the door.

Mummy pushed against it. 'Tell me this at least, why you've let her go inside?' she asked.

'She's always welcome.'

'Why?'

'She used to live here.'

Mummy looked startled. 'Lived here? When?'

'When she was a child,' said the guard and slammed the door shut.

Vikas Gupta had ordered out again – chicken tikka this time – and the family gathered around the TV in the living room.

This allowed for the same drill as before: Facecream was able to slip in through the gate courtesy of the delivery wallah, who was escorted by the guard and the family's mutt to the side door while she climbed up on to the first-floor balcony.

It was dark inside and, finding the sliding door open this time, she slipped into the bedroom unnoticed.

Gordon Gecko was positioned above the air-conditioner unit and Facecream flashed Flush a thumbs up.

'I'm in,' she said.

'I'm seeing you and I've got eyes on the family. They're watching that *Kyunki Saas Bhi Kabhi Bahu Thi*,'[31] he said in her earpiece.

It stood to reason that the cat dander was being distributed into the room either through a vent or an air freshener, and so Facecream first checked the walls and then around and under the bed for devices. Finding nothing of interest, however, she went on to examine the mattress and pillows for patches or pouches. That left the furniture, including a couple of side tables with drawers, the contents of which she examined carefully. Again nothing. She looked over the armchair, side table, and went through the two fitted cupboards. She turned her attention next to the side lamps and alarm clock, on the suspicion that perhaps they contained hidden dispensers.

'Zero,' she told Flush before moving into the bathroom.

The medicine cabinet above the sink contained the usual everyday stuff: creams for sores, chapped lips, conjunctivitis; blister packs of pills for headaches, colds, inflammation; powder for athlete's foot; some hair gel; some floss; a couple of bottles of prescription medication with long, unpronounceable names; a couple of boxes of plasters.

A shelf above the sink also held a can of shaving foam, a razor and a nearly depleted tube of Neem toothpaste.

---

[31] A popular Indian soap, entitled *Because the Mother-in-law Was Once the Daughter-in-law*.

She turned to the shower, but found nothing out of the ordinary there either, and then returned to the bedroom with nothing to show for her search.

Standing there, thinking it over again, she considered if perhaps she'd made an incorrect assumption; perhaps all that was required to trigger the snoring was to scatter the cat dander on the pillow at night. But that would require regular access. Also, there would be no need for the syringe and needle.

A thought suddenly occurred to her and she stepped back into the bathroom to examine the toothpaste.

Facecream unfurled the tube and found a puncture mark at the bottom.

'I've cracked it!' she exclaimed. 'She put the cat dander in his toothpaste.'

'Toothpaste, you're sure?' asked Flush.

'Don't you see? She injects a small amount into the tube and gives it a good massage to mix it in. There's just enough dander to ensure that when Gupta brushes his teeth before going to bed, his passages become inflamed and partially blocked and so he starts to snore.'

'Genius!' exclaimed Tubelight. 'Now what?'

Facecream considered her options for a moment or two, before deciding to take the tube with her.

If her theory proved correct, Vikas Gupta would sleep silently tonight – and the rest of the house, too. His marriage would be saved and Most Private Investigators Ltd. rescued from a potentially ruinous lawsuit.

As to whether to try and catch the culprit or present the evidence to Ram Bhatt and his tortured daughter, Tulsi, that was a matter for the boss.

Seventeen

It's *too* quiet, actually,' complained Puri as he headed down National Highway 19 in Subhrojit's new luxury sedan, which he'd borrowed to go and pick up Mummy. 'I like to experience the sounds and smells of a place. Otherwise there is no connection.'

'Should I put your window down, sir?' asked Handbrake, eagerly, his finger hovering over the central control panel.

They were fast approaching a lumbering old Leyland truck belching thick black fumes across the road.

'No, no, that won't be necessary,' answered Puri imperiously.

He stared out the window, trying to ignore how comfortable his reclining leather seat felt beneath him, and how capably the sedan's suspension dealt with all the potholes and ruts in the road. There were none of the violent jolts he was used to. The perennial shuddering that often made him sound as if someone was drumming on his back while he spoke on the phone was absent as well. He was also conscious of the fact that not once had he banged his head on the roof of the car

215

when it had gone over the many speed breakers placed along the road.

Not that he was ready to acknowledge any of this and remained doggedly unimpressed.

'One more problem is there,' he went on. 'All these fancy electronics will go haywire over time. Mark my words, so many of repairs will be required, costing the earth, whereas in thirty years the Ambassador was totally one hundred – *two hundred!* – per cent reliable. Come rain or shine my dear car never failed me.'

'Yes, sir, right, sir,' said Handbrake in a perfunctory tone.

'Must be you're missing her as well?' asked Puri, fishing.

'Yes, sir,' he said. 'I'm used to the old steering, this power steering is very sensitive. But, sir' – here Handbrake hesitated and looked suddenly sheepish – 'if you remember correctly, the Ambassador, now and again, well, it had some issues.'

'Minor ones, only. And each and every time they were easily remedied. Any mechanic across the whole of India is familiar with the working of the Ambassador and can make necessary repairs. That is the beauty of the thing.'

'Yes, sir, that's true, sir,' agreed Handbrake, with a nod of weary patience. 'You remember the time we drove to Patiala and the clutch started giving that loud grunting sound and smoke appeared and suddenly there was no acceleration and we got stranded and we had to get it replaced along with the gear box?'

'Within three to four hours, the mechanic got

hold of the parts and replaced them, and we were back on the road.'

'Right, sir,' said Handbrake with an unconvinced frown that suggested he remembered events differently. 'And then there was that time on the way to Madhya Pradesh when the exhaust fell off the back of the car and got crushed by a bus.'

'Again, on that occasion, the problem was remedied within a few hours, only. Besides, what car does not face wear and tear?'

They had come up behind a long line of lumbering trucks and buses and Handbrake could see the way was clear to overtake them. The sedan accelerated effortlessly, the engine giving little more than a purr as it slipped into fifth. Puri recognized unmistakable pride in the driver's eye as they shot past the other prehistoric vehicles (which would have condemned the Ambassador to a long wait and the indignity of having to take them one at a time).

'Speed is not everything,' said Puri once they were in the clear. 'The Ambassador has a certain character that cannot be matched.'

'It is what they call a classic car, sir,' affirmed Handbrake.

'A classic – exactly.'

'Some collectors keep them for special occasions like weddings and such. But when it comes to long journeys, they drive modern cars like this one, sir.'

'Is that so?' said Puri, sounding unconvinced.

'Main reason, sir, is safety, sir,' Handbrake continued. 'As well as the power steering, this car has an anti-lock braking system, collision air bags and an automatic dimming anti-glare rear-view mirror. Comfort is another factor. You're aware it has heated seating, sir?'

'Heated seating?' repeated Puri, sounding more intrigued than incredulous.

Handbrake did not waste a second in switching it on and then watched, with eager expectation, for the reaction in the automatic dimming anti-glare rear-view mirror.

'You're feeling it, sir?' he asked after a minute or so.

'Yes, yes, it is there,' confirmed Puri, struggling to keep his composure when all he really wanted to do was melt down into his seat with a long, abandoned, 'Aaaaaahhhhh.'

'And that's not all, sir. Listen to this!'

With the press of a switch on the stereo, the incomparable voice of Bhimsen Joshi soared through the car.

Puri felt the hairs on the back of his neck rise.

'Premium Bose Audio system!' bawled Handbrake over the haunting strains of the raga.

'Most impressive,' conceded Puri. 'Next you'll be telling me the car can produce a meal.'

'No, sir, but there are cup holders. This way you can bring chai with you in the car and not risk spilling it on your suit, like the other day.'

'It was a minor spill, only.'

'Yes, sir, right, sir,' said the driver, though they both knew it had necessitated an unscheduled visit to the dry cleaners, not to mention all the cursing.

*   *   *

It was past ten o'clock by the time the sedan reached the guesthouse where Mummy was staying. Puri arranged a bed for Handbrake in the drivers' quarters (though he seemed keener to sleep on the back seat of Subhrojit's car) and then went upstairs to find his mother.

The two wasted no time in swapping information, she divulging what she'd learned about Saanvi living in the widow ashram when she was a child and how the guard identified her as Jyoti; and Puri in turn shared the revelation that Dr Srivastava and his wife adopted Saanvi in Vrindavan in 1995, though without revealing his source.

'If Saanvi was adopted directly from the ashram, that would suggest she was a widow,' concluded Puri.

'It's possible, na? Could be she was married off as a child bride. After some time, tragedy struck and her husband died. From that moment she was seen as cursed. Probably she came from the village and thus family and neighbours, they would have avoided her shadow at all costs. No way she could have got married again. No family would take her. Thus, rejected by her in-laws and parents, she would have been cast out. Could be she was brought here and left on the street.'

'That scenario is rare these days but not altogether unheard of,' commented Puri gravely, before lapsing into silence.

A minute or so later he heaved a great sigh, then said, 'When we return to Delhi, I will go and see Saanvi's father and endeavour to learn

219

the whole story. Meantime, given that we are here, we might as well put our efforts into ascertaining what exactly has drawn Saanvi back to the ashram. That being said, and all things being considered, I am wary of getting side-tracked. After all, the point of all this is to find out what became of Riya Kaur.'

'I take it the so-called "accident" earlier today was nothing of the sort, na?' commented Mummy.

'A hit-and-run, no question about it at all. I've got my people following the would-be assassin.' Puri held up a hand in order to forestall a response. 'And, yes, Mummy-ji, Mantosh Singh is most definitely a suspect. Maybe he has come to know about my interest in the case.'

Puri stretched out his arms and gave a yawn. 'But enough of that. I went without my khanna and will require something before sleep.'

Given Vrindavan's status as a holy city where Krishna and Radha are believed to have walked (and are said to still visit after dark), it was slim pickings on the food front. Puri had to make do with a couple of vegetable sandwiches. These he doused in Maggi chilli sauce, grumbled a great deal about how he rarely went on pilgrimages for the lack of decent food (daal without garlic and onion was a particular bone of contention), and then he and Mummy headed back to the guesthouse.

Tubelight called to report in as Puri was settling into bed.

Thanks to Pawan the auto driver, he'd traced the hit-and-run driver to a studio apartment in Gamri Village, East Delhi.

'You want me to knock on his door, boss?'

'Not yet. First, I want to know his identity, then the names of his associates. After that, where he goes after dark, whether he's vegetarian or non-vegetarian, whether he wears Frenchies or Boxers. No one wrecks my Amby and gets away with it. Understood?'

'Right, boss, I'm on it.'

At five in the morning, the lanes of Vrindavan remained deserted save for the night *chowkidars* huddled around small fires fed by whatever refuse came to hand, and the odd cow feasting on peelings and leftovers spilling out from rank-smelling roadside tips.

There were sounds of life from inside the ashram, but the gates remained locked and, feeling the cold, Mummy and Puri decided to return to warm themselves in the guesthouse.

When they stepped outside again an hour later, the lanes were busy with pilgrims hurrying down to the steps on the banks of the Yamuna to take a ritual bath. Stands stocked with a vast array of *puja* paraphernalia, everything from incense sticks to fresh marigolds and plastic receptacles for collecting holy river water, had sprung up along tracks trodden by countless millions over the centuries before them. Guides claiming to know shortcuts to the best spots along the river-bank now proffered their services volubly to the crowd. The city's robber monkeys were out in full force, too, positioned on the tops of walls and balconies, waiting for any opportunity to swoop and grab free breakfast *prasad* out of the hands of unsuspecting worshippers. And widows, easily discernible in their white[32] saris, were taking up position outside the city's temples, crouching down among beggars with deformities and ash-smeared *sadhus*.

There was no age limit when it came to suffering the indignity of begging here. Some of the women Puri and Mummy passed were in their eighties, others perhaps older. Ancient and shrunken with shaven heads and eyes clouded by cataracts, they stared up imploringly at the blur of countless, anonymous visitors hurrying past, their routine appeals for alms all but lost amidst the hubbub – though now and again a coin dropped into a steel begging bowl or lap, and, occasionally, a note.

Puri and Mummy discovered several dozen more widows from Saanvi's ashram gathered in an adjacent prayer hall where, led by a pandit, they had begun chanting the name of Radha and singing *Bhajans*, a daily routine for which they would receive three rupees and a cup full of rice.

Saanvi was not among them, however, and the ashram's administrator, an individual who clearly relished his authority, would not allow them inside to find her.

No visitors were permitted, he insisted, without prior written permission from the director and the director was away.

'He's out of station owing to illness in the family.'

---

[32] The colour of mourning in Hinduism and most other Indian communities.

Puri could see that nothing was going to work on this man: not persuasion, bribery, threats, and certainly not an appeal to his better nature given that he seemed to have none.

Another approach was needed. And for this, Puri suggested they visit the local bazaar.

There they were able to purchase a simple white cotton sari, a necklace of sandalwood beads, some ordinary leather chappals, a walking stick, and a container of sandalwood paste.

It was proving a happy morning in the Gupta household: as Facecream had predicted, Vikas hadn't given so much as a snort during the night and the members of the family gathered around the breakfast table were cautiously optimistic.

'Was it the tongue-stabilizing device? Is that what helped?' the mother was heard asking her son excitedly over one of Flush's microphones.

'You know I hate that thing, Mother,' answered Vikas.

'Did you do your *pranayama* nostril-breathing technique and chant *"Om"*?'

'I've told you: all that makes me light-headed.'

'Did you have the humidifier on?' asked the father.

'Look, I just went to sleep in the same way I usually do.'

'Maybe all my visits to the temple have finally paid off,' reflected the mother.

'My bet is on the chicken tikka,' said Vikas Gupta. 'It's about the only thing we haven't tried.'

'We shouldn't rule anything out!' agreed the mother, her son's sarcasm apparently lost on her. 'Have some more chicken tonight and let's hope! I'll call Tulsi meantime and tell her.'

'I don't want to get her hopes up. It's just been one night.'

'Vikas is right, we don't want to jump the gun,' said the father, who had the final word.

In her white sari and with a flawless sandal-wood *tilaka* running down her forehead and the bridge of her nose, Mummy blended in seamlessly with the crowd of widows as they left the prayer hall – this after receiving their meagre remittance for their daily hours of imposed worship – and covered the short distance to the ashram.

In entering through the door, she took the extra precaution of leaning heavily on her cane and keeping her head bent down, and thus slipped by the guard unnoticed. None of the widows paid her any heed either (this probably had to do more with poor eyesight rather than the efficaciousness of Mummy's disguise and posture) and, having passed through the entrance hall and director's office, Mummy found herself free to move around the building.

What she discovered was shocking – and suggested that the management's real reason for turning away visitors was to hide the appalling conditions in which the widows languished. The toilets, of which there were only a few serving more than a hundred residents, were filthy. There were no bathrooms and the widows had to wash fully clothed at a communal pump in a central courtyard. No kitchen was provided either and all cooking had to be performed on the concrete floors of a couple of rooms set aside for the purpose, their walls and ceilings blackened by wood and cow-dung smoke.

Mummy made her way methodically down dark, dank corridors, checking each room without success, and in asking some of the more coherent residents where to find the young woman known as 'Jyoti', she fell into conversation.

One woman, who was in her sixties and like many of her fellow widows hailed from West Bengal in eastern India, claimed to have been living in the ashram for thirty years.

'My husband was ten years older than me and died from tuberculosis. We were poor farmers and I had no land or income of my own. I had one daughter and her husband would not take me in, so I came here.'

Her neighbour told a similar story. 'All I can hope is that when I die in this place I'll achieve *moksha*,' she said. 'I pray that it will not be long. They don't even feed us in this place. We're lucky to eat once a day.'

Mummy went up to the second floor where she was told she would find Jyoti with a widow named 'Maa'.

None of the rooms along the corridor had doors, though the lengths of cloth hung in some of the doorways provided a little privacy, and she was able to look into each without disturbing any of the occupants.

Finally, Mummy spotted Saanvi in one of the last rooms on the right.

She was standing behind a chair as she oiled

225

and combed the long, white hair of an elderly widow.

The sunlight falling into the room through a single small window was enough for Mummy to make out a scene of touching intimacy.

From the vantage point of the dark corridor, she observed the two women chatting quietly, sharing the odd giggle, as Saanvi rubbed coconut oil into the long tresses and made neat furrows with a comb.

This widow, surely, was the reason why Saanvi had come to Vrindavan.

No doubt, she could provide the missing details about her past.

With the intention of introducing herself and striking up a conversation, Mummy knocked softly and stepped into the room.

The widow turned in her chair, sunlight falling on her face. She looked to be in her sixties and Mummy realized she had suffered a stroke. The left side of her face was slack, as if made of wax that had become pliable, pulling her mouth in an 'S' and causing the eyelid to sag. There was a jagged scar, too, across her forehead. Still, the combination of her prominent nose and the contours of her thick, distinctive eyebrows marked her out as Punjabi.

More revealing still, she wore a *kara*, or steel bracelet, on her wrist. Without doubt, she was Sikh.

The sight of it caused Mummy to stare.

'Is it possible?' she murmured to herself, and then spoke up, asking urgently, 'Are you Riya? Are you Riya Kaur?'

226

The widow stared back at her with a frown. 'Everyone calls me Maa,' she replied, her speech badly slurred.

'But your given name, what is it?' Mummy half demanded.

'I can't remember,' the widow replied lightly, as if this was something she had long ago come to terms with.

Eighteen

This is Jyoti, I call her my daughter,' said Maa, who spoke slowly and paused frequently in the middle of a sentence, struggling to maintain her train of thought.

'She's my mother,' said Saanvi with a childish giggle.

Mummy had perched herself on the edge of an old, sagging charpai heaped in musty-smelling blankets.

'Jyoti was brought here from a village somewhere in UP.[33] She was a child bride, but her husband died,' continued Maa. 'They called her Anchahee.[34] That was her given name. I chose Jyoti because it means light.'

'You took her in?' asked Mummy.

'The poor child was all alone in the world.

---

[33] Uttar Pradesh, a northern state, India's most populous.
[34] Hindi for 'unwanted'.

Alone and afraid. Night after night she had night-mares. She would wake screaming, in a sweat, not knowing where she was. I cared for her, gave her a place to sleep, made sure she ate properly. It wasn't always easy though. She can be so different from day to day.'

'How do you mean?'

'She's like a goddess with different avatars,' said Maa, with a role of her eyes. 'Sometimes she's Kali, dark and angry; other times Sita, happy and ready to help others.' She smiled. 'Today she's Sita. But usually when she comes to see me she's frightened or she's had an argument with her new father, the man who eventually adopted her and took her from this place.'

'It's true, sometimes we fight,' said Saanvi, with a shrug.

'The man who adopted you, what's his name?' Mummy asked Saanvi.

'I call him *Dad*,' she answered with a smile. 'Why?'

'Does the name *Saanvi* mean anything to you?' asked Mummy.

'Sure, Saanvi lives in Delhi, too.'

'In the same house with you?'

'Yes, we share a room. She's very kind and sweet. We talk a lot.'

'And you, Maa? You remember anything about your life before you came to this place?' asked Mummy.

'For a long time there was nothing, just black-ness,' she said. 'Then bit by bit, things started coming back to me. Faces, places, episodes.'

Maa paused and then added, tantalizingly, 'I

remember the birth of a child, my first, I think. I remember my wedding day. And I remember that night, that last night in the house.'

'The night you escaped?' asked Mummy, barely able to contain herself.

Maa's face twitched with anxiety. 'I don't like to talk about it,' she said. 'It would be better if some of those memories hadn't come back to me at all. The pain is too great to bear.'

Saanvi came and crouched down next to her and held her hand. 'When she remembers the past, Maa becomes sad,' she said.

'She's described these memories to you, told you about what happened to her?' asked Mummy.

'We've shared everything together, all our secrets.' Saanvi grinned. 'There's nothing the two of us don't know about one another.' She stood. 'Now, Maa needs her rest,' said Saanvi.

She helped her to her feet and over to the charpai.

While their backs were turned, Mummy seized the opportunity to pick up a few of the hairs that had fallen on the floor. These she tied into the end of her sari.

This would have to be enough for now.

'Let us not jump to conclusions without all proper and necessary proof,' was how Puri greeted Mummy's excitement, concealing his hope that she was right.

'I'm telling you, Chubby, it is her – *Riya!* – in the flesh. Must be she escaped the house during the riots and ended up here in Vrindavan. She's been living in the ashram since.'

'Mummy-ji, please remain calm,' said Puri, hurrying her away from the entrance to the ashram for fear she'd be overheard by the guard. 'Take a moment to consider what you're saying. Until yesterday, only, you were insisting Saanvi was the reincarnation of Riya Kaur.'

She flung him a defiant glance. 'Had I dismissed Saanvi all together, we would not be here today,' she insisted. 'And Saanvi is the link as it happens. Her real name is Anchahee, a child bride widowed at an early age and brought here and abandoned. It was Riya who cared for her – that is until she was adopted by Dr Srivastava. Don't you see? Saanvi and Riya lived together for some years and thus they shared past memories. That is how Saanvi knows Riya's story and under hypnosis recalled events as if she experienced them herself!'

Puri made a face. 'I'm not following, Mummy-ji. Does this woman answer to Riya Kaur?' he asked as they reached the entrance to the guesthouse.

'No, she does not remember her name. Some part of the brain must remain damaged.'

Puri still looked unconvinced. 'Allow me to remind you, Riya's father searched for her high and low across Delhi after she went missing and no trace could be found.'

Mummy gave a loud tut. 'Chubby, you're forgetting, na, for three, four days during the rioting, he could not so much as leave his home without risking his life. When, eventually, he went to the police to file a missing person report, he was dismissed out of hand. By then hundreds of Sikhs were dead. It was only thanks to Papa-ji that the case was taken up.'

She continued: 'Think about it. Riya had no memory, no ID, thus it is entirely possible she ended up on the street or in a mental ward. Later maybe a charity or some charitable person transported her here and she was provided with a room. After that who was to question whether she belonged or not? There is no programme I'm aware of for reuniting widows with nearest or dearest. Thus she has remained hidden all these years, a non-person.'

'Without definitive proof, all this is mere speculation,' insisted Puri. 'We'll need to find a way to test for DNA and all.'

'Some hairs from her head will do, na?' asked Mummy.

She started to untie the knot in the end of her sari. 'Here, I brought these. Get them tested and then we'll see who is right.'

'We'll need a match with one of her relatives.'

'Her children will do, na?' said Mummy as if the answer was obvious.

'We'll need to establish their whereabouts.'

'The son works at his father's company. He goes to the office in CP.[35] As for the daughter, she married a 1979-batch IAS neta by name of Naresh Rai. Lives in Golf Links.'

Puri didn't deign to ask how she'd come by this information (though he suspected that it had been part of the Auntie Network), but took out his notebook and pen and asked for the relevant names and addresses.

[35] Connaught Place, New Delhi.

'I'll assign one of my people to do the needful,' he said, meaning they would get hold of DNA samples from the son and daughter. 'Now we had better get a move on, actually.'

Puri had promised Subhrojit he would return his car by the afternoon; he also wanted to eat on the highway beyond the city limits where he could hope to get a non-veg lunch.

'I've gone without my breakfast, and dinner last night was not at all satisfactory,' he said, sounding hard done by.

'And Saanvi? We leave her here?' asked Mummy.

'Better she remains out of harm's way while we confirm the facts,' he said.

While Mummy was changing out of her widow garb, Puri made a couple of phone calls. The first was to Facecream, who was now waiting for developments on the snoring front, and to whom he assigned the task of capturing DNA samples from Mantosh Singh and Riya Kaur's two children.

The second was to Tubelight, who was in Gamri Village, keeping an eye on the hit-and-run driver.

'He's got a woman in there, a *kasabi*. If she works by the hour, he's proving a good customer.'

'You've got enough manpower?'

'Sure, boss, no tension. I've brought three others. Wherever he goes, we go.'

Puri and Mummy emerged from the guesthouse to find Handbrake parked in front of the entrance, lovingly polishing the sedan's gleaming silver bodywork with a cloth.

The car drew an admiring coo from Mummy.

'This is more like it,' she said as Handbrake held open a door.

'Compared to what exactly?' asked Puri.

'That old wreck you've been driving around in all this time, Chubby. It was long overdue for retirement, na. What your clients must think of you turning up in that thing, I don't know.'

'The Ambassador denotes a certain class,' said Puri high-handedly.

'You're right, Chubby – third class, no AC.'[36]

She climbed inside on to the back seat, thrilled by the luxury of it all and pointing out all the automatic features.

Puri sat next to her, arms crossed in a position of resentful repose.

'*Dilli chalo*,'[37] he told the driver gruffly, but a moment later called a halt and pointed to a figure coming down the lane towards them.

It was Saanvi – and she was no longer twirling her hair.

'Think she's switched back to . . . *normal*?' speculated Puri, who'd read that this could happen quite suddenly.

He had his answer a moment later when Saanvi spotted Mummy and approached her window with an astonished smile.

'Auntie-ji! I don't believe it! What are you doing here?' she squealed.

[36] Air-conditioning.
[37] 'Let's get going to Delhi.'

'Um, well, just we wanted to come and do *aarti*,' said Mummy, thinking fast.

'And you, child?' asked Puri.

'Me? Oh, well, I've been visiting an old friend. She's a widow who I became very much attached to when we lived in Vrindavan when I was a kid,' she said.

'You lived here?' asked Puri, playing dumb.

'Right. Dad moved us here when I was around eleven,' she said, now apparently unconscious of her earlier life. 'So what's up? You're heading back to Delhi?'

'That's the plan – and you?' asked Puri.

'I'm going to visit my mother's tree,' she said.

'Tree?'

'Right, we planted it when she died and put the ashes underneath. It's in a garden, a beautiful, peaceful garden. I like to be there close to her, to think and reflect. Would you like to see? We can drive there. It's not far.'

Puri's stomach groaned. 'We were on our way to—' he said, but was cut short by a jab to the ribs.

'We'd love to, *beta*, thank you,' Mummy interrupted.

After visiting Saanvi's tree and then stopping for a late lunch at a Punjabi restaurant on NH 19 where Puri gorged himself on *murg mussalam*, *paneer kofta* and *makki di roti*, the heated front passenger seat lulled him into a deep sleep.

His dreams were fragmented and surreal – one moment he was back in the galli behind Mantosh Singh's house, watching Riya Kaur's yellow

234

chunni floating up through the air, the next he was being chased by widows through a bank. He found himself standing before the angel again as blood bubbled up from the ground at her feet, and then exiting his house in the morning to find his car parked there, as good as new – only when Handbrake opened the door, Puri found that the seats had been replaced with a hot tub.

Puri woke to find they were in Okhla, south Delhi, nearing the end of their journey.

He sat up, irritated with himself for his lapse of self-control – more so when he heard Mummy ask from the back seat, 'Oh, good, finally you're awake, na.'

'I nodded off for some time,' Puri grumbled and gave a yawn. 'Not enough sleep was there last night, what with the early start and all.'

'Chubby, you can keep a secret?' she asked, in a contrived tone that suggested she was playing to the gallery.

'You'll not find a better keeper of secrets than yours truly.'

'In which case there's something exciting Saanvi wishes to tell you.'

Puri turned in his seat to find Saanvi grinning from ear to ear. 'I'm going to be on TV!' she said.

'TV, is it?' he asked, smiling back at her.

'I'm going to be featured on this programme about people finding out about their past lives and solving crimes!'

'So exciting, Chubby, na?' enthused Mummy.

'Definitely, yaar!'

'Seems that Maaya has got an agreement with

a big station here in Delhi. They want to start shooting in a week or so,' said Mummy.

'But she told me not to tell anyone because there's like some clause in the contract,' Saanvi hastened to add.

'My lips are sealed one hundred and ten per cent,' promised Puri, and turned around to face the front, his eyes dwelling briefly but appreciatively on Mummy's reflection in the mirror.

Facecream arrived at the office at six thirty, bearing two specimens.

The first, a few strands of hair taken from the head of Surinder, Mantosh Singh's thirty-five-year-old daughter, had been plucked from her head. This had been accomplished with a minimum of fuss when Facecream had passed her in a doorway in a mall and the operative had managed to get a diamond ring caught in her hair.

The second exhibit was a damp jockstrap, which she'd been good enough to place in a manila envelope.

This begged the question as to how she'd got hold of it.

'Turns out Gajan Singh is bald – hasn't a hair on his head – so I had to improvise,' she explained.

'Meaning?'

'After work, I followed him to his health club where he played squash.'

'Don't tell me you entered the men's changing rooms?'

'When he was taking a shower,' she said, nonchalant. 'I'd hoped to get his T-shirt but this was the first thing that came to hand.'

'You're sure it's his?'

'It's not the kind of item anyone shares,' said Facecream with a grimace.

Nineteen

Puri returned home by taxi, taking a meandering route, and keeping an eye out in case he was being followed.

He reached the house to find his wrecked Ambassador sitting in the driveway where the garage had deposited it earlier in the day.

'Did they catch the driver who hit your car?' asked Rumpi after he stopped by the kitchen to greet her and check on dinner.

'By *they* you must be meaning the police?' Puri asked with a scoff.

'Come now, Chubby, they're not *completely* useless. They have been known to solve the occasional crime,' she said.

'From what I can gather, they've seen fit to charge the owner of the SUV.'

'Didn't you say the SUV was stolen?'

'Precisely, my dear. Any charlie with half a brain could tell this was so, owing to a screwdriver sticking out of the ignition. But seems the owner had not reported his vehicle stolen. Most probably this was because he had not noticed it missing from outside his office, thus our police, being not at all concerned with details, assumed him to be guilty.'

Rumpi was making *karhi*, one of Puri's favourites, and was in the process of slowly adding buttermilk to the masala. Malika, one of the servants, was chopping spinach for the gram-flour dumplings, and carried on diligently with her work.

'Well, all I can say is I'm glad you and Mummy weren't hurt. Sounds like you acted in the nick of time.'

'Given the habits of Dilli drivers these days, what with so many lunatics on the roads, I remain vigilant at all times,' he said.

Rumpi turned from the stove with a look of concern. 'It was *just* an accident, I hope, Chubby? No one's trying to kill you again, are they? I do worry about you.'

'Rest assured, my dear, it was a joyrider, only, nothing to be concerned about at all. Also, some good came from it.'

'Oh?'

'Mummy's phone got broken and now there can be no excuse for not getting a new one.'

'I'd have thought you'd know Mummy better than that by now.'

Rumpi returned to her cooking. 'Dinner will be ready in twenty minutes and I have some good news.'

Puri went upstairs, freshened up and put on a fresh kurta pyjama, his monogrammed slippers and swapped his Sandown cap for the tartan one he often wore around the house. Then he called down to Sweetu to bring him his drink on the roof.

Owing to his absence for the past twenty-four hours, he found the leaves of his chilli plants coated in a thin layer of dirt and pollution and, with a quiet apology to his plants – 'my dears' – he set about gently and methodically cleaning them with a spray bottle of water and a damp cloth.

When Sweetu appeared bearing his two pegs of Royal Challenge, Puri grilled him for information on the comings and goings in the house and for any gossip in the neighbourhood, and quizzed him on how his studies were progressing.

'Sir, you'll be buying a new car?' the houseboy soon asked, all eager expectation.

'Might be. What does madam have to say?'

'She wants you to get a Skoda. Monika prefers Toyota. But those are average cars, sir. For you, Audi is best.'

'Is it?' asked Puri with the faintest hint of a smile.

'Yes, sir, very smart, with hands-free parking and LED headlights.'

'We'll see,' intoned Puri, amazed at how much time everyone (even a houseboy who could not hope to own more than a bicycle) dedicated to thinking about fancy cars these days.

He dismissed Sweetu and went about murdering some aphids that had appeared on his young piri-piri plants (his weapon of choice being a little watered-down neem oil), spent a few quiet minutes sipping his drink while taking in the view of the new Gurgaon skyline with the lights of its office blocks blinking in the darkness – a sight that always stirred mixed feelings about where the country was headed – and then returned downstairs.

There was an awkward moment when Rumpi pointed out that he had left his phone on the kitchen table, that it had rung and the name *Dingo* had appeared on the screen.

Her words hung alarmingly in the air as Puri wondered if she'd recognized the number belonging to Kolkata.

'Isn't that a Bengali pet name?' Rumpi commented as she placed the food on the table.

'A car dealer,' said Puri, thinking fast. 'I spoke with him earlier.'

'Ah, good, so you're considering purchasing a new car. I'm glad to hear it.'

'Yes, an Audi. You know, the ones with the LED headlights. Most impressive.'

'An Audi?' Rumpi sounded somehow surprised and encouraged. 'They're good cars, no arguing with that. But are you quite sure, Chubby? They cost a fortune. And they're very . . . flashy. I'm not sure I can see you riding around in an Audi. You'd feel far too self-conscious.'

'You don't see me as being flashy, my dear?' he asked, playing wounded.

'I think a Skoda is more your speed, Chubby. In fact, that's what I wanted to talk to you about.'

Rumpi served him a small helping of rice and a more generous portion of thick karhi.

Puri wasted no time in devouring one of the spinach dumplings.

'You know the Lekhis – Prateek and Anjali – in the big house down the road?' she asked, as she joined Puri at the table. 'He's got a factory, manufactures rubbers or something?'

'A range of rubber parts for the automotive industry,' corrected Puri, who made it a point of keeping abreast of his neighbours.

240

'So they're shifting to Dubai. Their youngest has developed asthma due to the pollution, and they've got a Skoda sedan. It's two years old, good condition, low mileage, white, which I know you approve of because it doesn't stand out, and they want to sell it off. They're asking six lakh – and Chubby the best thing is they'll accept your old notes.'

Rumpi put up a hand to pre-empt his reaction.

'I know your concerns, but hear me out,' she went on. 'I spoke with Anjali and she assures me that Prateek declares everything – pays every last *paisa* in income tax. In other words, they can deposit it in their account and declare the whole amount without any issues.'

'And claim they sold us the car before the demonetization in other words.'

'There's nothing illegal in that – and everyone gets what they want.'

Puri carried on eating. 'This means we condemn the Amby to the scrap heap, I suppose,' he said.

Rumpi reached across the table and took his hand. 'Chubby, listen to me. I know how much the car meant to you. You've grown attached to it. But all good things come to an end. It's time to retire the car.'

'The mechanic told me he could fix it up for three lakh, only.'

'You'd be investing in a car whose days are numbered. Surely, it makes no sense to carry on with a model that has been discontinued. Eventually you won't find the spare parts.'

'You wouldn't miss the Amby, my dear? It is a blast from the past, so to speak. We drove to Nanital for the first time with it? You remember?'

'What I remember most is the precious days we had together in the hills, young and carefree as we were,' she said, smiling. 'Perhaps you could take me there again? Make some new memories in a new car?'

'I take it the Skoda has hands-free parking and heated seats and all,' said Puri.

'No, Chubby, I believe the hands-free parking is only available in the later models,' answered Rumpi. 'But, yes, heated seating, definitely. And it also has height-adjustable three-point seatbelts.'

Puri emerged from the house the next morning to find that Handbrake had, as per his orders, collected Mummy's little Maruti, which she'd agreed to loan him for a few days.

Strangely, Tubelight was there, too.

Stranger still he had a young man, bound and gagged, in the dickie of the car.

'The *supari* who tried to run you down,' explained the operative nonchalantly, as he held the boot open.

'What the bloody hell?' was Puri's natural response.

'We followed him here in the middle of the night, boss. He was carrying this.'

Tubelight showed him a country-made .38 revolver.[38]

---

[38] An improvised or homemade firearm, usually manufactured using scrap metal, such as gun barrels fashioned from truck steering wheels.

'The plan was to shoot you as you exited the house. Up close and personal.'

'Thank the God you were watching him.' Puri sighed. 'But why you didn't inform me right away?'

Tubelight gave a shrug. 'Didn't want to disturb your sleep, boss. Didn't want to cut into your breakfast, either. Plus, our friend here needed some time to think things over, reflect on his decisions and consider his future. Going around trying to shoot people, run them over, it's bound to have consequences.'

'Question is which ones?' said Puri.

'Right, boss, that's what I've been trying to explain to him. But I think he needs more time. Better we get back to him later.'

The young supari stared up at them, his eyes cold, unrepenting.

'It would seem that way,' said Puri, before addressing the would-be killer directly. 'Enjoy the accommodation. Should room service be required, kindly knock.'

With that, he closed the boot.

Puri set off for south Delhi with the hitman in the dickie and encouraged Handbrake to drive over as many potholes as possible. But in this endeavour, he was spoilt for choice and, what with all the swerving and the car's shot suspension, Puri himself started to feel queasy and countermanded his own order.

Besides, he still hadn't called back Dingo (not wanting to risk the conversation while still in the house). After rolling down the window and letting in a bit of air, Puri tried his number.

'Anything?' asked Puri, getting straight to the point.

'I've the total picture,' answered the Bengali detective, though there was a hint of nervousness in his voice, quite unlike him. 'Turns out Bishwanath Ganguly is the black sheep of the family. Relations between father and son are up and down – mostly down. His father wanted him to study literature and sent him to United States to the Stanford University, but he wasn't into mugging. His first love is motorsports.'

'He's a college dropout?'

'Not exactly. He passed out of Delhi and was working on his master's. After he dropped out, he remained in US and for two years his father would not speak with him.'

'Any girlfriends in US?'

'One. Her name is Ange-lee-nia Scowtt,' He paused. 'Sir, one more teeng.' Dingo gave a nervous giggle. 'Bishwanath Ganguly visited his father few days back in Kolkata. His purpose was to inform him that he wants to marry. I came to know the girl's name is Radhika Puri from Delhi.'

'My daughter,' said Puri, now understanding Dingo's nervousness.

'Yes. I understand she is a very beautiful girl, very accomplished. You must be proud.'

'The father did not react well to his son's wishes, I take it.'

There came a long 'Ummm' down the line.

'He objected on what grounds, exactly?'

244

There was another pause. 'Such a family as this, sir, academics with PhD . . . you know the type . . . they can make problems.'

'Yes, yes, very much so,' said Puri, calmly, though he could feel his anger simmering.

'Anything more from me?' asked Dingo.

'Get back to me if there's more regarding the girlfriend,' he said. 'And Dingo, one more thing: don't call me during evening time at home.'

Puri rendezvoused with Tubelight by the Defence Colony flyover where the supari was put into the back of another car and driven away.

The detective's next stop was the private DNA-testing laboratory, a swanky new building clad in reflective glass on the ring road in South Extension.

He was shown straight into the director's spotless, minimalist office where Dr Prasher, a short, efficient, softly spoken man, welcomed him with his usual patter. 'It's wonderful to see you again, sir. You're looking well. I trust you weren't kept waiting. Do make yourself comfortable.'

Opening a file on the desk in front of him, Dr Prasher went on mechanically: 'You sent us two specimens for analysis, one from a female, the other a male, both of similar age, and you asked us to compare their sequences with those of an elderly woman, whom I will refer to as Subject A. I have the result here for the younger female, Subject B. You provided a sample of her hair, I see. But I must inform you that the results for the male, Subject C, will take some time. We have extracted sweat from the, um, *article* you

245

provided, but the test is more advanced and will take a further twenty-four hours. For future reference, we do recommend a mouth swab or blood test if available.'

He was about to go on but there came a knock at the door and a secretary entered, bearing a cup of tea for Puri, though on this occasion he hadn't asked for one.

It was a good long minute before the secretary left the room and Dr Prasher returned to the file.

'Regarding Subject B's results,' he continued methodically.

'Please,' urged Puri.

'The result is positive. The maternity is not in doubt. Subject B is the daughter of Subject A.'

Puri blinked. 'Come again?'

'To clarify, the older woman is the younger female's mother.'

'No question?'

'There is no margin for error, sir. The test is definitive.'

Puri stared at him in disbelief, not sure if he wanted to laugh or cry.

Mummy was right! As incredible as it seemed, she was right! And suddenly he regretted not having brought her along.

'I take it the result has come as a surprise?' Puri heard the director saying.

Puri didn't answer. His mind was racing ahead, considering the implications of Riya being alive and the challenges it posed in helping to rehabilitate her into mainstream society and seeing justice served.

There was no stopping Riya leaving the ashram of course – it wasn't as if she was kept there under duress – but there was no guarantee that she would do so. It had been her home for some thirty years or so and she might not want to leave. Just speaking with her presented a problem in itself given the ashram's strict rules on visitors – and he could hardly call up Mantosh Singh and tell him, 'Good news, your first wife is alive and well, kindly pick her up from the widow ashram in Vrindavan where she's been stranded for thirty-plus years.' Puri was now certain that Mantosh Singh had locked her in her room and left her to die that night in 1984, and that if he knew she was alive, he might try to get rid of her once and for all.

Dr Prasher repeated his question. 'The result, sir, it has come as a shock, it seems? We do have a counsellor standing by should you require one.'

'No, no, it's nothing like that. This is regarding a case under investigation. But you're right: I was not expecting a positive. It was a long shot. The woman in question has been missing and everyone was under the impression she'd been murdered, actually.'

The director's face showed a moment's surprise before he gave a perfunctory nod and then repeated his concluding-the-meeting patter.

'We do appreciate you have a choice of facilities and welcome your custom. Let me see you to the door. My secretary will issue you with an invoice and the cashier is there to take your payment.'

*   *   *

247

At the same time that Puri exited the building, the Gupta family sat down for breakfast, all of them being late to bed, late to rise.

A second snoring-free night had left them all in a happy, optimistic mood and Vikas, who had identified the Ayurvedic herbal remedy he was taking as the cure, decided to call his estranged wife and share the good news.

Flush monitored the conversation and promptly called Facecream at home to inform her that a hopeful-sounding Tulsi had agreed to return to him.

The marriage was saved.

But how best to warn Gupta about the cause of his snoring without confessing to breaking into and bugging his house? And should they attempt to catch the perpetrator of the cat dander in the toothpaste, the chief suspect being Ruchi, the jilted ex-girlfriend?

'Better we keep silent for now and meantime place a camera in the bathroom. With any luck the ex-girlfriend will come to know Gupta has stopped his snoring and return to spike his toothpaste again. Meantime, I will meet with Tulsi's father, Ram Bhatt, and inform him that his son-in-law has been the victim of a vicious campaign to wreck the marriage.'

Over a cup of tea in the quiet of the Gymkhana Club, Puri also drew up a plan to bring Riya out of the ashram and put her in a place where she would feel safe and cared for. There was only one individual he could think of who could make it happen. And though Puri didn't relish the prospect of seeing him again, he went straight from the club to explain everything and ask for help.

The conversation lasted more than an hour and, though not easy, ultimately proved successful.

Afterwards Puri drove to Punjabi Bagh to pick up Mummy.

She was just finishing her morning puja in her room and joined him in the kitchen. 'What did I tell you, Chubby, na?' she exclaimed, beaming with happiness when he shared the result of the test.

'Heartiest congratulations are in order, Mummy-ji,' Puri said in all earnestness. 'Frankly speaking, some doubts were there on my side. But had you not entered the ashram and done a sterling job, we would be none the wiser with regard to Riya's status. Papa-ji would be proud.'

Mummy looked touched. 'I could not have done it without you, Chubby, don't forget.'

'I've played my part, keeping us on an even keel, that is certain,' he acknowledged unashamedly. 'Now we should celebrate. We'll go round the corner.'

'You mean it, Chubby?'

'Come, I'm buying.'

They walked through Puri's childhood neighbourhood, past shops unchanged since he was a kid, stopping here and there on crowded pavements to greet neighbours, waving across the street to familiar faces, until they reached the Mother Dairy.

Though the shop, one of dozens of outlets across the National Capital Region, stocked

249

mostly milk, yoghurt, paneer and ghee, it also sold especially good ice lollies, and Mummy and Puri had long been partial to them. His favourite flavour was cola, hers orange, and after they haggled over who should pay the bill – a sum total of twenty rupees (Mummy won) – they stood on the pavement in a welcome burst of sunshine, licking away until their lips were dyed brown and orange respectively, as Puri began to outline the plan he'd already put into place for getting Riya out of the ashram.

'I've arranged for her to be examined by an eminent psychiatrist once she reaches Delhi,' said Puri. 'Let us hope she can answer a few simple questions and fill in some blanks. *Daal mein kuch kaala hai.*'[39]

'Regarding the blood and shovel Bobby found in Mantosh Singh's dickie, for example,' said Mummy.

'So far I don't see where they fit in. Also, while we know with some certainty that Riya escaped the house and reached the park as the mob closed in, we've no clue as to what happened next. I've suspicions, only.'

'There's one way to find out meantime, na.'

'Saanvi?'

'Her next session starts in one hour,' said Mummy.

---

[39] Literally: 'There is something black in the lentil'. By this Puri means that something is not right, maybe even fishy, but he can't pinpoint what exactly.

Twenty

The diyas were flickering in their alcoves, the piped New Age music playing in the background, the video recorder rolling, and Saanvi was lying again on the mattress with her eyes closed in a hypnotic state.

Puri and Mummy were there too, and in Puri's case as uncomfortable as before on a floor cushion with his back to the wall, while Maaya knelt next to her client, the lappets of her silk kurta spread evenly about her.

'Who are you?' she asked, in her soft, affected voice.

Saanvi's lips were dry. They clung together as she formed her answer. 'I'm Riya Kaur,' she said.

'Where are you?'

The reply came slowly. 'I don't know . . . I'm alone . . . it's dark . . . I'm lying down . . . wait.' Here her eyes tightened. 'I'm weak, exhausted, and I feel pain – down there. I think I've just given birth. Yes, I can hear the baby crying now . . . but it's in the other room. My mother-in-law has taken it.'

'Is this your first or second child?'

'My second.'

'Are you in hospital?'

'No, I'm at home, in my own bed. The baby came suddenly.' She paused. 'I'm thirsty. I need water,' she said, her voice cracking.

'Where is your husband?'

'I don't know. I'm trying to call out to him but he's not answering. Why hasn't he come?'

A few seconds passed, her expression tense, and then Saanvi said, 'Wait, I can hear footsteps approaching. The door's opening. It's him.'

'Your husband?'

'And a doctor. They're standing in the doorway, talking.' She paused. 'Now the doctor's entering the room. He's taking something out of his bag. It's a syringe and a needle and a little bottle. He says he's going to give me something for the pain.'

Maaya took Saanvi on to the next significant event and then the next until eventually she was back locked in her room as the mob reached the house on 1 November 1984. Puri found it remarkable how her description of the key being pushed under the door, of climbing over the wall, of losing her chunni in the galli and of reaching the park matched her last account so precisely, at times word for word.

Soon, she was standing on the far edge of the park, looking out over the road.

'I can see a few cars burning . . . there are people running back and forth . . . and there's a group of men coming towards me. They're armed with clubs and bars . . . carrying cans of kerosene. They're shouting. "Blood for blood!" Oh God, they're getting closer. I've got to hide. There are some bushes. I get behind them and wait.'

Puri, before the session, had asked Maaya to try to bring Saanvi back to this moment and

252

ascertain what happened to Riya next, and the therapist was good to her word.

'Have they gone?' she asked.

'Shh, they're close,' whispered Saanvi in alarm.

A minute passed before she declared the coast clear.

'I step out from the bushes and as I do, I catch my hair on a branch. I realize my *kangha* is gone and look down and try to find it, but it's useless in the dark. It doesn't matter. I've got to reach the police station across the road. When the coast is clear, I run.'

'You reach the entrance?'

'Yes, but it's locked, so I start to bang on it.'

'Does anyone answer?'

'No, so I go to the window and look in, but I can't see anyone inside. Wait, a police jeep is pulling up. There are a few men inside.'

'Can you describe them?'

'The man in charge, an officer, is young. I tell them that I escaped from my house, that I need to call my father. He says I can use the phone in the station. He bangs hard on the door and shouts to someone inside. The door opens and he escorts me into the station, telling me I'm safe now.'

Saanvi fell silent.

'Are you inside now?'

'I'm in a room, but I can't move. My arms are tied, I'm lying . . . on a charpai, I think, face down. The string is rough on my skin. A door opens behind me. A couple of men come in. One of them grabs me!'

'I've heard enough!' said Puri, suddenly. 'Snap her out of it.'

Maaya fixed reproachful eyes on him. But his intervention had disrupted Saanvi's hypnotic state and she was left with little choice but to bring her young client back slowly to full consciousness.

Within a couple of minutes, Saanvi was sitting up with an innocent smile and Maaya was assuring her cheerily that they were making good progress.

'I'm so pleased,' gushed the therapist. 'We know now what happened to you, who was responsible for your murder in your past life, and can move on to the healing process. In our next session we will begin to use your current life resources to help repair the damage done to your soul consciousness by the trauma you've experienced. We will start to unblock your emotional energy field of the negative, intrusive impact of your past life memory and this will improve your mental health. Your outlook will improve and you can start to look to the future, free of the past.'

'Sounds great,' said Saanvi cheerily. 'I can't wait. Same time tomorrow?'

Puri needed to be alone after the session to collect his thoughts.

He asked Handbrake to take Mummy home while he made his way to Drums of Heaven, his favourite Chinese restaurant, which was close by.

By now it was half past two and, being the only customer, he had the choice of his favourite table next to the big tropical fish tank.

He ordered his usual, though he was not in the

least bit hungry. Saanvi's session had left him anxious, and in a way he wished he hadn't gone. Her account might be second-hand and almost certainly it had been embellished by her imagination, but he was sure it was the crux of the truth. Riya Kaur fled to Rajouri Garden Police Station to demand protection and, instead, the guardians of the law, men sworn to protect her, robbed her of her dignity and future. This was the reason why the Riya Kaur file was destroyed. And it raised the painful possibility that Bobby knew more than he had let on.

The tenacious investigator Puri knew and admired could not, surely, have concluded that Riya was taken by the mob? He would have understood that she escaped from the house, would have considered the possibility that, with her knowledge of the neighbourhood, she had fled to the nearby police station.

Puri's starter was brought to the table and he picked up one of the veg spring rolls, soaked it first in soya and chilli sauce, and took a bite.

The food tasted insipid and he pushed the plate away with lament.

Puri was staring blankly into the fish tank, watching the bubbles streaming up hypnotically from the small ornamental pagoda, when the waiter brought him his hot dragon chicken and vegetable fried rice.

'No appetite today, Mr Puri, sir?' asked the owner, who appeared after the waiter, showing a mix of concern and surprise. 'Something wrong, you're sick? There's brain fever going around – change of season, you know.'

'Something on my mind, only.'

'Ahh, you've got brain itch?' The owner knew his customer well.

'Facing a hard decision, actually.'

'Ahh, no wonder – too much thinking!'

'Should I let sleeping dogs lie, that is the question?'

'You want I bring you a fortune cookie, help you decide?'

Puri smiled. 'Somehow I doubt it will help with this one.'

'Try! You never know!'

The owner called to the waiter loitering by the bar and the plates were removed and soon a fortune cookie and a pot of jasmine tea arrived.

'What does it say?' asked the owner, watching with eager anticipation.

Puri read aloud, 'Watch till clouds part to see moonlight.'

'Good advice! Don't run into decision!'

'Doesn't it mean every cloud has a silver lining?'

'Hmm, depends on you,' said the owner.

Puri never got personally involved with torturing anyone. He was too squeamish. And though Tubelight didn't relish the work, he accepted it as an occasional and necessary part of his job description. When dealing with a certain kind of individual, extreme forms of persuasion were sometimes unavoidable.

The supari killer, who, for the past few hours, had sat bound with thick, strong rope to a metal chair clamped to the floor in the middle of the basement that served as a storage room for Most Private Investigators' old files, was such a case. What's more, Tubelight was beginning to relish the prospect of taking the gloves off and properly getting to work on him.

Lord knows the usual stuff wasn't working.

He'd played it nice, offering his guest chai, a cigarette, even some biscuits, and pointed out that there was no need for it to get nasty if he spilled the beans on who had hired him to knock off the boss. He didn't owe his client any loyalty, surely? Why not save everyone time?

All the while, Tubelight's accomplices kept up the pretence that someone else was being tortured in the next room. Over the strains of death metal band Napalm Death, played very loud, came blood-curdling shrieks and screams, and demands for information delivered in a deep, gruff voice.

At one point, Munnar, a great bear of a man with one drooping eyelid, stepped out of the room wearing overalls splattered in blood while holding a saw with some fatty (mutton) gristle clinging to the teeth, and took out his earplugs. The subject had passed out from blood loss, he reported nonchalantly, and he wanted permission to go and have his lunch.

Tubelight told him that was fine but not to be too long, suggesting that he might have more work for him.

'Make sure the battery is fully charged,' he added. 'Oh, and bring me a chicken kathi roll, extra chutney.'

The supari remained defiant, however.

The discoloration of the patch of concrete floor

in the area in front of him was testament to all the oaths of retribution and profanities that had shot from his mouth along with a considerable quantity of spittle.

After three hours, Tubelight had nothing to show for his efforts, he was out of cigarettes and, with the front of his kurta now moist, he would have welcomed a change of clothes.

Tubelight considered bringing in Mangal, a snake charmer, whom he'd used a few times to great effect. This technique involved sitting the victim on a chair stripped of its seat, placing his basket containing a big, black cobra underneath and getting him to play a little tune. But he decided to try a different tactic. All the rings and talismans that the supari wore spoke, despite his bravado and swagger, of a superstitious nature.

Billy might just prove the answer.

Before going to collect him and letting him loose in the basement, Tubelight sprinkled a quantity of a certain dry herb into his captive's lap, down his legs, and even put some in his hair.

When he returned twenty minutes later, it was with a pet carrier containing a kitten, black in colour save for a patch of white beneath his chin and a splash on the tops of both paws.

Having always been scared of cats himself, especially black ones, Tubelight didn't dare handle the animal.[40] Instead, he opened the door to the storeroom ajar and let Billy inside.

---

[40] Among Indians, Tubelight is hardly alone on this score.

It took the herb, *vidaalaparnassa*, commonly known as catnip, a few minutes to take full effect.

The supari's shrieks began as the kitten began to climb up his legs.

Having Billy rolling around on his lap and gently clawing his thighs engendered screams.

And when the kitten clambered up onto the hired killer's shoulders, he started begging for mercy.

Puri was appraised of the full confession as he was on his way back to the DNA laboratory to pick up the second result.

The supari, who was called Jaggu, worked for Hari Dev, aka Hairy Toes, mostly helping run extortion rackets and doing away with people.

'He'll never testify,' said Puri, though he was pleased with his operative's success. 'He would not last five minutes total in the jail.'

'No need for him to testify, boss,' said Tubelight. 'He knows everything about Hari Dev's operation. Says his boss is laundering several crore though the bank – going there every day to deal with the transactions personally.'

'Can he identify the inside man in the bank?'

'He's got no idea, boss. Believe me, he would have told me if he knew.'

Puri couldn't bring himself to believe it was the mild-mannered branch manager, Mr Dhawan. He had always been so polite and helpful and seemed almost painfully honest. Then again no one else knew that he had been in the next stall to Hari Dev in the toilets. It must have been Dhawan who told him – perhaps just in passing and in all innocence – and old Hairy Toes had deemed Puri an immediate threat.

'What to do with Jaggu?' asked Tubelight.

'Keep him on ice for now. And tell me one thing: where did you get the cat?'

'My cousin's daughter. She likes cats, keeps them in the house. She doesn't seem to realize how dangerous they are.'

Dr Prasher came to greet Puri again at his office door.

'It's wonderful to see you again, sir. You're looking well. I trust you weren't kept waiting. Do make yourself comfortable. May I get you anything? Some tea, coffee, water?'

Puri took his place in front of his desk with a feeling of déjà vu that for once did not seem misplaced.

This time he passed on the coffee and made a point of saying he was pressed for time.

'Of course,' said Dr Prasher, sounding languid nonetheless.

He opened the file, studied the contents for a moment and looked up with a little frown.

'Interesting, sir,' he said. 'You sent us two specimens, one for a female, the other for a male, both of similar age, and you asked us to compare their sequences with those of an elderly woman, whom I will refer to as Subject A. A more advanced test had to be conducted to analyse the sweat retrieved from the article belonging to the male, Subject C.'

'Yes, yes,' said Puri, impatiently. 'It was a match, also, I take it? Correct?'

'In point of fact, no, sir. It was not,' said Dr Prasher.

'That cannot be.'

'I can assure you, our results are one hundred per cent accurate. There is no question that Subject C is *not* related to Subject A.'

'You would not want a saliva swab or blood test to confirm?' asked Puri.

'Should you or the subjects require peace of mind, we would have no objection to confirming the results. However, I can assure you there is no need.'

Dr Prasher passed Puri a copy of the file and began his concluding-the-meeting patter.

'I believe that concludes our business. We do appreciate you have a choice of facilities—' Dr Prasher began.

But Puri was out the door.

Twenty-One

The blood, shovel and dirt Bobby discovered in the dickie – it all made sense now. Grim and terrible sense.

Gathering the hard evidence needed to put Mantosh Singh away for life, as he no doubt deserved, was another matter altogether, however. There were only two people alive who might ideally be able to tell Puri what he needed to know and testify in a case, and one couldn't remember her name, while the second wasn't ready to talk, let alone testify in court.

Still, when Puri and Mummy had gone to speak with the retired cook, Surjeet, three days ago, they hadn't known that Riya was alive and that Gajan Singh wasn't her son. Armed with this information, perhaps the use of shock tactics would persuade her to come clean.

Inconveniently, however, Puri couldn't go and speak with Surjeet right away: he'd arranged to meet Ram Bhatt at home at six thirty and dared not cancel for fear of antagonizing his former client. Also, Mummy, whom he felt obligated to take along, was back at home, and, without his own car, he could envisage spending most of the evening criss-crossing Delhi in the traffic, picking her up, driving to Tilak Vihar and so on.

There seemed nothing for it but to send Handbrake in the Maruti to pick up his mother and endure a ride in an auto.

The journey through the madness of Delhi's rush hour, which any stranger would have been forgiven for thinking was part of a mass attempt to get into the Guinness Book of Records for the most noise created by tens of thousands of cars stuck in gridlock traffic all at once, proved a wholly unpleasant experience.

After forty-five minutes crawling in an open vehicle, assaulted by choking diesel fumes and blaring air horns, and feeling like his skin was being eaten by acid and his hearing had been impaired by a fair number of decibels, the detective staggered out of the vehicle in front of the

Bhatts' luxury villa with its voguish sliding laminated-wood gates, all polished and spot-lit.

The security guard, who promptly ticked off the auto driver for blocking the gates and insisted he push his unseemly looking vehicle out of the way, looked unconvinced when Puri explained that he had an appointment with Ram Bhatt himself, asking a couple of times for confirmation of his name and the time of the meeting, before returning to his sentry post to use the phone to the house (though keeping an eye on him all the time).

Puri suffered a further humiliation when he realized that he had miscalculated how much the auto ride would cost and his last sixty rupees, all in grubby five- and ten-rupee notes, didn't quite suffice. The driver demanded another twenty and the only way to avoid an argument and a scene was to ask to borrow the amount from Ram Bhatt himself after Puri was allowed inside.

'It's not enough that you ruin my daughter's life, but now you want to borrow money from me?' he said, only half-joking, checking his wallet for change as they stood in the entrance hall of the house. 'Fortunately I think I have a few notes left myself.'

'Apologies, sir, but you see my Amby, it—'

'Broke down by any chance? You know you really should get yourself a decent car, Mr Puri. I mean the Ambassador, it's ancient.'

'The car was in an accident. A hit-and-run. I was fortunate to escape with my life.'

'That sort of thing must all be in a day's work for you,' said Bhatt without empathy.

'Not every day, fortunately, sir. It is the eleventh attempt on my life to date.'

Bhatt called for one of the servants to take the cash out to the auto wallah waiting in the street.

'Come, we can speak in here,' he said, leading Puri into a reception room that looked like a cross between an airport first-class lounge and a hothouse, with water trickling down glass panes framing jungle foliage and white leather couches arranged on a rink of highly polished Italian marble.

'I don't know if you're aware, but Tulsi is trying to make another go of it. Apparently Vikas hasn't snored for the past couple of nights. Maybe something has finally cured him. Let's see. But either way this doesn't change anything between us. You didn't do your job properly, pure and simple, and it caused my daughter incalculable trauma and damage,' said Bhatt.

'Sir, kindly hear me out if you will,' answered Puri. 'I've been making some enquiries and have come to know that your son-in-law was not a snorer before marriage. It seems someone found a way to "tamper with him", so to speak, meaning they caused him to start snoring in this way.'

Bhatt regarded Puri sceptically. 'I find that hard to believe.'

'Well, sir, you may be aware that he is allergic to—'

Puri stopped mid-sentence. Something under the couch in front of him had caught his eye.

It was a tail. A striped, furry tail. And it was swishing back and forth.

He pointed. 'That is a cat,' he said.

Bhatt looked down at the tail. 'Yes, Mr Puri, very good, you're not a detective for nothing. That is a cat. Now you were saying?'

The cat came suddenly scurrying out from beneath the sofa, chasing a piece of fluff.

Puri drew back in alarm, pulling his legs up on to the couch.

'Really, Mr Puri, it's just a cat. Only minutes ago you were telling me that people are always trying to murder you.'

The detective kept his legs up off the floor all the same. 'Problem is you don't know what they're thinking,' he said.

'Nothing malicious, I can assure you. We call him Shah Rukh. Amir and Salman are somewhere around the place as well,' said Bhatt.

'You've *three* cats?' asked Puri, eyeing the animal as it rolled around on the floor, batting the fluff with his paws.

'Tulsi's a soft touch when it comes to animals. She's got that female fostering kind of nature going on. The dogs we have outside – you would have seen them – she rescued them. The cats she got from the street also as kittens.'

Bhatt lowered his hand and clicked his fingers, and the cat scurried over to him.

'I have to admit that at first I was reluctant to have a cat in the house,' he went on. 'Like you, I was suspicious of them. I suppose we Indians grow up believing cats are bad news, don't we? All that superstition – backward village thinking, Tulsi calls it. Then again, there are people who are genuinely allergic to cats. Vikas is one of them. The first time he came

265

here, he started wheezing and sneezing all over the place. He's banned Tulsi from bringing pets into the house.'

The detective had a knowing look in his eye. 'The cat – cats – they shed fur around the place, I suppose?' he asked, as if speaking to himself.

'Sure, if one of them sits on your lap it always leaves hair on your clothes.'

Puri blinked. Was this the source of the cat dander rather than Ruchi's laboratory? Had Tulsi engineered the snoring?

Bhatt broke into his thoughts with an impatient snap of his fingers. 'Hello, Mr Puri, are you still with me?' he demanded. 'We were discussing Vikas and his snoring.'

The detective gave a start. 'Yes, sir, apologies. As I intimated, I believe Vikas's snoring began after marriage and he's been manipulated in some way.'

'And you've evidence to prove this?' demanded Bhatt.

'Not as of yet,' said Puri cautiously, in view of the revelation about Tulsi's cats. 'It is a theory, only. Meantime, a question: can you think of any person with motive enough to try wrecking the marriage?'

Bhatt threw up his arms in despair. 'Who would do such a thing? And if there was any such person, it was your job to find them out before the marriage!'

'It seems we might have been looking in the wrong quarter,' Puri admitted. 'Kindly give me a day or two and I'll revert.'

* * *

266

By eight o'clock, Puri and Mummy were back in Tilak Vihar and searching for Balwant, the young man who'd helped them find Surjeet, the retired cook, the first time.

They found him lazing in a local barber's shop near to the gurdwara, watching Twenty20 cricket on TV while the owner, apparently his relation or friend, swept up around him.

'I can't help you people,' said Balwant after listening to Puri's request for help. 'Auntie was very distressed by your last visit. She even called her old employer, the one you were asking about, Mantosh Singh, and told him you'd been to see her. He said you were after money, that you're trying to blackmail him. He said she shouldn't talk to you again if you show up.'

'Listen, na,' said Mummy. 'Mantosh Singh tried to murder his wife and we can prove it.'

'Then why do you need Auntie's help?' asked Balwant.

'Because she was a witness. And we need her to provide one or two missing pieces,' said Puri. 'If she refuses to cooperate a guilty man could escape justice.'

Balwant gave a shrug. 'Don't speak to me about justice,' he said. 'How about our fathers' murderers? Some of them are MPs sitting there in the parliament today. They brought the mob to our doors, handed out kerosene and matches, and now they sleep in comfortable beds and ride around in courtesy cars.'

'Two wrongs don't make a right,' said Mummy.

'We are talking about hundreds of wrongs,' said Balwant.

267

'By that measure, I should simply steal all this barber's money and shoot him down at the same time, and I should not face charges because such crimes are common and plenty of crooks get away with it,' said Puri.

'It's not like that,' said Balwant.

'It is precisely like that. The law is not perfect but we cannot give up on it if and when it suits us. I for one would see each and every person responsible for the killings in 1984 put behind the bars. Many of them should be served capital punishment, actually. What occurred remains a great shame for India. It is a stain upon each and every one of us. Thus we must ensure the law is upheld at all times and evildoers are served the maximum penalty. Responsibility lies on my head to set a good example for future generations. Had the police not acted in such a cowardly fashion in 1984 and instead done their duty to protect each and every citizen, hundreds of innocent citizens would be alive today. Were I to walk away from this case and not pursue the truth, I would be guilty of doing the same.'

Balwant, who had listened respectably to Puri's impassioned soliloquy, gave a nod.

'Grief and bitterness poisons and hardens the heart. When you have faced such injustice, soon you lose faith in everything. Family, authority, your god.' He jumped down off the barber chair. 'But you're right, ji,' he continued. 'If Auntie knows the truth then she has a duty to tell what she knows. Come, I'll take you to her now.'

Tilak Vihar was experiencing load shedding and the lanes and alleys were filled with residents sitting out in front of their properties, huddled in blankets, faces lit by lamps, lanterns and the odd mobile phone.

When the party reached Surjeet's door, Balwant suggested he go inside alone first.

Ten minutes later, he emerged looking defeated, and explained that Surjeet had demanded that they go away and leave her alone.

But Puri wasn't having it and, stepping up to the door, bellowed, 'Auntie-ji, listen to me! We have found Riya alive! You hear me? Alive! I have a picture of her here on my phone. She's on her way to Delhi as we speak! Open the door and I'll show you!'

He waited a moment, his ear to the door before trying again. 'We know you helped Riya escape from her room,' he lied, though by now he was convinced this was the truth. 'She told us you brought her the key, pushed it under the door. Had you not acted, she would have died for sure. You did the right thing. You understood right from wrong. You did not abandon her to die as her husband did. Do the right thing again now. Help us.'

Puri waited.

A few seconds passed.

The door opened slowly and a pair of haunted eyes appeared in the light cast by the light of Balwant's mobile phone. Tears trickled down the crags of her face.

'Alive?' she asked.

'Riya suffered memory loss and has been in Vrindavan in a widow ashram,' explained Puri.

Surjeet cupped her hands over her face and

gave a whimper. 'All this time, all these years, I thought ma'am was dead,' she said. 'There had been so much killing, so much suffering, I never spoke of what happened. What was the point? It could only lead to more pain.'

She wiped away the tears and dried her eyes.

'The picture of her, I want to see it,' said Surjeet as Balwant fetched a few chairs from inside and placed them in the alley.

Puri showed her the image on his mobile phone that had been taken earlier in the day of Riya by Dr Srivastava after he secured her release from the ashram and persuaded her to come and live with him and Saanvi in Delhi.

'Yes, that's her, that's ma'am,' said Surjeet, smiling in surprise through the tears. 'But why has she stayed away all these years?'

Puri explained the circumstances and that her memory was patchy.

'What about sir? If I cooperate, will he face arrest?' Surjeet asked.

'Do you think he deserves to be punished?' asked Mummy.

Surjeet handed back the phone to Puri. Her face was a picture of conflicting emotions.

'What sir did was wrong,' she said. 'I taught myself to forget. But it was wrong. He's not a good man. I know that. I have always known that.'

'Fortunately it is not too late to make amends,' said Puri. 'Now, I suggest we make some chai and then you tell us everything that occurred that fateful night – every detail. No stone should be left unturned.'

*   *   *

270

Surjeet described the night the mob closed in and the panic in the household as Mantosh Singh and his father took the extraordinary step of shaving their beards and long hair and shedding all remnants of their religious identity.

'Riya was where exactly?' asked Puri.

'In her room. Sir and his mother were keeping her locked inside. She'd been sedated with tablets.'

'For how long?'

'Since giving birth to her second child a few days earlier.'

'You'd visited her in her room when they were out of the house?'

'Twice, yes. I took her some food. She had always been kind to me, given me a little extra salary here and there. We used to talk. I could always see she was unhappy. She missed her home, her parents. Mantosh-sir was cruel to her from the start.'

'How did you get hold a copy of the key?' asked Mummy.

'I borrowed it from sir's drawer.'

She went on to describe how, the night they fled, the family members and the servants gathered at the back gate, but she sneaked back into the house unnoticed.

Making her way quickly up the stairs, she slipped the key under Riya's door and fled.

'That was as much as I could do. I was worried sir would realize I had gone back inside. After that I didn't know what happened to ma'am. As time went by and she wasn't found, I just assumed she'd been killed . . . along with all the others.'

271

'You told the police at the time that Mantosh Singh left the cinema where you were hiding in the middle of the night,' Puri reminded her.

'For that he became very angry with me and said that if I didn't take back my statement then I would lose my job. I had to do what he said. My husband had gone and I had to work.'

'You knew he'd gone back to the house to check that ma'am had been taken,' said Puri.

'Yes, I knew.'

'But with the house burned to the ground, your secret was safe.'

Puri added, almost casually, 'Had his car been burned, also, all the evidence pertaining to the killing of his girl-child would have been destroyed, also.'

Surjeet gave Puri a startled look. 'How could you know about that?' she asked.

'Meaning how did I come to know that Riya gave birth to a second girl and they took it from her, swapping it for a baby boy? That is of no importance at the present time. What matters is whether or not you were in the house at the time of the birth.'

'I was there,' said Surjeet, who sounded almost relieved to have the opportunity to finally speak the truth. 'The baby came suddenly, a month early. I stayed that night to help.'

'You saw the girl-child?' asked Puri.

'I took up towels and warm water several times, but I was not permitted to enter the room.'

'When did the baby come?'

'At around two in the morning. I heard it crying.' Surjeet's hands were clutched tight in a convulsion of restrained emotion as she continued. 'Thirty minutes later, Mantosh-sir left the house in his car,' she said.

'How long was he gone?'

'The first time, one hour. Then he came to the kitchen to say ma'am had given him a boy.'

'But Riya came to know the boy did not belong to her,' guessed Mummy.

'A mother knows,' said Surjeet. 'The boy didn't take to her. She had a lot of trouble feeding him. Later, I heard whispers of a mother in the *jhuggi* who'd sold her baby to a rich family in Rajouri Garden.'

'You've any idea where he buried the little girl?' asked Puri.

'It can't have been far,' she said.

'Why do you say that?'

Surjeet hesitated. 'I had to stay in the house the following night and Mantosh-sir drove away again at two o'clock. I saw him through the kitchen window. He was carrying something in his arms . . . a small bundle. He returned at around three thirty. The sound of the engine woke me. In those days there were not so many cars. The next morning he had a cut on his left hand. It had to be bandaged.'

Twenty-Two

Puri had often observed that the motive for most crimes was easy to comprehend. Jealousy, greed, poverty, stress, madness and conditioning could all play a part. If a husband murdered his wife in the hope of starting afresh with his lover it could be fathomed, though condemned. There were certain other crimes, however, which no rational, normal, feeling person could fathom. Such hideous acts of pure evil undermined the very notion of what it meant to be human, the idea that we had progressed beyond eating one another in the primeval mulch.

Snuffing out a tiny, innocent life just because it was deemed to be the wrong sex was one such act – and left even the most experienced of detectives struggling to contemplate the horror of it all.

Indeed, Puri spent most of the journey back to Punjabi Bagh staring silently out the window, past his own reflection, taking no interest in the route taken by Handbrake, which was far from the usual state of things.

When they were about halfway across Vandemataram Marg, which runs along the Delhi Ridge (an uninhabited twenty-one-mile-long section of the one-and-a-half-billion-year-old Aravalli Range)[41], however, Puri found himself considering that it was probably here along this road, somewhere amidst all the trees and shrubs, that Mantosh Singh had buried the body.

'In the wee hours, he could have reached an isolated spot here in fifteen minutes, only,' he said, finally breaking the silence.

---

[41] India's oldest range of fold mountains. The Himalayas are a mere fifty million years old.

'What is your thinking, Chubby? That he disposed of the body on the second night?'

'That seems the most likely explanation, going by Surjeet's testimony. The first night he had to procure the boy child from the slum and make the swap and soon after he and or his mother did away with the girl baby. The body was kept hidden away for twenty-four hours and the following night – when Surjeet spotted Mantosh Singh through the kitchen window with a bundle in his hands – he placed the body in the dickie of the car, took a shovel and drove to some predetermined location where he could be sure he would not be spotted.'

'Surjeet said he was gone for one hour and a half.'

'Plenty of time to do the needful – including changing the tyre on his car.'

Mummy threw him a puzzled look.

'Apologies, Mummy, I neglected to tell you about the flat,' said Puri before explaining that Bobby had remembered finding a sweet thorn sticking out of the spare tyre.

'There are plenty of acacia trees on the Ridge,' she said with a sigh.

'But there is no question of finding the remains out here, if this is where he placed them,' said Puri. 'It would be like searching for a needle in multiple haystacks. We are talking hundreds of hectares.'

Mummy considered for a moment and then said, 'What if he led us to the spot, Chubby?'

'Trick him into thinking we might get to the remains first? That is how things work on TV,

Mummy-ji, but not in the real world. Number one, Mantosh Singh is not a man to panic. A cool customer all round, I would say. Second thing, I doubt he himself could again find where he put the body.'

Mummy crossed her arms. 'Why you're sounding so defeatist, Chubby, ha? Someone might have seen something. A chowkidar, maybe? We should check the police reports. Could be his car was spotted by a patrol and written down in the record.'

'I've other cases pending, a business to run, Mummy-ji. I don't have the man hours.'

'Man hours are not required, Chubby,' she protested. 'Mummy hours will suffice!'

Puri stayed up late laying out his plans for the next day and reached Khan Market the following morning at eight.

Thankfully everything was back to normal in the office with a full complement of staff at his beck and call. Door Stop soon brought him a cup of strong chai and a few biscuits, followed by Elizabeth Rani with his post and messages.

By nine, Puri was ready to receive Inspector Singh, who was out of uniform, in jeans and a regular shirt.

Their first order of business was the plan to catch Hari Dev, aka Hairy Toes, in the act of laundering his money.

'It's simple, sir,' explained the officer. 'I've got a plainclothes unit watching Delightful Marble Emporium. They'll alert us when Hari Dev leaves for the bank. I will enter ahead of him, posing as a customer, and endeavour to identify Dev's collaborator among the staff. A second unit will then apprehend Dev as he exits the bank.'

'Have you considered putting on a disguise?' asked Puri.

Inspector Singh stood out, after all. Even without the uniform, he looked and moved like a cop.

'I don't really go in for that kind of thing,' he said. 'You really think it's necessary, sir?'

'I'm not one to tell others how to go about their business, Inspector-sahib, but you don't exactly blend into the crowd.'

'Perhaps some glasses would help?'

'It would be a start.'

Puri moved on to the Riya Kaur case, though decided not to mention his suspicion regarding the Rajouri Garden Police Station, wanting first to speak with Bobby and also to Riya to ascertain what she herself remembered.

Inspector Singh paid close attention, asking the odd question here and there, and, at the end, blew out a long breath that denoted doubt and gave sail to a couple of pieces of paper on Puri's desk.

'Hard to get any of it to stick,' he said. 'On the charge of infanticide, it's a non-starter as you say. On the attempted murder, a lawyer will argue that her husband didn't leave her behind intentionally, that there was no way of reaching her. Our only hope is if Riya proves a reliable witness.'

'As I intimated earlier, Dr Srivastava has brought Riya to Delhi and offered for her to remain under his protection for as long as she wishes. He told me when we spoke late last night that her memory is fractured. Some of her past she recalls vividly, other parts remain blank. We've agreed that the way forward is for her to be examined by a psychiatrist and she plans to see Riya later today. I suggest we speak again once I know more.'

Inspector Singh stood to leave. 'You really think glasses will help, sir?' he asked.

'You might care to switch your boots for everyday shoes, also,' said Puri.

'Or perhaps I should consider assigning someone else into the bank altogether. I don't suppose your mother is available?'

Puri stared up at him in alarm and Inspector Singh misinterpreted his reaction.

'I know, sir, she's busy with other pressing matters. No doubt she's out there now, trying to figure out where Mantosh Singh buried the girl-child,' he said. 'I envy you having her as your partner. She is the most remarkable woman – a natural detective. To have entered that ashram posing as a widow and found Riya Kaur and to have the presence of mind to collect some of her hair for analysis . . . well, she deserves recognition. Truly. Once the case is done with, I intend to put her name forward for a civilian award.'

Inspector Singh reached for the door and missed the daggers Puri shot at him with his eyes.

Facecream arrived about ten minutes after Inspector Singh had gone on his way.

Gupta had snored again all night – 'Sounded like a hurricane' – and Tulsi had fled at first light, swearing never to return, she reported.

278

'Meaning his toothpaste got doctored again,' said Puri.

'Right. So I went back and checked the video for the couple of hours before he went to bed and we've got them,' said Facecream.

'Them?'

'Better if you see for yourself.'

She found the relevant video file on her smartphone. It showed a grainy image of Vikas Gupta's bathroom from the perspective of a pinhole camera placed inside the light fitting above the sink.

The time on the bottom of the screen read *21.03.*

Facecream forwarded it to 21.06 and a figure appeared. It was a young woman.

'That's not Tulsi,' observed Puri.

'No, it's Ruchi.'

'So she was the one after all.'

'Wait and watch, boss.'

Ruchi took a syringe with a needle attached out of her handbag, injected a solution into the tube and massaged the contents vigorously before placing it back next to the sink.

'Bingo!' said Puri. 'Caught red-handed!'

'There's more,' said Facecream.

The video cut to the perspective of Gordon Gecko positioned up on the wall in the bedroom. It showed another woman standing in the door, keeping watch on the stairs.

'That's Tulsi,' said Puri.

When Ruchi emerged from the bathroom they exchanged a few words, shared a sneaky smile and went on their way.

'They've conspired together.' He frowned. 'But why?'

'I'm guessing Ruchi told Tulsi about Vikas jilting her and they decided to have bit of fun and make his life a misery,' said Facecream.

'It's a little more than fun, surely. The marriage would seem to be over. Tulsi will not find a new husband easily,' said Puri.

'Actually, boss, I'm not sure that's the case. I did a bit of checking earlier today and it seems Tulsi had a boyfriend herself while she was at university. Seems they were smitten with one another. And he himself is now divorced and available. In fact, it just so happened they met for coffee together this afternoon.'

Puri shook his head slowly from side to side in disapproval. 'What to do with these young people today,' he said. 'Respect for the institution of marriage is going out the window.'

'That may be, boss,' said Facecream, though she sounded less than convinced, 'but we're not out of the woods yet. How are we going to tell Ram Bhatt the truth? He's still going to blame us for the breakup of the marriage. And we can hardly admit to all the illegal surveillance, not to mention the breaking and entering.'

Puri had planned to drive over to see Bobby at home around ten thirty, by which time he was sure to have washed and finished his breakfast. When the time came to set off, however, the detective found plenty to get on with in the office. He had several prospective clients to contact. One said his wife was sharing details of their private life on Facebook and he wanted it stopped (this was a domestic matter, Puri pointed out), and another woman wanted him to investigate the death of her husband, who had suffered a fatal heart attack when a neighbour lit a strip of loud firecrackers outside his bedroom window in the middle of the night during Diwali celebrations, knowing full well that he had a weak heart.

He discussed replenishing the petty cash with Elizabeth Rani.

Puri even called Rumpi to speak about arrangements for Saturday when Radhika planned to bring Bishwanath Ganguly to the house. She also reminded him about the second-hand Skoda on offer from the neighbours.

'I would look it over just as soon as I've finished inspecting the boyfriend,' he said.

But as midday fast approached, he knew that he could procrastinate no longer. He was duty-bound to find out whether Bobby had conspired to cover up what happened to Riya at the Rajouri Garden station house. And as he told himself, 'Not knowing would be worse than knowing the worst.'

Half an hour later, with a knot in his stomach, he found himself standing at his old mentor's front door with his finger hovering over the buzzer.

At that precise moment, purely by coincidence, Bobby opened the door.

Both men gave a start, and in that instant showed in their own ways an unmistakable apprehension that had never existed in their relationship until now.

'VP!' exclaimed Bobby, trying to recover. 'You gave me a shock.'

'I was coming to see you, actually,' said Puri, stating the obvious. 'We need to talk, Uncle-ji.'

His formality engendered a quizzical look. 'Yes, of course, anything, let's walk over to the park.'

They sat on the same bench where they had chatted the other day.

Bobby reached into his shirt pocket and, just like last time, removed a slightly sad-looking cigarette.

'So how's the case going, any progress?' he asked.

Puri came straight out and said it: 'I – we – found Riya. She's alive.'

'*Alive?*' Bobby repeated. 'But how, where?'

'She's been in Vrindavan all this time. In a widow ashram. She's suffered partial memory loss – can't remember her name, where she's from.'

'Alive,' Bobby repeated again, clearly amazed by the news. 'Well, congratulations are in order. You've succeeded where I failed. Sir always said you would be the best of all of us.'

'Without Mummy I would not have located her,' Puri acknowledged.

'Well, we all need a helping hand now and again, VP,' said Bobby.

He started to knead the cigarette between his fingers, trying to get out the chinks.

'Vrindavan.' Bobby gave a light, ironic guffaw. 'It makes sense, if she was suffering from shock and amnesia. God knows I searched everywhere else. For three, four days. I went with her father to the hospitals, to the camps for the displaced and of course we looked in the streets. By then, they had dumped a lot of the bodies in the river so we searched along the banks. There were more bodies piled up at the vegetable market in Okhla as well. Many of them were burnt beyond recognition. Men, old women . . .' Bobby's voice cracked. It took him a few seconds before he got it back. 'Finally we had to accept she was gone. Riya's father cried in my arms. But what do you tell a father? "It will be OK? You'll get over it?" If only he'd lived to see this day.'

They sat in silence for a while, watching a few crows hopping around on the grass.

'I need to know everything, Uncle-ji,' said Puri eventually. 'If there's a chance of bringing charges, then I cannot turn a blind eye.'

Bobby gave a nod and, though his cigarette was still slightly bent, he put it between his lips, lit the end and took a long, hard drag.

Smoke spilled from his nose and out of his mouth as he said, 'VP, listen to me, I would not blame you for thinking the worst. And God knows I've been a coward. But I was not involved in a cover-up. It was not *I* who doctored the file.'

'You'll need to testify,' said Puri.

'Willingly,' he said. 'Not a day has gone by when I don't regret lying to sir, not sharing my suspicions.'

'Good, then I suggest we start at the beginning. At what point did you know for sure that, firstly, Riya had not been murdered by her husband prior to the riots, and second, she had escaped from the house on her own accord?'

'When the cook told me Mantosh Singh had left the cinema in the middle of the night, I grew suspicious – more so when she retracted the statement, of course. Why risk his life? It could mean only one thing: that he was searching for his wife, either out of concern for her safety or because he wanted to ensure she was dead.'

Bobby took another drag and went on: 'Then there was Riya's chunni found by her father in the street in front of the house. That placed her at the scene. Of course, there was every chance that she'd been taken by the mob or killed in the street and her body cleared before we came to investigate. But there was another possibility: that Riya escaped from the house and tried to reach the police station. That led me to the park and, at the far end, I spotted a piece of yellow cotton material caught on a bush. On the ground beneath the branch, lying in among the leaves, there was a kangha.'

'You showed it to Riya's father?'

'I did not,' Bobby answered, frankly and clearly, as if addressing a judge in court. 'I kept it to myself while I made discreet enquiries. I went and looked around the station house, checked the daily diary register though there was nothing, and established who was on duty that night. Soon I had three names. I knew them for what they were – that they had been instrumental in encouraging the killings, had helped direct the mob to homes owned by Sikhs. I knew they were guilty

284

as hell. I also knew the investigation would go nowhere and that if I told sir he would not hesitate to call for an internal investigation and that we'd be transferred or suspended, or worse. So I let it go.'

By now, his hand with the cigarette poking out between his fingers was resting on his knee, smouldering.

Bobby continued in a quiet voice, 'There is only one time in my career that I suppressed evidence, VP. That doesn't make it right – and I should have told you the whole truth. I should have known you would figure it out anyway. But I wasn't involved in any cover-up. I wasn't bribed or cajoled to drop the case. It wasn't *I* who gutted the file. They must have done that later . . . to make sure.'

'The men – they're still around?'

'Retired.'

'Then with any luck you will have your chance to make amends,' he said. 'That is if Riya is able and willing to testify.'

Puri went on to explain her condition and the steps he was taking to ascertain her full mental state and capacity.

Bobby finished his cigarette in silence and stubbed it out on the side of the bench.

'How about Mantosh Singh? Do you have enough to charge him?' he asked.

'On the charge of attempted homicide, I'm hopeful.'

Bobby turned suddenly and studied Puri's expression. 'You mean you believe there might be the possibility of other charges?' he asked.

'The other evidence – the blood, the shovel – is it related to another crime?'

Puri laid out the chilling facts of how Mantosh Singh and his family had murdered Riya's baby, not forgetting to mention that somehow he'd cut his hand when he'd gone to bury the body, which possibly explained the blood Bobby had found in the dickie.

'He cannot be allowed to get away with this,' stated Bobby resolutely.

'All we have to go on is the sweet thorn in the tyre, assuming it went flat the night he disposed of the child. If it was the Ridge, then we will never locate the body.'

'The Ridge?' Bobby sounded doubtful. 'Singh wouldn't have risked it. There were still jaguars roaming around then, even the odd tiger and *dacoits*.'

Puri threw up his hands in a gesture of helplessness. 'Mummy wanted to check police registers and logs and all. Personally, I've not the time or the resources. For a week now I've been missing in action and there is no other work getting done.'

'Deputy Commissioner of Police (Retired) Madhur Sharma at your disposal, sir,' said Bobby. 'You can rely on me.'

Puri reached out and held his arm and gave it a gentle, reassuring squeeze.

'I know, Uncle-ji. Forgive me. I had to be sure.' He paused. 'You've been like a second father to me. Over the years I've learned more from you than anyone could imagine.'

Bobby scoffed. 'Listen, we're sitting too close

to the fires of self-congratulation and if we're not careful we'll get scorched. Enough of all this talk. There's a crime to solve here. Let's put our heads together.'

Bobby sat forward on the bench and stared down at the ground between his shoes in deep thought.

'The fact that Mantosh Singh buried the body tells us something important,' he mused. 'He could have placed it in a bag and thrown it in the river weighed down by a brick or stone.'

'He didn't want to get his hands dirty in other words,' said Puri.

'Exactly. I'd bet he, or his mother if she was the one, opted for opium. A few drops on the tongue and the baby would have gone off to sleep.'

'Most humane,' said Puri bitterly.

'There's a strange dichotomy at play here – he murders his own innocent child but then wants to place the body somewhere safe, very possibly somewhere familiar.'

'If not the Ridge, then he had the pick of farmland to the west, and if not there, then riverbanks and so forth.'

Bobby pulled a face. 'Head off into some farmer's field and you might just be noticed. Someone is out late drinking, or suffering from insomnia, or returning from a wedding, or just hears the car engine and comes to investigate.'

Bobby paused.

'Never forget, VP, people are creatures of habit and repetition, and what's more, they're lazy,' he said. 'Woe betide the detective who has to deal with the creative murderer using his imagination. Fortunately for us, the average person in such circumstances will often come to a quick decision based on a limited number of choices within the scope of their own limited experience. In the case of Mantosh Singh, he lives in the same house and from what I understand goes to the same place of work every day. He probably takes the same walk, goes to the same club, has the same breakfast even after all these years. Habit. Never underestimate how much people are ruled by it.'

'That's all well and good, Uncle-ji, but where to begin?'

Bobby slapped him on the thigh. 'I've an idea,' he said. 'But first I'm going to need another cigarette. In fact, I'm going to need a pack. Come.'

Twenty-Three

Puri never needed much of an excuse to treat himself to a very large lunch. And the relief he felt at knowing that Bobby hadn't conspired in a rape cover-up (and that he would help ensure that whatever transpired at the Rajouri Garden Police Station was brought to light) provided the perfect excuse to head straight to (the suitably named) Punjabi By Nature where a veritable feast was promptly ordered.

The sight of it would have made a vegan faint. First came a plate of *kakori* kebab of minced lamb flavoured with cloves and saffron, and as a second course the *nihari gosht*, lamb shanks slow cooked in various spices, yoghurt and rose water, served with hot butter naan.

Before deciding on dessert, Puri made a few phone calls, the first to Inspector Singh, who said that he was still waiting in Khan Market, where he had bought himself 'a disguise', and Hairy Toes was still inside Delightful Marble Emporium.

The second call was to his lawyer, Balbir.

'At your disposal, et cetera!'

Puri, having formulated a plan for putting an end to the legal threat from Ram Bhatt once and for all, needed an indemnity agreement drawn up and to be signed by one Vikas Gupta, 'whereby he waives all liability on my part for bugging his house and breaking and entering and so forth.'

'What if he doesn't go for it?'

'Most definitely he'll sign.'

'And your client, Bhatt? Are you so sure he still won't sue, et cetera?'

'He won't risk the video of his daughter falling into the wrong hands.'

The third call was to Mummy, who by now had replaced her broken phone with the same outdated model.

She was at the Pusa Police Station to the west of the Ridge, searching through old records.

'It's useless, na,' she fumed. 'Everything is getting mouldy and disintegrated or missing altogether.'

Puri had to break it to her that Bobby had ruled

out the Ridge, anyway. 'Says there were tigers and dacoits and all.'

'He had any other suggestion?' asked Mummy.

Puri hesitated, loath to share Bobby's plan with her, which could very possibly put them in danger.

'He advised studying Mantosh Singh's habits and past and all,' he said. 'Could be something there that will lead us to the body.'

'He's planning to speak with Mantosh Singh himself, no doubt,' said Mummy. 'That's very much Bobby's style. Try to entrap him. Hope he leads him to the grave.'

Puri stopped eating. 'Mummy-ji,' he said with a sigh. 'I'm the first to acknowledge that without you we could not have come so far with the case but—'

'What you're talking, Chubby? You want me to stay home and do knitting, is it? This is no way to treat your mummy! You're giving me so much *chakkar*!'

With that, the line went dead.

It took Puri a second or two to confirm that his mother had hung up on him and a couple more seconds to consider that she was probably calling Bobby – and that no plan had been discussed regarding how best to handle her.

Another couple of seconds was lost in finding Bobby's mobile number in his address book and dialling it. And by then he was too late: it was engaged.

Puri slammed down the phone on the table. 'Here we go again!' he cursed. 'Give her one inch and she takes ten miles.'

* * *

The document was ready to be collected an hour later at Patiala House and, after checking on Vikas Gupta's whereabouts with Flush and learning that he was at home, Puri headed straight over to Mayfair Gardens and sent in his card.

Gupta was still in his bathrobe and his hair was dishevelled.

'Vish Puri, Most Private Investigators: Confidentiality is our watchword,' he read from the detective's card in a half-believing voice. 'Didn't I read about you in the paper?'

'I'm in and out of the news,' said Puri, obviously well pleased with the recognition. 'Many of my cases grab headlines and eyeballs.'

'So? What's this all about?'

'It has come to my attention that you've something of a snoring issue.'

Gupta pulled a face. 'Did the Aroras send you?' he demanded.

'The Aroras, sir?'

'Our neighbours. They've complained about the noise. Say they can hear the snoring through the wall.'

'No, no, nothing like that. Allow me to explain: you see, I know how to put a stop to your snoring once and for all.'

'Let me guess. You want me to eat dry bat-wing powder? Or sleep upside down in an oxygen bubble while listening to the sound of a waterfall?'

Puri smiled. 'You're not following, sir,' he said. 'I happen to know your snoring has been started by someone with a grudge against you. You are being *made* to snore, in other words.'

'You're saying someone has done this to me? How?'

'First things first.'

'You want money.'

'No, sir, not at all. What I'm proposing is this: I'll share with you certain information that's in my possession and your snoring will come to an end. Guaranteed. One hundred per cent. But in return you must agree to waive all liability against my good self.'

He produced the agreement, but the young man took one look at it and refused.

'I don't know you. Why should I trust you?' he asked.

'Because I know you, sir,' said Puri. 'I know your wife has left you. I know you have an allergy to cats. I know you're fond of mutton biryani from Urban Village.'

Gupta eyed him with a mix of surprise and suspicion.

'Sign it and I'll reveal everything and your snoring days will be behind you, I assure you,' reiterated Puri. 'When challenged as to how you got hold the evidence, you can claim you arranged for surveillance to be done yourself, suspecting foul play.' He held out a pen and added, 'Believe me, sir, you'll thank me later. Do the right thing.'

Gupta hesitated for a moment longer, then grabbed the pen. 'I guess I've got nothing to lose?' he said, signing with a flourish. 'This whole thing is so weird.'

'That much is certain,' said Puri, and then called Flush and told him to transfer the video.

*   *   *

At around the same time that Puri was driving back to Khan Market nursing tingling ribs thanks to the big, enthusiastic hug Gupta gave him when he realized that his snoring days really were over for good (and that he was rid of Tulsi, whom he revealed didn't seem interested in him physically), Inspector Singh got the call confirming that Hari Dev had left Delightful Marble Emporium.

'He's carrying a sports bag,' one of his men reported.

This was Inspector Singh's cue to enter the bank.

He did so without difficulty by discreetly showing his badge to the security guard on the door.

By now, he'd swapped his boots for a pair of cheap chappals in Khan Market, but he still stood head and shoulders above the other customers and as he waited in line faced no difficulty in surveying the layout of the bank.

The Exclusive Platinum Account members area was at the back, sectioned off by a couple of glass partitions. Just as Puri had described there was a waiting area, a desk with a receptionist and to the left of this a door to the General Manager's office with his name and title prominently displayed, and to the left of that the famed toilet reserved for the exclusive use of Exclusive Platinum Account members.

The little red couches with the free coffee machine positioned in between were occupied by a few customers at a time and, every so often, the door to the manager's office would open and someone would emerge along with Mr Dhawan, who would shake them by the hand before showing the next person inside.

At around three forty-five, however, the manager bid good day to his last customer and, after a brief exchange with the receptionist, went back inside the office and closed the door.

At three fifty, with just ten minutes to spare before the bank was due to close, Hari Dev entered.

In black wraparound shades, with his thick hair combed back and a smug, proprietorial swagger, he was hard to miss. And, yes, as Inspector Singh could not help but notice as Dev passed through the main part of the bank towards the Exclusive Platinum Account members area, the man did have extraordinarily hairy toes.

'Sir, how can I help you?' came a teller's voice as Dev approached the receptionist's desk and then went and occupied one of the red couches.

The voice came again but weary this time. 'Sir, kindly approach.'

Inspector Singh realized that he was next in line and was left with no choice but to step up to the counter.

'Um, well, I'd like to open an account,' he said.

'You're not an existing customer?' asked the exasperated teller.

'No, I should like to become one.'

Inspector Singh didn't hear her answer. His eyes were fixed on Dev, who was now making his way into the toilet with his bag.

'Sir, to open an account you'll have to revert in the morning and speak with the relationship manager.'

Inspector Singh said with his eyes still fixed on the toilet door, 'OK, so just give me the form.'

'As I told you, you'll have to see the relationship manager, Mrs Srinivasan.'

'Sure, I'll see her now.'

'As I've intimated, she is not available. Kindly stand aside for the next customer,' said the teller through clenched teeth.

The toilet swung open and Dev emerged, carrying the bag over his shoulder.

Inspector Singh waited for him to leave, then turned back to the teller who was glowering at him.

'I've just realized I want an Exclusive Platinum Account,' he said. 'I'll apply over there?'

Without waiting for an answer, he went over to speak with Mr Dhawan's receptionist and engaged her in a similarly farcical conversation.

Fortunately he didn't have to keep this up for long before the manager himself emerged and went straight into the toilet, taking with him a couple of large envelopes.

Inspector Singh waited around twenty seconds and then burst into the toilet, expecting to find Mr Dhawan retrieving cash left for him by Dev.

Instead, when he looked over the top of the first cubicle, he found the manager relieving himself into the toilet.

'Sir, this facility is for Exclusive Platinum Account holders only,' he protested.

Ignoring him, Inspector Singh looked behind the cistern, searched the second cubicle and prodded the roof tiles in case the money had been placed there. But he could find nothing.

* * *

'Tell me,' said Puri when his phone rang a minute later and Inspector Singh, who was now out on the pavement in front of the bank, quickly summarized what had happened. 'Where's Dev now?'

'My men are following him.'

'Pick me up in your vehicle at the backside,' said Puri.

A few minutes later, Inspector Singh collected him from outside the temple and pulled out of Khan Market with the jeep's emergency beacon flashing and the siren wailing. Neither made much of an impression on the drivers blocking the way, however – even with the horn honking constantly as well – and it was a good few minutes before they reached the main road.

A voice came over the walkie-talkie on the dashboard.

'Garuda One, this is Garuda Two, over.'

Inspector Singh grabbed the handset. 'Garuda Two, what's the target's position, over?'

Hairy Toes was heading south past 'hospital', meaning the junction next to the All India Institute of Medical Sciences, Singh's man reported.

'Keep on target, we're five, six minutes behind you, over,' said Inspector Singh as he turned left on to Sri Aurobindo Marg and sped down the Jor Bagh service road and then over the bridge next to Safdarjung Airport.

Some fancy slaloming and a short stretch along a pavement got him through the hospital junction in record time and soon they were speeding south towards the airport.

Five minutes later, Garuda Two came back over

the walkie-talkie reporting that Dev had stopped outside the new Sun Temple in Chhatarpur.

'Target's now on foot, heading inside. Awaiting your instructions, over.'

'Has he got the bag with him?' asked Puri urgently.

Inspector Singh relayed the question and the answer came back: 'Affirmative.'

Puri thought for a moment and then exclaimed, 'We've had this thing back to front. Faster, Inspector-sahib, or we'll miss the whole thing!'

'Had what back to front?'

'Just drive, jaldi *karo*!'

Inspector Singh did as he was told and reached the temple just four minutes after Dev had gone inside.

Puri advised him to proceed with caution.

'We need to catch him in the act,' he explained.

'What act?'

'Laundering money from the bank. Bring your men and hurry.'

Inspector Singh signalled to his subordinates and they all hurried inside.

A pandit tried to bar their entry but was ordered to one side.

With Puri leading the way, the group went straight to the office.

Inspector Singh pushed open the door to reveal Dev emptying his sports bag of wads of old one-thousand-rupee notes onto a table while the head priest sat operating a counting machine.

'You're both under arrest,' shouted Inspector Singh, as he and his men pushed inside. 'Hands where I can see them.'

'On what charge?' Dev demanded coolly. 'I'm making a donation to the temple, nothing more.'

'I'll be the one asking the questions. Sit down and if you know what's good for you, keep your mouth shut,' said Inspector Singh.

But the truth was he didn't know what charges to bring and had to step out of the room for a moment with Puri to consult.

'I'm not following, sir. Where did the money come from?'

'The bank. He wasn't dropping off, he was picking up.'

Inspector Singh thought for a moment. 'You mean when he went inside the toilet?'

'Exactly. The cash had been left there for him earlier.'

'But whose money is this? And why take it out of the bank? And then why bring it here?'

'My guess is Mr Dhawan is offering to launder money on behalf of clients for a fee but is unable to do so through the bank because it will invite scrutiny. So he and Dev are conspiring to wash it through the temple.'

'Right, sir, I'm with you. Temples are eligible to receive anonymous *hundi* donations and can deposit the money with no questions asked.'

'Thus the priest can deposit the cash and later return the amount to the donator in white – minus some commission, naturally.'

'Then the charges should be framed under the 2002 Prevention of Money Laundering Act,' said Inspector Singh.

'Not forgetting attempted murder, also. And destruction of property. I hold Mr Dev personally responsible for the damage done to my beloved Amby,' said Puri.

Twenty-Four

Puri wanted to speak with Dr Anjali Mittal, the psychiatrist, on a clear landline that could be relied on not to 'give call drops', and hurried straight back to Khan Market from the temple.

As he pulled up, he saw Mr Dhawan being escorted from the bank by Inspector Singh's deputy and a couple of jawans.

The man was sobbing as he was put into the back of a jeep and driven away.

Puri watched him go with a heavy heart. The circumstantial evidence suggested he had been up to his neck in a massive money-laundering scheme.

'Greed can act like acid to the mortar of a person, no matter how strong their moral fibre might appear,' he told Madam Rani, who was still behind her desk though she seemed eager to be on her way. 'In Mr Dhawan's case it seems like the prospect of easy money turned his head. I wonder if it was the shoes that did it.'

'Shoes, sir?'

'His shoes were gifted to him from an uncle in America. They had little leather tassels on them. Perhaps he got too used to the idea of such luxury items.'

'Not Mr Dhawan, sir. He's always been so

299

polite and courteous. I cannot believe he would break the law and risk everything.'

'Let us hope you are correct, Madam Rani. My faith in humanity has taken something of a knock over the course of the past few days,' said Puri.

Halfway through his conversation with Dr Mittal, Mummy arrived at the office.

Finding Puri's door ajar, she entered without so much as a knock and came and sat down in front of his desk.

'Mummy-ji, you can't just walk in when I'm on the phone!' he protested the moment the call ended.

'Your door was very much open, na,' she said.

'That is not the point. This is my private office. I can't have everyone entering when they feel like it.'

'I'm *anyone* now, is it? You've forgotten I trained you to use a potty or what? Now tell me: what is the verdict from Dr Mittal?'

'Not until you give me your assurance – total, one hundred and ten per cent, no argument – that you'll do as I say when we do the stakeout tonight,' countered Puri. 'Bobby messaged me to say he'd given his consent for you to come along as an observer only, meaning you are not to leave the car under any circumstance. This thing could turn ugly, actually. Bobby is advising me to bring my pistol as a precaution.'

'Fine, fine,' said Mummy brusquely, 'now what is the verdict on Riya?'

Puri stared back at her. 'Pinky promise,' he said, holding out his hand.

'*Mera beta mera dimag kha raha hai,*'[42] she murmured before leaning over the desk and entwining one little finger in his and giving it a cursory shake.

'Done,' she added. 'Now tell me.'

Puri tipped back in his leather executive chair. 'It's bad news and on-the-fence news, so to speak,' he said.

'Meaning?'

'It is Dr Mittal's considered opinion that Riya suffered a severe trauma. She found a scar from a deep wound at the back of the head,' he continued. 'Consequently, her cognitive abilities were affected. Her eyesight, also. As for her memory, the events that occurred in the hour or more before she sustained the trauma have been wiped clean away. Last thing she remembers was hiding in the bushes in the park and then approaching the police station. Dr Mittal is certain Riya will never be able to identify whoso-ever assaulted her. But Riya's memory of earlier events are intact on the whole. She remembers giving birth, being locked in her room, escaping the house, losing her chunni and so forth.'

'So it's as we thought: Riya was able to describe the events to Saanvi when they were living together in the ashram, and Saanvi, under Maaya's influence, related those same events under hypnosis as if she experienced them first-hand. Meaning Riya will be able to testify against Mantosh Singh, na?'

[42] Literally: 'My son is eating my brain', meaning: 'You're talking too much, going on and on'.

'Not exactly, Mummy-ji.'

'Why?'

'One major catch is there. Riya cannot remember her name or where she came from. She's forgotten the name of her own father and mother, even.'

'Those details will come back for sure, now she's again in Delhi,' suggested Mummy optimistically.

'Could be, with the proper treatment and all, but that is by no means certain. The truth is, Mummy-ji – and one we must accept – the case against Mantosh Singh remains weak.'

Mummy brushed aside his worries with a gesture of the hand. 'Don't do tension, Chubby. Have faith. It is meant to be, you'll see.'

'A case does not get solved by faith alone,' said Puri.

'So sure, Chubby?'

Puri took a deep breath and slowly exhaled, determined to not be drawn into another pointless argument.

'I'm going to take a cup of chai before I send everyone home,' he said. 'Can I fetch you anything?'

'Just one glass of water,' she said. And then added, as if the two thoughts were connected, 'Regarding tonight, what has Bobby got in mind exactly?'

Puri threw up his hands in a gesture of ignorance. 'All I know is he thinks he knows a way to get Mantosh Singh to lead us to the grave. How exactly he would not say, and he's my senior so I cannot challenge him.'

'Bobby has never been one to share his plans,'

reflected Mummy. 'He learned the hard way while on the force.'

'Well, we should know shortly if tonight is a go. Bobby was due to meet Mantosh Singh at eight o'clock.'

Mummy cast around the office and found the sofa. 'Chubby, I want to take rest. Just I'll lie down for some time.'

'Actually, Mummy-ji, I've got a new client coming to see me shortly, so I'll be needing some privacy,' insisted Puri.

'Don't mind me, I'll not get in the way,' she said, and before Puri could object, she had laid down and closed her eyes.

By eleven o'clock, Puri, Mummy and Bobby sat in the latter's old, beaten-up, cramped and uncomfortable Maruti, which was parked in the dark beneath a defective streetlight three doors down from the gate to Mantosh Singh's home.

Bobby anticipated a long wait, perhaps as long as three or four hours, and warned that the odds of success were 50-50.

'Well, maybe 70-30 to be honest,' he said, correcting himself. 'I've placed doubt in his mind, but that may not be enough. Mantosh is as cautious as a hyena.'

Bobby was behind the wheel with Puri next to him and Mummy in the back. The street was deserted save for the odd street dog and a couple of chowkidars who were sleeping soundly at their posts.

'You had no trouble meeting Mantosh Singh?' asked Puri.

'He remembered me, of course, and couldn't risk turning me away. Men like him trust no one and expect the worst from others precisely because they're as slippery as well-oiled wrestlers themselves.'

Bobby went on to explain how, for a price of ten lakhs, he'd offered Mantosh Singh information on Puri's renewed investigation into the Riya Kaur case.

'I managed to imply that I had debts – cards and so forth. At first, he was doubtful that you could have come up with anything new. When I told him you had proof that his son was not his, he changed his tune. Not only did I get the ten lakh but he offered me double to arrange a meeting with you for tomorrow and to name the price.'

'You took the money?'

'Sure, why not? It's been a while since Pammi and I enjoyed a holiday. I've promised her a cruise.'

'But what makes you think he'll lead us to the grave?' asked Puri.

'Well, after he handed over the money, I spilled my guts – told him everything.'

'About Riya being alive?' asked Puri, sounding concerned.

'OK, not *everything*. As far as Mantosh is concerned she's dead. That's the beauty of my plan. Never forget, the most effective lies are based on truth.'

'I'm not following,' said Mummy.

Bobby smiled to himself, evidently revelling in the suspense he'd created.

'Better I don't reveal the finer details in case things go against us. *Nazar na lag gayi.*'[43]

They all stared out the window in silence for a few minutes.

Puri had a plastic bag at his feet. He reached down to feel if the box inside was still warm. 'Anyone want some pakoras?' he asked.

His mother gave a tut. 'How you can eat at a time like this, Chubby?' she asked.

'A stakeout is not a stakeout without pakoras. You would not go to watch a movie and not order the popcorn.'

'The pakora is to the Indian cop what the doughnut is to his American counterpart,' affirmed Bobby.

'And it would be sacrilege to have them without a nice cup of chai,' said Puri, producing a thermos.

'Come, ma'am, take some, this is part of the initiation,' Bobby told Mummy as he poured her a cup.

She accepted it graciously and reached for a pakora dipped in tamarind chutney.

'Now this is shaping up to be a proper Indian stakeout,' said Puri, biting into a pakora of his own soaked in tangy mint chutney. 'You have to pity those Americans with their doughnuts and Twinky.'

By half past two, when the automatic gates to Mantosh Singh's property slowly swung open

---

[43] Broadly, 'Let no one's malevolent look be cast upon us.'

with a low mechanical hum, Puri had been sleeping for at least an hour. Mummy, on the other hand, having enjoyed a long restful nap on the sofa earlier, was fully alert and gave her snoring son a nudge from behind.

'There, it's him, he's leaving,' she said, as the BMW turned left into the street and she caught a glimpse of Mantosh Singh behind the wheel, his bearded face and turban lit by the glow of the car's dashboard.

Bobby, who'd stayed awake by smoking half a packet of cigarettes, reached for the small tracking device that was linked to the tracer he'd managed to attach to the bottom of the BMW when he'd gone to speak with Mantosh Singh. He switched it on, and it started to beep intermittently every few seconds.

'Here, take this and watch for the turns,' he said, handing it to Puri and starting up the car. 'It's got a range of just half a mile, so we'll need to keep up.'

Bobby waited until Mantosh Singh reached the end of the street and then followed after him.

They left the colony and reached Mahatma Gandhi Marg.

The wide boulevard, so busy during the day with heavy, noisy traffic, seemed to belong to another dimension, one surreally silent and cast in other worldly yellow-tinted neon light.

'He's heading into town,' said Puri with surprise. 'He's accelerated. Moving fast. Very fast, in fact. Must be sixty, seventy. Hurry or we'll lose him.'

Bobby flicked on his hazard lights and floored the accelerator.

He tore through the red light at Raja Garden Chowk and took the turn with a screeching of wheels. Puri and Mummy were pressed against their windows. For a moment it felt as if the car might flip but Bobby maintained control, and though the car rattled and shuddered and his hands shook on the steering wheel, he came out of the turn and managed to get the Maruti up to sixty miles per hour.

It was a straight run down Shivaji Marg, where dozens and dozens of unmoving figures, adults and children alike, all cocooned in blankets, lay on the pavements as if waiting for collection from the morgue wagon after some terrible plague.

They sped past the odd fire where heavily swaddled night guards stood warming their hands. Packs of dogs appeared, patrolling their territories, testing the air with their noses, barking warnings into the night. The odd truck thundered past, high beams on, throbbing music and pulsating neon lights coming from their cabs.

Beyond Shadipur Flyover, which served as a veritable dormitory of auto- and bicycle-rickshaw drivers all sleeping in various contorted positions on their vehicles, fog began to creep over the road and soon Bobby was forced to slow a little. Presumably Mantosh Singh had done the same as the tracking device continued to emit its beep, keeping time, more or less, with the passing of the long row of numbered concrete Metro pillars in the middle of the road.

'Where's he going? Doesn't make sense,' said Mummy. 'Could be he's just going back to the office, na.'

'Wait,' answered Puri, throwing up a hand, 'he's stopped suddenly.'

Bobby slowed down accordingly, one eye on the road, the other trying to get a look at the screen himself.

'Where is he?' he asked.

'Close to Lady Hardinge Medical College.'

The Maruti was down to a crawl now.

'Looks like he's turning,' said Puri. 'Yes, he's turned around . . . and now . . . wait . . . by God, he's heading back in our direction.'

Bobby pulled over to the side of the road and killed the lights and engine.

Less than a minute later, Mantosh Singh's BMW rocketed past. They caught a glimpse of him, eyes ablaze with anger.

'He's had second thoughts,' said Bobby and reached for the tracking device. 'Show me where he stopped.'

Puri pointed to the position on Panchkuian Marg.

Bobby gave a shrug. 'Well, ladies and gentlemen, we tried, but it seems that he hasn't taken the bait. We should follow him back. I suppose there's always a chance he might have a change of mind.'

Puri had spotted something on the map and a thought had struck him.

'Uncle-ji, wait, something is there, drive on,' he said.

'What is it?'

'Indulge me.'

Bobby started up the car again and passed though Veer Chand Singh Garhwali Chowk and under the elevated Ramakrishna Ashram Marg Metro station.

They were moving closer to the river and the fog was growing thicker by the second, but Bobby spotted the fresh black tyre marks on the road where Mantosh Singh had braked suddenly and then appeared to have performed a furious U-turn.

Bobby stopped. To the left, beyond the pavement, stood a set of gates with a whitewashed archway above with the words *The Indian Christian Cemetery* in big black letters.

Puri thought suddenly of the angel he'd seen in his dream and a strong urge came over him to go inside the cemetery.

'I . . . *think* this could be the place,' he said.

'How do you know?' asked Bobby.

'You wouldn't believe me if I told you.' He pointed. 'There. Park under that tree. I have to go and look.'

He retrieved his flashlight from the glove compartment though left his pistol behind and alighted from the car.

Bobby did the same, as did Mummy, and was promptly reminded of the agreement.

'Lock the door,' Bobby told her. 'We won't be long.'

They found the gate to the cemetery unlocked and unguarded, and passed through a second archway.

Confronted by the sight of a jumble of stone crosses and tombstones surrounded by swirling fog, they both stopped and exchanged a look.

It went without saying that graveyards were

309

full of ghosts and possibly witches as well and it suddenly seemed like a bad idea to continue.

'Perhaps we should come back in the morning,' said Bobby.

'Mummy-ji will never let us hear the last of it, believe me.'

'Worse, she'll insist on coming to look herself. Come, we'll stick together.'

'I suppose we're looking for a grave dated October 1984,' said Bobby as he moved tentatively forward into the cemetery.

'Yes, right, that would make sense,' said Puri.

They passed a sign that read, *Notice. This cemetery is full to its capacity. Only family graves (doubling) are allowed*, and then took a path through the graves with Puri directing his flashlight on each one, first left, then right.

Most were old, the words on the gravestones wiped clean by the elements, time and moss. Some had crumbled or lay in pieces. But dotted here and there were stones marked with dates from the past half-century, and even a few marble ones from the past few years.

They had no joy on the first path, however, and had to turn back and take the second.

They passed a freshly dug grave – a heap of fresh earth with flowers laid upon it.

And then Puri spotted her.

The angel.

She was just as she had appeared to him in his dream, her sad face cast down, her great wings unfurled behind her shoulders. One arm was pointing down at the ground, though the hand had broken off.

He approached her slowly, wondering how it was possible that he could recognize her when he had never, as far as he could remember, set foot in this graveyard before.

Had he seen a picture of her in the newspaper, perhaps, and it had lodged in his memory? Was his mind playing tricks on him? Was he about to make a huge fool of himself?

He directed the torch at the gravestone below. The words were covered in moss and he scratched some of it away.

Bobby read the date: '22 October 1984.'

'This is it,' said Puri.

'It makes sense – the burial probably happened a day or so before his girl-child was born,' said Bobby. 'He might have passed the funeral on his way to work and when he needed a place to bury the baby, he thought of here. The one place someone is never going to be disturbed in the middle of the night is a graveyard.'

'It was probably foggy like this. It was the same time of year, after all.'

'The grave had already been dug; the earth was loose.'

'The stone slab would have been placed on top later, sealing the evidence.'

'And it's going to remain that way,' spoke a man's voice from behind them.

Puri and Bobby gave a start and wheeled around.

'Put your hands up and don't move,' said Mantosh Singh.

He had an old army revolver levelled at them.

'You shouldn't sneak up on people like that,'

said Puri. 'You could have given us a heart attack.'

'Shame I didn't. It would save me a job,' said Mantosh Singh.

He motioned upwards with his revolver. 'I said to get those hands up where I can see them,' he said, and then gave a nod in Bobby's direction.

'I thought we had a deal,' he said. 'You were going to deliver the girl to me for cash.'

'Girl?' asked Puri.

'Saanvi,' Bobby answered. 'Sorry, VP, I should have explained. You see, when I went to see Mr Singh earlier I told him that she's the reincarnation of his former wife Riya and that's how we know all about him murdering his own child and swapping her for a boy and how, knowing that his wife had figured out that the boy didn't belong to her, he left her to die when his house was attacked by the mob during the riots.'

'The word *riot* is something of a misnomer, actually. It was more like a pogrom,' said Puri.

'You're right, sorry, *pogrom*. Anyhow, the bottom line is that I lied to him.'

'Achcha! So you intended to spook him, in other words,' said Puri, sounding impressed. 'Genius!'

'Well, I knew that if I revealed that Riya *is* alive and that's how we know about his crimes, then he would never lead us to the grave, that the secret was safe. He'd hidden the body on his own. No living person could possibly know. The best chance was to make him think there was some kind of supernatural phenomenon at work – that his wife had been reincarnated and was out for revenge. I put worry into his mind and that led him to come to the grave to check that it was still intact and hadn't been tampered with.'

'Wait!' interrupted Mantosh Singh with a scowl. 'What are you saying? Riya's *alive*?'

'Very much so,' said Puri. 'My Mummy-ji located her in a widow ashram in Vrindavan. She's been suffering from partial amnesia all these years. But yes, before you ask, she remembers everything and will make the star witness at your trial.'

'It's over,' said Bobby. 'Put down the revolver. Don't make this any worse for yourself.'

'I don't think so. You tell me where Riya is and I won't shoot the two of you and dump you in that new grave back there.'

'I've got a better idea,' came Mummy's voice from behind.

She was holding Puri's pistol and prodded the barrel into the small of his back.

'Stick 'em up, na,' she said.

Inspector Singh had only managed a few hours' sleep when he got the call from Puri. But he came quickly all the same, and soon Mantosh Singh was taken away to be charged.

'First thing, I'll find a judge to provide an order to exhume the grave. Just as long as you're sure,' he promised.

'Rest assured, Inspector-sahib, you'll find the baby's remains inside.'

They were now standing out in the street in front of the entrance along with Bobby and Mummy.

'One thing I don't understand,' said the

tired-looking officer. 'Was he, the accused, planning to dig up the remains himself?'

'If need be, he would have done so, yes,' answered Bobby. 'But I believe he came here tonight to check whether the grave was intact. I doubt very much he has visited this place in all these years, and for all he knew the spot had been disturbed. Quite a lot of graveyards have fallen into disrepair and grown over.'

'Then why did he turn around at first?'

'When I told him that a young woman was claiming to be his reincarnated wife and that she had revealed certain details that only Riya could have known and that she was being assisted by her spirit guides, he didn't question it. Not for one second. And he looked worried. The worry gnawed at him, as I hoped it would, and turned to doubt. A part of him wondered, *What if this Saanvi identifies where I buried the body?* Of course, another voice countered this, telling him he was being ridiculous, that he was the only one to know where the baby lay. It was that voice that caused him to turn back – but ultimately it lost out. He returned to the graveyard.'

'I knew he was reverting when that thing started beeping again,' said Mummy.

'For once I'm glad you did not do as instructed and came to the rescue,' acknowledged Puri.

'But one thing I'm wondering, Chubby,' said Mummy, giving him a strange look. 'How you knew how to find the spot?'

Bobby, too, regarded him with curiosity.

'I knew it had to be a gravestone from October 1984, so when I saw the date, then I knew.'

'It was covered in moss – you had to scratch it off,' Bobby reminded him.

'But before that, na, when we stopped in the car . . . you said you thought this was the place, Bobby asked why and you said that we wouldn't believe you if you told us. What was the meaning, Chubby?'

There was no way Puri was going to reveal his dream. Not to Mummy, Inspector Singh, Bobby, not to anyone. But especially not to Mummy. It would be a tacit admittance that not every solution in crime fighting involved proof and reason and logic. Sometimes, just sometimes, the unexplained – the miraculous – did indeed play a part.

'It was a hunch, gut instinct, nothing more,' he said. 'Now come, we require some shut-eye.'

Inspector Singh went on his way and Puri, Mummy and Bobby returned to the Maruti, still parked under the tree outside the cemetery.

They had not driven far when they realized something was wrong with the car. There was a thudding noise coming from the front and the whole thing was lurching from side to side.

Bobby pulled over with a sigh. 'Stay where you are, I'll take a look,' he said, popping the hood to see what the matter was.

A half-minute later, he leaned in through the window with a big, ironic smile that seemed inappropriate to the circumstances.

'We've got a puncture,' he said. 'I discovered this sticking out of the tyre.'

And he showed them a big, thick, sweet thorn from an acacia tree.

315

Epilogue

'How you do it, sir, I don't know,' gushed Elizabeth Rani. 'My mind would get caught up in knots dealing with so much all at once.'

It was Saturday morning, three days after Mantosh Singh's arrest, and Puri was in the office catching up with the paperwork. He had just spent the best part of an hour dictating every last detail of the Reincarnated Client case, as his secretary had dubbed it, and then provided her with a summary of Hairy Toes' money-laundering affair.

'An investigator's work in India is never done, Madam Rani,' said Puri. 'One cannot succeed in this place without the capacity to keep multiple balls in the air at the same time. So much juggling goes on, I tell you. And what with the population reaching epic proportions and the police stretched to breaking point, responsibility falls constantly on my head.'

Elizabeth Rani collected up all her notes, which now needed typing up for the case files. 'I understand you went to have tea with Riya Kaur finally yourself yesterday,' she commented.

'I did indeed, Madam Rani – along with Mummy-ji and Bobby, also. For Uncle-ji, it was a memorable moment with some old ghosts laid to rest once and for all. Furthermore, it was most reassuring to see Riya and Saanvi happy together.

The bond between them is extra strong, like mother and daughter. Given the many years of pain and suffering they've both endured, it's a happy ending all round, I'm pleased to say.'

'And Mantosh Singh's family, sir?'

Puri gave a great heave of a sigh. 'I cannot imagine what Gajan Singh must be going through,' he said with pity. 'His life has literally fallen apart around him. He has come to know that the man he considered to be his father is an impostor, so to speak, and also a cold-blooded murderer.'

'How could anyone do such a thing, sir?' asked Madam Rani.

'What goes on in the minds of such people we can never fully understand,' said Puri. 'But if one thing holds true, it is this: we human beings are capable of justifying any action when need be, believe me. In the case of infanticide, people condone their actions by telling one another it is for the good of the family, to make it stronger and so forth, by ensuring they have sons and not daughters. Nowadays, of course, such acts are rarer, but with ultrasound readily available, feticide is rampant.'

Madam Rani gave a slow shake of the head. 'I suppose so, sir,' she said, still struggling to reconcile it all. A thought then seemed to pop into her head and she added, 'There is one positive thing to come out of it, I suppose. On the bright side, Mantosh Singh's daughter has gained a mother.'

'True, Madam Rani. The two are due to meet next week. Saanvi's father, Dr Srivastava, has made all the arrangements. He's turned out to be

317

a thoroughly decent fellow all round, I must say. In fact, I don't mind putting up my hand and admitting I had him all wrong. In my defence, my misjudgement was hardly surprising what with him tearing his daughter away from us in the street and then confronting me right here in the market. But he was distressed at the time and under so much of pressure. Since then, I've witnessed for myself how deeply he cares for Saanvi. He rescued her from that ashram in Vrindavan, after all, and has been trying to help and protect her all along.'

'Does Saanvi know she was a child bride?'

'Who knows what Saanvi knows or understands about herself, Madam Rani,' said Puri. 'Our so-called reincarnated client is complicated to say the least.'

'I do hope she's not going to see the past life regression therapist again.'

'That is my hope, also,' said Puri, though he sounded far from convinced. 'Maaya is nothing but trouble, causing so much confusion in people's minds.'

'Sir, there is one thing I don't understand,' said Elizabeth Rani, puzzled. 'How was it that Riya could not recall her own name, but when Saanvi underwent her past life regression therapy with her spirit guide and so forth, she identified herself as Riya Kaur?'

'I believe I already explained how that came about earlier, Madam Rani, but I'll explain this thing again,' he said, a touch condescendingly. 'You remember I told you Maaya sent me a DVD to watch of Saanvi's sessions?'

'Yes, sir, you called that day when you were facing difficulties with the computer.'

'Yes, well, those sessions on the DVD were not the first. Saanvi had at least two or three prior to those ones. It was during those first exploratory sessions that Saanvi's subconscious started to recall Riya's life experiences as if they were her own. And it became obvious to Maaya that the events related to 1984—'

'Hence the file in Maaya's study that Mummy spotted,' interrupted Elizabeth Rani.

'Precisely. At that juncture, Maaya did her homework on unsolved cases from 1984 and came across newspaper reports about the original investigation. After that she hired another private investigator to provide her with more background information on Mantosh Singh and his family and so forth. At that point she contacted Mummy, also, hoping to gain more insight into the case. And then with Saanvi in her power, it was child's play for Maaya to slip the name Riya Kaur into her subconscious.'

'Not knowing all along that Saanvi suffered from multiple personality disorder and had met Riya herself. Amazing,' concluded Elizabeth Rani with an air of wonderment.

She paused. 'I take it Maaya's plan for a TV show featuring Saanvi will not go ahead?'

'The project would seem to be dead in the water, yes.'

'Good! And with any luck Maaya will be out of business altogether,' she added.

'I would not be so sure, Madam Rani,' said Puri cautiously.

319

'But didn't you tell her that Riya is alive, sir?'
'Yesterday, only, I called on her to do just that.'
'And?'
'By then Mummy had beaten me to it, thus I was robbed of the satisfaction of breaking the news that her reincarnation theory was a total nonsense,' said Puri with an undertow of frustration.

'Was Maaya not embarrassed, sir?'
'Quite the reverse, in fact. She's found a way to explain the whole thing away, naturally – to vindicate herself, in other words.'

'How, sir?'
'Is it not obvious, Madam Rani?'
His executive secretary gave a blank look. 'I'm afraid I don't have much of a head for these things, sir.'

Puri cocked an eyebrow in her direction. 'Saanvi is the reincarnation of Riya's lost daughter, of course. That is why the two found one another and share such a special bond,' he said mockingly.

Outside in the market, the lines at the banks were shorter. But by now long queues had formed in front of the ATMs, which had been calibrated to provide the new five-hundred and two-thousand-rupee notes, though as one shopkeeper Puri passed on the pavement put it, the machines 'kept running dry'.

'Some persons are waiting three, four hours at a time to do the needful,' the man told him. 'Tomorrow being Sunday with the banks closed, there will be no let up.'

320

Puri anticipated that it would be at least another week before the country returned to normal and he was not alone in wondering whether the disruption to the economy and people's daily lives had not been worth it. The whole policy now appeared reckless. In fact, rather than nurturing confidence in the state, the entire episode had helped enforce an impression of callousness and ineptitude. It had only invigorated people's motivation to bypass the system.

Puri himself had been fortunate enough to secure a few thousand rupees in new notes by getting Door Stop to stand in line from early morning at his bank's ATM with his cash-withdrawal card.

It was a couple of these notes he now used to purchase three bouquets of flowers ordered by Rumpi.

In this way he was able to return home and justifiably claim to everyone working busily in the kitchen for Radhika and Bishwanath Ganguly's much anticipated arrival that he'd 'literally come up smelling of roses'.

With his own hearty guffaws sounding in his ears (though not anyone else's), Puri retired upstairs to freshen up.

He was still undecided whether or not to wear an everyday safari suit, which would not fail to present a business-like message to this possible future son-in-law ... or whether to adhere to Rumpi's request that he change into kurta pyjama. It took him a few minutes to decide – and perhaps owing to his good humour and the fact he was feeling well pleased with himself at all he'd achieved in the past few days, Puri adhered to his wife's wishes. Once changed, he also picked out the tartan Sandown cap he liked to wear at home, tweaked his moustache in the mirror, and dabbed on a little of his Sexy Men aftershave for good measure.

A honk from outside the gate brought Puri downstairs as Mummy's Maruti pulled in front of the house. Her new driver sat behind the wheel. Though evidently in his early twenties and only in the job for two days, he already wore a harried look.

'Yes, madam,' Puri heard him answer as she ordered him to wait with the car out in the street and warned him not to 'do dozing on the back seat'.

'How's his driving?' asked Puri after helping her out of the car, knowing full well that his question would enlist complaint.

'Last one was driving so slow, now this duffer is going fast over speed breakers. I'm getting chakkar and feel like doing *ulti*!'

Rumpi greeted Mummy at the door and then Puri led her into the living room. As tea was served, he turned on Action News! hoping to catch Inspector Singh being interviewed about the money-laundering case. Instead the news stories, blizzard of graphics and headlines that whooshed across the screen like the credits of a Superman movie were all focused on the effects of demonetization. Ordinary people across India were bearing the brunt of the hardship the policy had caused, just as they dealt with more familiar, everyday hardships caused by corrupt or inept governance. Various think-tanks, banks and economists were pointing to a slowdown in the economy and forecasting a reduction in the country's GDP growth rate. A commentator was interviewed, casting doubt on the effectiveness of the move in tackling India's enormous black cash economy.

'Mind turning it down, Chubby?' asked Mummy. 'I wish to speak with you regarding Radhika.'

Puri turned off the set and gave her his full attention.

'Rumpi tells me she wants to go in for a love marriage,' Mummy continued.

'You know he's a Bengali boy,' said Puri, not altogether sure of Mummy's feeling on this score. A marriage in the family to a non-Punjabi was a first, after all.

But Mummy gave a wave of the hand. 'Bengali, Tamil . . . British, what is the difference? Main things are love and trust. Two go hand in hand. For the love part, only Radhika can answer. As for trust . . . before marriage that is the parents' department.'

'I've had a full background check done,' said Puri, knowing Mummy was the only person in the family with whom he could confide in on that score.

'*Aur?*' she asked.

'He studied in America and for a while there was a *gori* girl.'

'How long?'

'Some months, it seems.'

'He wished to marry her?'

'He proposed, yes. She rejected him.'

'Why?'

'Seems she didn't want to leave US.'

'So he returned to India. Good. And his parents?'

'His father has come out against Radhika.'

'On which grounds?'

'Her being Punjabi and non-Bengali and all.'

'And the mother – she's also opposed to marriage?'

'She, it seems, is more easy-going.'

'Ah, then he'll come around,' said Mummy with a gentle smile.

'I suppose so.' Puri gave a pensive sigh.

'What's troubling you, Chubby?' Her tone was soft, motherly.

'This is not the proper way to go about these things, actually,' he said. 'A daughter bringing her boyfriend to meet her parents to discuss marriage . . . what has the world come to?'

Mummy reached out and patted him on the hand. 'Chubby, come, don't do tension,' she said. 'Everything will be fine, you'll see. Radhika is not going away; she wants to remain in the family. And what is more, she's smart and a good judge of people. It's in her blood. She's a Puri, after all.'

Despite Mummy's reassurances, Puri was stiff and formal during tea with Bishwanath Ganguly – and was content to be so.

This was about his daughter's future and he made no bones about asking the young man straight questions about his past, family, qualifications, work, plans for the future and where he intended to raise a family.

'Bish', as Radhika called him, made a good account of himself, and Puri gave him full marks for respect and cordiality. His ease at being within a nuclear family environment went in his favour, too, and he was upfront about having had a girlfriend in the US, an episode of his life that he said had taught him a valuable lesson about knowing where he belonged, or so he claimed.

By the time the teacups had been drained for the second time, Puri had formed a favourable impression of the young man.

When it emerged that Bish had spent some years in Chandigarh when his father had taught at the university and he spoke passable Punjabi, Puri warmed to him all the more.

In suggesting that he, Rumpi and possibly Mummy should travel to Kolkata to meet Bish's parents, however, Puri remained scrupulously formal.

It was only after the tea was over that he let his guard down.

Puri and Rumpi had seen Bish to the door when the young man asked about what had happened to the Ambassador.

'An accident, so to speak,' said Puri.

'Looks pretty badly bashed up. Mind if I take a look, sir?' asked Bish.

'Surely.'

Puri, Rumpi and Radhika followed him to the spot where the Amby was parked.

'It's a Mark 4,' Bish said, with fondness. 'This was my first car. I used to take it apart and put it back together on the weekends.'

He popped the hood and looked at the engine.

'Luckily the damage is all cosmetic.'

'I'm told spare parts are hard to come by,' said Puri.

Bish slammed down the hood. 'Not really, sir. You'll get everything in Mayapuri.'

'But all the work will be costly, surely,' said Rumpi.

'A lakh at the most, including labour.'

Puri's face lit up. 'The garage told me three times that amount.'

'I'd be happy to get the parts for you, sir,' offered Bish.

'He's an absolute genius at fixing things,' gushed Radhika.

'But the car's so old, surely investing even one lakh is a waste of money in the long run?' stuttered Rumpi, her dream of the comfortable Skoda sedan slipping away. 'Besides, what about all the cash you've been left with, Chubby? You might as well buy the other car. How are you going to spend it, otherwise?'

'Actually my dear I was thinking of donating it to charity – a certain widows' ashram comes to mind,' said Puri.

'Either way, I wouldn't part with the car,' added Bish. 'It's a classic.'

'That is my feeling exactly. It has broken my heart to think of life without it,' said Puri.

'Then you should keep it, sir,' said Bish.

And Puri resisted an urge to hug him.

Author's Note

According to a 2018 report from the Reserve Bank of India, approximately 99.3% of the country's demonetized bank notes were deposited in the banking system in the days after the prime minister's surprise announcement on 8 November 2016. This has led many leading analysts to conclude that the effort failed to remove much black money from the economy.

Glossary

AARTI
a Hindu religious ritual of worship, a part of PUJA, in which light is offered to one or more deities.

AAM ADMI
Hindi for 'common man'.

AUR
Hindi for 'and'; also used to ask 'what's new?' or 'what else?'

ACHCHA
Hindi for 'OK', 'good' or 'got it'. Can also be used to indicate surprise and as a form of reproof.

ALMIRAH
a cupboard or chest of drawers, nowadays mostly made of steel.

ALOO
potato; ALOO TIKKI is a fried snack made out of boiled potato, peas and spices.

AMCHOOR
mango powder, made from unripe green mangoes.

AMLA
Indian gooseberry.

ARREY	Hindi expression of surprise, like 'hey!'
AMBASSADOR	until recently India's national car. The design is similar to the British Morris Oxford.
ATTA	wholemeal wheat flour used to make flatbreads.
AUTO	a common abbreviation of auto-rickshaw, a motorized version of the traditional pulled or bicycle rickshaw.
AUTOLIFTER	a car thief.
AYURVEDA	a system of medicine with roots in the Indian subcontinent.
BADMAASH	a bad guy, crook.
BAINGHAN BHARTA	smoky, grilled eggplant mince mashed with tomato, onion, ginger, garlic and spices.
BANIA	generally used to refer to a merchant or anyone involved with commercial enterprise, but more specifically within the Hindu caste system an occupational community of merchants, bankers, moneylenders.

BARFI	a dense milk-based sweet.
BEEDI	a thin cigarette or mini-cigar filled with tobacco flake and most commonly wrapped in a leaf from the East India ebony, commonly referred to as Tendu.
BENAMI	property that is transacted under the name of a proxy to conceal the identity of the buyer; can also refer to a person owning such property.
BHAI	Hindi for 'brother'; a BHAI FRIEND is a friend who is like a brother to a girl or young woman.
BHAJAN	literally 'sharing' but more generally used to refer to a song with a religious or spiritual theme, usually performed in a group and accompanied by music and sometimes dancing.
BHINDHI	okra or ladies' fingers.
BILKUL THEEK	absolutely right.

BUCKS	often used to mean rupees, a 100 bucks being equivalent to 100 rupees.
CHAAT	a savoury snack, usually fried dough or boiled potato and various other ingredients, typically yoghurt, chopped onions and coriander, Sev (thin dried yellow salty noodles), and spicy Chaat masala. Often served in a dried banana leaf bowl.
CHAI VAI	informal colloquialism in which the first word is followed by a nonsense rhyming word. Another common one is 'egg vegg'.
CHAKKAR	a feeling of giddiness or disorientation.
CHAKU	a knife.
CHALO	Hindi for 'let's go'.
CHALTA HAI	broadly, 'It's all right, that's the way it goes', usually said with a shrug.
CHAPPALS	Indian sandals, usually made of leather or rubber.

CHARPAI	literally, 'four feet', a woven string bed.
CHARSOBEES	Indian English slang for a person who is known to be a trickster or a fraudster. Translates literally as 420, a reference to the old Indian Penal Code Section 420, which relates to cheating and dishonesty.
CHATTRIS	an elevated, dome-shaped pavilion. Common in Rajasthani and Mughal architecture.
CHAWAL	rice.
CHUDDIES	underpants.
CHUNNI	see DUPATTA.
CHHURI	knife.
CHOWKIDAR	guard.
CRORE	a unit in the Indian numbering system equal to 10 million.
CROREPATI	a rich person, similar to referring to someone in English as 'a millionaire'.
DAAL	spiced lentils.
DACOIT	a bandit, armed robber.

DANGA	a riot.
DARBAR	the room in a Sikh temple where the holy scriptures are kept on an elevated throne.
DESI	a loose term that refers to the people, cultures and products of the Indian subcontinent.
DHABA	a roadside eatery on highways serving local food.
DHAI	curd, usually made with buffalo milk.
DHALAO	a structure on the side of the street where household rubbish is deposited before being sorted and taken away.
DICKIE	Indian English for 'a boot' or 'trunk of a car'.
DIDI	respectful term of address meaning elder sister.
DILLI	local pronunciation of Delhi.
DIYA	an oil lamp, usually made from clay with a cotton wick dipped in ghee or vegetable oil.

DUPATTA	a shawl-like scarf, traditionally worn around the shoulders and head.
FUNDA	Indian English slang, contraction of fundamental, meaning situation or understanding.
GAANDU	Hindi slang for 'asshole'.
GALLI	an alley, narrow lane or passageway.
GAPPU	a talkative person, a chatterbox.
GHAT	a flight of steps leading down to a river.
GHEE	a class of clarified butter that originated in ancient India.
GOONDA	a hired thug or miscreant.
GOPI	a milk maid.
GORI	a white person, female.
GRANTHI	the individual who organizes the daily services and reads from the Sikh scriptures in the gurdwara. He is not a priest but a reader and custodian.

HARINAM CHADAR	a shawl worn by worshippers of the Hindu deity Krishna, usually coloured saffron or white.
HAVELI	a traditional town house or mansion.
HAWALA	an informal monetary transfer system operated by a vast network of brokers, primarily in South Asia, the Middle East and North Africa. It is a parallel alternative remittance system that operates outside traditional banking channels.
HING	*Asafoetida*, the dried latex exuded from the rhizome or tap root of several species of the herb Ferula, part of the celery family. A standard spice in lentil and chickpea soups or curries.
HOLI	Hindu spring festival.
HUNDI	literally a cash collection box, but the word is used generally to

	refer to donations made at places of worship.
INCHARGE	Indian English for 'the person in charge, the boss'.
JALEBI	a sweet made from batter fried in swirls and then soaked in sugar syrup.
JALDI	Hindi for 'fast', *Jaldi Karo* means, 'make it fast'.
JAPA BEADS	a string of prayer beads.
JASOOS	a spy or private detective.
JAWAN	a police constable.
JEERA	cumin.
JHARU	a broom made of reeds.
JHUGGI	a slum.
JI	a gender-neutral honorific used as a suffix in many languages of the Indian subcontinent, such as Hindi and Punjabi. Commonly used to show respect.
KACHORI	a spicy snack comprising a round flattened ball of flour stuffed with a

	variety of fillings, usually a mix of *daals*, beans, gram flour and chillies.
KAKORI	a type of SEEKH kebab, very soft.
KANGHA	a small wooden comb that Sikhs usually use twice a day, supposed to be carried at all times.
KARA	iron bracelet worn by all initiated Sikhs.
KARHI	a popular Punjabi dish consisting of fritters in a sour yoghurt gravy flavoured with spices including cloves, fenugreek and coriander seeds.
KASABI	Hindi for 'prostitute'.
KATHAK	a form of Indian classical dance.
KATHI ROLL	a type of street food similar to a wrap, usually a roti or paratha stuffed with chicken tikka or lamb, onion and green chutney; originated in Kolkata.
KHANNA	Hindi for food.

KHATHAK	one of the forms of Indian classical dance.
KHOKHA	slang term used by the Indian underworld for a CRORE; often used in Bollywood movies.
KHEER	milky pudding often made with rice vermicelli and raisins.
KHICHDI	a simple, popular dish made from rice and lentils.
KIDDAN	Punjabi for 'how are you?'
KIRANA-STORE	a small neighbourhood retail store, selling household essentials.
KITTY PARTY	a regular social gathering of women in which each member contributes money to a central pool and lots are drawn to decide which member will get the entire sum.
KULFI FALUDA	Indian ice cream with noodles made of cornstarch or arrowroot.
KURTA PYJAMA	a long collarless shirt worn with loose,

lightweight trousers fitted with a drawstring waistband.

LAKH	a unit of the Indian numbering system equal to 100,000.
LANGAR HALL	an area in a Sikh temple where worshippers and visitors are fed for free. The food is always vegetarian.
LOAD SHEDDING	Indian English for 'a power cut'.
MALI	a gardener.
MANDIR	a Hindu temple.
MASALA	any blended mix of spices or herbs. A Bollywood masala film has a heady mix of ingredients, i.e. action, love, tragedy and plenty of song and dance.
MASSI	a term in the Indian family system for mother's sister.
MAZDOOR	an unskilled labourer.
METER DOWN	Indian English for 'taking a break'.
MOKSHA	a term used in Hinduism,

Buddhism, Jainism and Sikhism which refers to various forms of emancipation, enlightenment, liberation and release.

MOMO

a type of dumpling popular across South Asia, thought to be Tibetan in origin.

MOONG DAAL

daal made with the green mung bean.

MUGGING

Indian English for 'studying hard for an exam, cramming'.

NAAN

a leavened, oven-baked flatbread.

NAMASTE

a customary Hindu form of greeting and leave-taking. Usually spoken with a slight bow and hands pressed together, palms touching and fingers pointing upwards with thumbs close to the chest.

NAXALITE

a member of any political organization that claims legacy of the Communist Party of India (Marxist-Leninist).

The term *Naxal* derives from the name of the village, Naxalbari in West Bengal.

NETA	a politician.
NIHARI GOSHT	lamb shanks slow cooked in various spices and rose water.
NIMBOO MIRCHI	a string of lemon and chillies, an evil eye averter.
NOTEBANDI	a Hindi colloquial term meaning, literally, 'the closing down of the currency'.
OYE	comparable to 'Hey!'
PAGRI	a turban.
PAKAU	slang for a very annoying person.
PAKORA	a popular deep-fried snack. They can be made from pretty much anything dipped in gram flour batter.
PANDIT	a Brahmin scholar or a teacher in any field of knowledge in Hinduism.
PANEER	a cheese made by curdling milk with a

	fruit- or vegetable-derived acid such as lemon juice.
PARATHA	a flat wheat bread pan-fried, often stuffed with spiced potatoes, cauliflower or cottage cheese and eaten at breakfast.
PATAKA	Punjabi slang for firework or firecracker and a 'hot' or attractive girl.
PEELU TREE	a species of Salvadora. Also known as a toothbrush tree.
PEEPAL TREE	a sacred fig tree.
PRASAD	a religious offering in Hinduism and Sikhism.
PUJA	an act of worship.
PUKKA	a Hindi word meaning 'solid, well made'. Also used to mean, 'definitely'.
PULAO	a popular rice dish, usually comprising rice cooked in stock or broth, with either meat or vegetables added along with various spices.

RAGA	a chapter from the principal Sikh scripture, *Guru Granth Sahib*.
RAJMA	a Punjabi dish, rajma are red kidney beans cooked with onion, garlic, ginger, tomatoes and spices.
RANDI	a prostitute.
ROGAN JOSH	Kashmiri dish made with lamb or goat and a rich gravy flavoured with garlic, ginger and aromatic spices.
RUMBLE TUMBLE	referring to eggs – scrambled.
SADHU	a holy man, sage, ascetic.
SAFARI SUIT	a safari jacket is lightweight, usually khaki in colour with a self-belt, epaulettes, four or more expandable bellows pockets and sometimes cartridge loops. Worn with paired trousers.
SALAA	a term in Hindi for wife's brother, but also a common insult, the use of the word implying that the user is sleeping

343

	with the insulted person's sister.
SALAA KUTTA	a common insult that doesn't make much sense, KUTTA meaning 'dog'.
SEEKH KEBAB	kebab made with minced or ground meat.
SEPOYS	a private in the Indian army, the lowest rank.
SINDOOR	a traditional vermillion red or orange-red cosmetic power worn by married women along the parting of their hair.
SPEED BREAKER	Indian English for 'a hump' or 'ridge constructed across the road', often by local people to slow down traffic travelling through their area.
SABZI	vegetables.
SUPARI	slang for 'contract killer' or 'hitman'.
TARA	a flat pan or plate for pan-cooking flatbreads.
TEMPO	a generic term for a van or small vehicle used to transport general goods.

THALI	a round platter for serving food; also a meal made up of a selection of dishes served on a platter.
TILAKA	a symbol or mark worn (mostly) on the forehead by Hindus. The symbols, which are applied using paste or mud, vary according to the various traditions within Hinduism. As worshippers of Krishna, the Vrindavan widows wear long, vertical *tilakas* with a narrow leaf-like symbol on the nose pointing downwards and two lines running up the forehead like a tuning fork.
TIMEPASS	Indian English for 'spending time doing something that doesn't require effort' like watching TV.
ULTI	vomit.
VELLA	a Punjabi word for 'a person who is lazy, a layabout'. Can also mean the equivalent of 'loser'.

WALLAH a person concerned or involved with a specified thing or business i.e. sabzi wallah, rickshaw wallah.

NOTE

The exchange rate at the time of writing is:

$1 = 70 rupees
£1 = 88 rupees